GOOD THINGS
COME
IN THREES

Other Ellora's Cave Anthologies
Available from Pocket Books

DOING IT THE HARD WAY
by T. J. Michaels, Shiloh Walker, & Madison Hayes

OUT OF THIS WORLD LOVER
by Shannon Stacey, Summer Devon, & Charlene Teglia

BAD GIRLS HAVE MORE FUN
by Arianna Hart, Ann Vremont, & Jan Springer

ON SANTA'S NAUGHTY LIST
by Shelby Reed, Lacey Alexander, & Melani Blazer

ASKING FOR IT
by Kit Tunstall, Joanna Wylde, & Elisa Adams

A HOT MAN IS THE BEST REVENGE
by Shiloh Walker, Beverly Havlir, & Delilah Devlin

NAUGHTY NIGHTS
by Charlene Teglia, Tawny Taylor, & Dawn Ryder

MIDNIGHT TREAT
by Sally Painter, Margaret L. Carter, & Shelley Munro

ROYAL BONDAGE
by Samantha Winston, Delilah Devlin, & Marianne LaCroix

MAGICAL SEDUCTION
by Cathryn Fox, Mandy M. Roth, & Anya Bast

GOOD GIRL SEEKS BAD RIDER
by Vonna Harper, Lena Matthews, & Ruth D. Kerce

ROAD TRIP TO PASSION
by Sahara Kelly, Lani Aames, & Vonna Harper

OVERTIME, UNDER HIM
by N. J. Walters, Susie Charles, & Jan Springer

GETTING WHAT SHE WANTS
by Diana Hunter, S. L. Carpenter, & Chris Tanglen

INSATIABLE
by Sherri L. King, Elizabeth Jewell, & S. L. Carpenter

HIS FANTASIES, HER DREAMS
by Sherri L. King, S. L. Carpenter, & Trista Ann Michaels

MASTER OF SECRET DESIRES
by S. L. Carpenter, Elizabeth Jewell, & Tawny Taylor

BEDTIME, PLAYTIME
by Jaid Black, Sherri L. King, & Ruth D. Kerce

HURTS SO GOOD
by Gail Faulkner, Lisa Renee Jones, & Sahara Kelly

LOVER FROM ANOTHER WORLD
by Rachel Carrington, Elizabeth Jewell, & Shiloh Walker

FEVER-HOT DREAMS
by Sherri L. King, Jaci Burton, & Samantha Winston

TAMING HIM
by Kimberly Dean, Summer Devon, & Michelle M. Pillow

ALL SHE WANTS
by Jaid Black, Dominique Adair, & Shiloh Walker

GOOD THINGS COME IN THREES

ANYA BAST

JAN SPRINGER

SHILOH WALKER

POCKET BOOKS

NEW YORK   LONDON   TORONTO   SYDNEY

Pocket Books
A Division of Simon & Schuster, Inc.
1230 Avenue of the Americas
New York, NY 10020

First Pocket Books trade paperback edition July 2009

POCKET and colophon are registered trademarks of Simon & Schuster, Inc.

For information about special discounts for bulk purchases, please contact Simon & Schuster Special Sales at 1-800-456-6798 or business@simonandschuster.com

Manufactured in the United States of America

10 9 8 7 6 5 4 3 2 1

Library of Congress Cataloging-in-Publication Data

Good things come in threes / Anya Bast, Jan Springer, Shiloh Walker. — 1st Pocket Books trade pbk. ed.
    p.   cm. — (Ellora's Cave anthologies)
 1. Erotic stories, American. I. Bast, Anya. Tempted by two. II. Springer, Jan. Edible delights. III. Walker, Shiloh. Voyeur.
  PS658.E7G67 2009
813'.60803538—dc22   2008039376

ISBN 978-1-4391-0294-7

These stories have previously appeared in Ellora's Cave anthologies published by Pocket Books.

CONTENTS

TEMPTED BY TWO

Anya Bast

ONE

Theo watched the glass slip from Miranda's fingers and crash to the floor as the goblin walked into the restaurant.

"Oh, my God," she breathed.

He exchanged a quick glance with Miranda's best friend, Olivia. It was clear that Miranda could see the goblin and that only meant one thing.

She possessed fae blood.

For Theo, it explained everything. He understood then that, on some level, he'd already known Miranda had fae heritage. He simply hadn't realized it. From day one he'd felt a strong pull toward her. In fact, he'd never felt drawn to a woman this way, not this powerfully. Not even once in his very long life.

He should've realized it earlier.

Miranda stared with wide eyes at the greenish-colored creature in the doorway. Her blue-green eyes were like a sea, emotions ebbing and flowing within them. Theo clenched his fists in his lap, wanting nothing more than to comfort her. He wanted to reach over and tangle his fingers gently through her blonde curls, draw her close to him for comfort. But that would seem strange to her since Miranda didn't know about her heritage yet. She didn't feel the pull like he did. Not yet. She was attracted to him, Theo knew that much, but the attraction was shallow.

For the moment.

If he nurtured it, it would bloom.

"What's going on?" asked Will. He was one of Olivia's mates and was also a Gaelan warrior. Olivia's other mate, Mason, sat on her opposite side.

"The doorway," Olivia replied tersely. The goblin turned and fixed his gaze on the table. "There's a full-blood here who wants to see you and Mason."

Mason and Will both centered their gazes on the goblin, and then slid from their seats.

"Want me to come?" Olivia asked.

Mason shook his head and looked meaningfully at Miranda. "You better stay." Will and Mason walked toward the goblin. The three of them talked quietly, and then left the restaurant. They'd been working on a case for some time now and this was possibly related to it. Olivia was in training, learning how to wield her newfound abilities as a seer and find her place as third in a Gaelan partnership, but she wasn't yet ready to fully engage in Gaelan business yet.

Olivia exhaled slowly and examined the remnants of the Chinese food on the table. "That's either a break . . . or it's trouble."

Miranda stared blankly at the large fish tank behind Theo's chair. "Guys, I think I-I might be sick. Maybe I need to go home and sleep for a while. I'm seeing things."

Olivia covered Miranda's hand with her own. "You're not sick, sweetie. I saw it too."

Miranda's wide eyes snapped to her friend. "You saw that-that thing?"

"It was a goblin," said Theo, "a full-blooded adult goblin. A servant to a kingpin, most likely."

Realization swept over Miranda's face. She laughed. "This is some kind of practical joke! You hired that guy to come in here all dressed up and you're acting like he's real."

"No, honey," Olivia answered. "We didn't—"

Miranda turned to the waitress who'd come to clean up the shattered glass. "Miss, did you see that man who just came in with that mask on?"

The waitress' brow furrowed. "Uhhh."

"He was wearing a blue shirt, tan pants and a black jacket."

"I saw a man dressed that way, miss, but he wasn't wearing a mask." She smiled. "Actually, he was pretty cute."

Miranda's face fell.

"It's glamour," Olivia said quickly in a whisper, letting the waitress finish cleaning up. "Goblins use a glamour, a type of magick, to disguise themselves as human. Only some people can see through the glamour. Hobgoblins, the smaller and less dangerous of the species, are skilled with glamour. The full-blood goblins are less skilled, but they're the ones you really have to watch out for."

"Okay, I'll play along. If only some people can see through the glamour, why could *I* see through it?"

Theo glanced at Olivia. "You're a seer. You have something in your genetic makeup that gives you that ability. It's very rare. Olivia has it too. The skill can come upon you at any time." He paused. "Now is apparently your time."

"What kind of *something?*" Miranda asked suspiciously.

Theo drew a breath. This was too much for her, too soon. "Fae blood, Miranda."

She laughed and clapped her hands with delight. "This is fun. You guys have great imaginations. So how is it my best friend just happens to have fae blood too?"

Theo paused for a moment in thought before speaking. "It's actually not that big a coincidence. On some level, you both sensed blood kinship and it drew you closer. In other words, subconsciously, like attracts like. You bonded as friends because on some level you knew you shared something."

If only she knew just how true that statement was. Theo had been attracted to Miranda in a deep way from the moment he'd first met her. It had been very strong, but he hadn't known until

Miranda had seen the goblin that it was because she had fae blood. That fact, coupled with the unusual attraction he had to her, meant that she was his mate. Theo had no doubt of that. Not only was she his mate, she was Marco's mate as well.

Miranda was their third.

Theo sat staring into Miranda's blue-green eyes. Confusion bled into anger. She was meant to link with him and Marco. Happiness and fierce possessiveness surged through him.

"Okay, joke's over," Miranda replied. "You've gone far enough. It's really funny and all, but come clean. You guys are starting to piss me off."

Olivia looked uncomfortable. "It's no joke, Miranda. Plus . . . there's more, but you need to absorb this before you hear the rest. We didn't have any idea that you would be able to see through glamour. I'm sorry we're not more prepared to explain things to you."

"I should have known," Theo said meaningfully. "I should've guessed."

Olivia's gaze snapped to his and held. Theo could tell she knew exactly what he wasn't saying out loud.

Miranda leaned forward and forced Theo's gaze to her face. "Look, I really like you, but I'm getting sick of this and you guys are scaring me half to death." She stood and grabbed her coat and purse. Before leaving, she leveled her gaze at Olivia. "And *you* just have no excuse."

Olivia and Theo watched Miranda leave. He wanted to follow, but Olivia was right, she needed time to think about what had just happened.

"She's pissed," said Olivia mournfully.

"No, she's not pissed, she's scared."

Olivia nodded, then leaned forward, rested her head in her hands and groaned. "What the hell just happened? I thought Miranda was normal, human . . . one hundred percent *human*." She lifted her head and stared at him. "And you! You thought she might not be completely human and you didn't say anything?"

"I wasn't sure. I only suspected because I'm strongly attracted to her. Now I know it's not just lust."

"God, this is wild." Olivia shook her head. Her brown shoulder-length hair slid over her shoulders. "That was her first time. Poor Miranda."

"If the blood is there, the skill can awaken at any moment. She's lucky we were here. Otherwise she might have gone for months not knowing what was going on and afraid to tell anyone. She might've ended up like you, thinking she was crazy."

Olivia nodded. "You're right." She bit her lower lip. "What are you going to do?"

Something clenched hard and fast inside within Theo as those words were spoken out loud. He felt elated and protective all of a sudden. "I'm going to make her mine."

"Don't you mean *ours*? There's Marco to consider too."

A feeling of possessiveness made Theo grit his teeth. He had to admit there was something inside him that didn't want to share. He didn't answer her.

Unseen by the shoppers around him, Theo leaned back and watched Miranda. As a full-blooded Tylwyth Teg, he had the ability to use glamour to disguise himself. He wasn't quite invisible in the formal sense of the word. He'd made himself unremarkable. When a person's gaze landed on him, he or she hardly noted his existence and then forgot him the moment they looked away.

Miranda allowed the salesperson to fasten the strap of the red high-heeled shoe around her ankle. Theo envied him. When the salesman—the *male* salesperson—smiled at her a little too long, masculine interest flickering over his face, Theo clenched his fists.

Theo wanted her, wanted her more than he'd ever wanted a woman. From the first time he'd seen her, the first time he'd scented her perfume, he'd wanted her. Now that he knew she was the third in his Gaelan partnership, he wanted her with a soul-deep hunger that nearly made him insane. The knowledge had triggered something primal inside him. After all, he had been waiting hundreds of years for her.

But he had to go slow. Miranda was being initiated into a world completely foreign to her. If he moved too fast, he'd only end up pushing her away.

He watched her walk across the floor to a mirror to admire the pretty shoes. The salesman watched her with appreciation in his eyes.

Theo wanted just a little time with her, watching her, when she was his alone, because he knew she wasn't. His partner, Marco, also had a claim on her, the same deep and inexorable claim that he had. Theo knew it was wrong to keep the knowledge of their third from Marco, but he just couldn't seem to help himself.

He just wanted one more day of her to himself. Of course, he'd said that yesterday and the day before that.

He *would* tell Marco soon.

Maybe tomorrow.

Miranda apparently had decided to buy the shoes. So Theo watched as she had the clerk box them up and she paid. He couldn't get the image of her in just the shoes and nothing else out of his mind. He could imagine her skin, soft peaches and cream, against the black comforter on his bed. The red shoes would look good against both his comforter and against her pale, pretty skin.

Her long legs would look good wrapped around his waist while he shafted long and hard into her.

Theo blew out a hard breath of frustration. He wanted her with everything he was. He wanted to keep her safe in the circle of his embrace, give her everything. Theo knew Marco would want the same—would want to cherish her, protect her, pamper her . . . love her.

As he followed her out of the store and down the mall to a

bar, he thought about the ways he'd take her when he finally had her in his bed. He wanted to hear her whispers; her sighs and moans in his ear. He wanted her silky skin under his hands, while he was buried root-deep inside her eager pussy. The mere thought of it made him hard.

In the shadowy entranceway of the bar, Theo disengaged the concealment spell he'd cast on himself and entered a good ways behind her. It was crowded. She took a seat at the far end of the bar and he took one near the entrance.

A black-haired man in his mid-thirties immediately took notice of Miranda as she crossed the floor, but she seemed unaware of the man's attention—to all men's attention. Miranda seemed to have no idea how lovely she was, how attractive she was . . . and how males responded to her.

It made Theo crazy. He didn't think he'd ever felt jealous over a woman in his life, but he felt it intensely whenever another man even glanced at Miranda.

She settled in and ordered a cosmopolitan, sipping it as she waited for Olivia to arrive. Olivia was keeping a secret from her best friend, Miranda. Olivia was a part-blood Tylwyth Teg with special abilities. And now that her mates had injected her with goblin blood, letting that blood transmute the fae blood she already possessed, she was immortal . . . or at least immortal by human standards. The fae did grow old and die eventually, but it took many, many centuries.

Theo knew how absolutely crazy all of that would seem to Miranda, yet she had a huge surprise coming. Not only was she the mate to two full-blooded Tylwyth Teg men . . . she was a part-blood Tylwyth Teg herself.

Theo ordered bourbon and sipped, keeping one eye on Miranda. Yes. This evening he would tell Marco. It was way past time.

Out of the corner of his eye, Theo noticed the black-haired man get up and approach Miranda. Every muscle in Theo's body went rigid. The man sidled up to the bar on her side and set his drink down. He said something and laughed, but Miranda just smiled politely and drew away from him a little. The man said something else and Miranda looked down at the bar and played with her glass, obviously trying not to encourage him. Her body language was clear, but the man seemed oblivious to it.

Theo couldn't take it any longer. He got up and crossed the floor toward them with his drink in hand. The black-haired man watched him approach with a belligerent look on his long face and a challenge in his eyes.

"Leave her alone," Theo growled as he walked toward them. "She doesn't want to talk to you."

"Theo!" Miranda cried, her beautiful eyes sparkling and her short blonde curls bouncing. "It's so good to see you." Theo could see she genuinely meant that. She turned to the man. "I'm sorry, could you please excuse us?"

The black-haired man looked chagrined and left them alone.

"Sit down," Miranda said, patting the seat the other man had vacated.

Theo slid in and set his glass on the bar.

"What are you doing here?" she asked.

Suddenly, he was at a loss, finding he couldn't lie to her. It wasn't like he visited the mall very often on his own. "I'm here to see you, of course," he answered with a grin.

She laughed. He loved the sound of it, so lilting and clear. There was something less happy in her eyes, however.

"Everything all right?" he asked.

She licked her lips. "You guys really weren't joking that day in the restaurant, were you? I've been . . . seeing things." She shook her head, letting her curls tumble around her face. "Strange things. I asked Olivia to come out with me today, so we could talk."

"You want to talk about this kind of stuff at the mall?"

"I wanted a little normality, I guess. I'm craving normality these days since I'm not sure exactly what normal is anymore."

She fell silent and studied her glass with serious intent. "There are strange things in this world, aren't there? Things I never would've dreamed."

Theo could see it in her eyes and on her face; Miranda was struggling hard to understand the way reality had changed in the last couple of days and her place in this new world. He'd seen it before, people struggling with the concept that most of what they'd been told during their lives wasn't true.

"I understand," he replied in all truthfulness and took a drink of his bourbon. "Can I buy you another drink?" he asked, glancing at her empty cosmopolitan glass.

She looked regretful and shook her head no. "Sorry, I'm meeting Olivia soon. We've got an appointment for manicures." She smiled sadly and rolled her eyes. "All in the name of normality. She should be here any minute. After that we're going somewhere quiet to talk about . . . everything."

"I'm willing to discuss things with you too, Miranda." He leaned forward a little. "Would you like to have dinner with me sometime this week?" The question was out of his mouth before he realized he'd been asking it. Just then he saw Olivia enter the bar and spot them. "We could talk then," he finished.

Miranda smiled. "I'd love to," she answered in a warm voice. "I'm free tomorrow night if you'd like."

"How about I pick you up at eight?"

Miranda nodded. "I'll look forward to it."

Olivia reached them and kissed his cheek. "Theo! It's so good to see you."

"You too, Olivia." They'd just seen each other that morning actually. Theo was training Olivia in her Tylwyth Teg powers in order for her to take her place in the Gaelan triad along with Will and Mason. Miranda knew about none of that. Not yet.

"It's too bad we can't stay and talk more, but the manicurist awaits. Unless you want a manicure too, Theo?" she asked with a raised eyebrow and a twinkle in her eye.

He was almost tempted if only to spend more time with

Miranda, but he sensed Miranda needed Olivia's company more than his right now. Theo laughed. "Uh, no. Thanks."

"I didn't think so." Olivia looked at her best friend. "You ready, Miranda?"

Miranda slid off her stool and gathered her packages. "I'll see you tomorrow night, Theo."

"Tomorrow night?" Olivia questioned with a smile. "What's happening tomorrow night?" Theo heard her ask as they walked through the bar toward the door.

"He's taking me to dinner," Miranda answered with a smile.

As they left, Olivia shot a meaningful look over her shoulder at Theo and smiled.

Theo turned back to the bar and sipped his drink, deep in thought. Someone slid onto the stool next to him.

"Why didn't you tell me?" The voice was deep, ragged and tormented-sounding.

Marco.

Theo briefly closed his eyes before turning to look at him. Marco's blue eyes looked pensive. "I was going to tell you tonight. I'm sorry I kept it from you this long."

Without a word, Marco turned his gaze to the bartender and ordered a shot of tequila. He downed it quickly. "Damn," was all he said. He ordered another shot, drank that and stared at the empty glass. His dark hair fell into his eyes. "Damn," he repeated. "I can't fucking believe it."

"Why are you here, anyway?"

Marco's jaw locked for a moment before he spoke. "I knew it. Somehow I knew you'd found her. I followed you today to find out if I was right."

Theo sighed. "I'm sorry I kept her to myself for this time."

"I understand. I really do." He shrugged and grinned at him. "I would've done the same. Still, just being near her, seeing her . . . *damn.*" He paused. "I have a powerful will to punch you out right now, friend."

"She has Tylwyth Teg blood. She just started seeing goblins, but it's all new to her and very confusing. That's why I didn't tell you. She needs time."

He let out a loud laugh. "Bullshit."

Theo played with his glass. "Yes, all right, perhaps there was an element of selfishness in there as well, but I'm serious. For all intents and purposes, she's human."

"So, basically, she knows nothing of our kind and she's mortal."

"Yes."

Marco gave a short, bitter laugh. "So, beyond the fact that there are two men bonded to her, there are some roadblocks."

"To say the least."

"I need to meet her, talk to her . . . touch her."

Jealousy flared in Theo. "I asked her to dinner tomorrow night. It wouldn't be good if you showed up. It might scare her off. She's in a delicate place right now."

"Theo." Marco was silent for several moments. "If you don't want to share her, expect competition." He got up and walked away.

TWO

Normality.

That had become her internal refrain. Ever since she'd been a child that's what she'd wanted. She thought she'd finally had it, that she'd tamed the chaos that had been her life.

But it appeared that wasn't the case after all.

Normality. Stability. These things just weren't destined to be hers.

She would embrace the small bit of normal she did have, though, and get ready for her date, if it could be called that. Miranda guessed it was a date, at least. The attraction between them seemed to be mutual.

She'd had the hots for Theo from the first time she'd ever seen him. Tall, broad-shouldered and leanly muscled, the man was like a living, breathing god. It wasn't just his looks or his bone-meltingly sexy Welsh accent, it was his personality she found attractive. Theo was intelligent and witty. Someone you could have long conversations with . . . after he'd made you come hard enough to see stars.

Theo seemed, in a word, *perfect.*

Miranda stared into the mirror critically, and then applied a little more lipstick. She'd decided on a red skirt and top for the evening, along with her matching pair of heels that she'd bought at the mall the previous day. The outfit was sexy, yet not *too* sexy. She wanted to entice Theo, not make him think she'd do him on the first date.

Okay, so she actually might do him on the first date, but she didn't want *him* to know that.

This was all wonderfully normal. It had nothing to do with goblins, or the Tylwyth Teg. It was just her getting ready for a night out. Something she'd done many times before. She'd just disregard the fact that the date was with a five-hundred-year-old fae, according to Olivia.

She was so nervous her hands shook as she applied a little gloss over her lipstick. It had been a long time since she'd accepted a date with anyone she really liked, least of all with a man like Theo. Mostly, she just went out with men she knew she could never be serious with, just for fun. Commitments weren't her cup of tea. Never had been and probably never would be.

The fact that Theo wasn't human? She shook her head. She wouldn't think about that right now.

Theo was the kind of guy she could actually see having a relationship with, despite the weirdness she was trying not to think about. Although why she'd said yes to him, she wasn't sure. The man scared her and excited her at the same time. Yet, when he'd asked her out she'd accepted so fast she'd barely known she'd done it.

The doorbell rang and Miranda practically jumped out of her skin. She primped one last time and went to answer it.

"Theo," she said smoothly, masking her nervousness. Wow, he looked good. He'd dressed in a well-tailored suit and wore a black dress coat. His long blond hair was tied at the nape of his neck, revealing the aristocratic bone structure of his face and his intense gray eyes. "You look incredible," she managed with a smile.

Olivia had told her that he and his partner, Marco, were the head honchos, the men in charge of the faction of Gaelans here in the city. Olivia hadn't met Marco, but Theo had the body and bearing to play such a role. He was the epitome of grace and power and emanated control and self-possession. She could easily see how men would respect and obey him.

His gaze swept over her as she ushered him into her living room. God, he had a great ass. "As do you, Miranda. Though you always look beautiful."

She laughed. "You've only ever seen me a few times. You should see me when I wake up in the morning."

He only held her gaze speculatively and smiled. She blushed crimson, realizing what he was probably thinking. Theo might like to see her when she'd just woken up . . . be there in the bed with her. Tingling excitement raced up her spine at the thought.

He leaned forward and inhaled near her throat. "You smell as good as you look too."

Had it suddenly grown hot in the room? "Thank you." She stared at him for a moment, and then went to the hall closet for her coat. "Well, I suppose we should get going."

He followed her and helped her on with her coat. His masculinity enveloped her and nearly took her breath away. His hands rested on her shoulders for a heartbeat before he moved away.

God, the man was a menace. The feel of his hands on her was enough to send her spiraling into every sexual fantasy she'd ever had about him. She'd had a bunch since she'd met him, when it was just her and her vibrator.

She turned and found him a breath's space away, looking at her with an intent expression. For a moment, she thought he would kiss her. Instead he went to the door and held it open for her.

Miranda felt a little disappointed that he hadn't kissed her, but she didn't let it show. She grabbed her purse from the nearby kitchen counter and walked out the door with Theo following.

They exited the building and got into Theo's silver BMW. On the way downtown they made nice chitchat—first date talk.

The restaurant he selected was very expensive, very high class. Miranda was glad she'd chosen the skirt, top and heels she wore. Just as they were opening the door another man approached them. He was tall, with dark hair and blue eyes. He wore a pair of black dress pants and a gray cashmere sweater under a long black duster.

The man was as drop-dead gorgeous as Theo. Miranda's mouth went dry, watching him approach. He walked with a sure, badass kind of swagger. Could this be Marco? It *felt* like Marco, but why she should think that escaped her.

"Theo!" the man said. "Hey, great to see you."

Theo pulled her against him a little and hesitated before answering. "Hey, Marco." He didn't sound incredibly enthusiastic. "Miranda, this is Marco Collins."

Marco stuck out his hand and Miranda took it. His touch sent shivers up her arm—honest-to-God vibrations skittering up her spine and through her body. "Nice to meet you, Miranda."

"Marco." She smiled. "I'm Miranda Davis." For some reason she felt compelled to make sure he knew her whole name. It was odd that she instantly liked this man. "I've heard a lot about you."

She had that same sense of *knowing* Marco, the way she'd had with Theo when she'd first met him. It was strange. Like she'd met him before and they'd been close, but she hadn't seen him in a really long time. She wanted to get to know him better, much more intimately, and not just on a physical level.

Miranda glanced at Theo, feeling the slightest bit guilty for being so attracted to his friend.

"Really?" He glanced at Theo. "I wonder what he's said." Miranda saw his eyes flash silvery and angry for a moment before returning to blue. "Are you two eating here?"

"Yes," answered Theo. He said no more.

Miranda frowned and shot him a look. How unfriendly he was being! "We have a reservation. I'm sure Theo wouldn't mind if we shared a table, would you, Theo?"

Theo glanced at her and hesitated, but recovered nicely. "No, of course not. You're welcome to share our table, Marco."

Marco shook his head. "No, I don't want to be a *third wheel*. You two are obviously on a date." He shot a hostile look at Theo, then took Miranda's hand and squeezed it gently. His touch sent shivers up her spine again. "I hope we meet again sometime soon."

"Uh, me too," Miranda managed to stutter out. She felt another twinge of guilt at being fascinated with the friend of the man she was currently on a date with, but she and Theo had no commitment. She liked Theo, but at this point, she had a right to feel attracted to anyone else she desired. Anyway, she didn't do commitments. She did affairs.

"Great, Marco. See you later then," said Theo as he guided her away with a possessive grip on her arm.

Miranda cast one more glance over her shoulder as Theo herded her through the doors of the restaurant. Marco stood on the sidewalk, watching her with a dark, intent gaze.

They were seated at a private table in the back that had been set with candles and flowers. A bottle of red wine already sat in a tall metal holder beside the table. It was beautiful and intimate. Obviously, Theo had requested this be done before they'd arrived. Miranda was quite flattered he'd gone to the trouble.

They settled in. The waiter poured the wine for them both then left them to decide what they'd like to eat. Miranda decided on salmon in a rich cream sauce and some steamed vegetables. Theo ordered a steak.

"So," said Theo as they waited for their food to arrive. "How are you?"

Miranda knew he didn't mean just in general. She pursed her lips. "Aside from thinking I'm going nuts, I'm okay."

"Olivia thought she was nuts too."

Miranda nodded. "She told me about everything yesterday. How when she'd started coming into her abilities she'd withdrawn from everyone, thinking she was insane. She told me about Will and Mason and how they helped her to accept what was happening to her." She shrugged. "It's just all a little . . . much. I've seen more, er, goblins since the night in the restaurant, but I guess I've been trying to ignore it all. It's so crazy and your mind can only take so much at one time."

"This world is filled with all kinds of things, Miranda, wild and unbelievable things. If you ignore your abilities and you ignore the truth, it will only make things harder for you in the long run. Do you understand?"

"Yes. I just wish for normality, I guess."

"Things will become normal again, but it will be a different kind of normal than you're used to."

Miranda laughed. "I guess."

"There are three kinds of goblins, did Olivia explain that to you?"

"A little."

"There are hobgoblins, who are always servants to the kingpin goblins. Those are the first two kinds. Last, there are the regular run-of-the-mill goblins. Sometimes they're servants to the kingpins and sometimes they just pass themselves off as humans, live under glamour their whole lives."

She frowned. "Why would they do that?"

"The goblins and the fae are vastly outnumbered by humans. It was not always so. Before this world belonged to the Other-Kin. However, war and sickness almost killed us all off long ago. Now we live in the human world and most of us have learned to live by human rules."

"And some goblins and fae then interbreed with humans?"

Theo nodded. "Fertility is vastly diminished in a coupling like that, but it happens. You're an example. So is Olivia."

"But you're a full-blood. So, tell me about yourself."

He leaned forward, his gray eyes sparkling. "I'd much rather hear about you, love."

Miranda shrugged. "I'm kind of boring."

Theo smiled. "Now I know that isn't true. Are you from the city?"

She shook her head. "I moved here with my mom from California when I was a teenager. She was escaping my father, who was abusive." She put a hand to her mouth. "I'm sorry, I wasn't going to tell you that. It just slipped out."

"Why wouldn't you tell me that?"

"It's a little heavy for a first date, that's all."

Theo leaned forward and took her hand. She had the same kind of reaction to Theo that she had with Marco. Little shivers of pleasure shook through her body at his touch. "I know we only just met, but I think we can skip the small talk and just be honest with each other. Let's both face the truth together."

A flicker of fear ran through Miranda. Wow. Theo was looking for something serious, wasn't he? She licked her lips and glanced away. "Okay."

It was true she did feel really comfortable with Theo. So comfortable, she'd let something slip that caused her a lot of pain, something she normally didn't tell anyone. That was odd.

"My mother had to run from my father," she continued, not even knowing why she did so. "We had to hide from him. He was very . . . violent."

"Were you successful? Did he ever find you?"

Miranda bit her lip and looked away, feeling her eyes fill up with tears. "Yes, he found us. That was how my mother died. I was eighteen and had pushed my mom to leave my dad. I convinced her to move all the way across the country, but he still found us." She dropped her gaze and studied the white tablecloth. "He, uh, killed himself afterward. I was there when it all happened."

Theo rubbed his thumb over the back of her hand to give her comfort. "I'm sorry, I can tell this gives you a lot of pain to discuss. We can change the subject, if you'd like."

Miranda shook her head and plunged ahead. "I was there when it happened," she repeated. She paused. "He kept saying he loved her." Her voice broke on the words as she remembered that day. "He told her he loved her while he . . . "

"I'm sorry."

"You never would've guessed it, looking at us as a family. Both my parents were professionals—my mother was a CPA, my father was an architect. People have a tendency to stereotype wife beaters, but my father broke all of them." She shook her head. "You never would've guessed."

"Did he ever beat *you*, Miranda?" Theo asked gently.

She shook her head. "No. My mother was always the focus of his anger, not me."

"You were eighteen when this happened. What did you do after that?"

"I was already accepted to Newville State. In the fall, I went to college. I ended up getting a masters degree in psychology. Now I counsel women down at the local shelter." She shrugged. "There's not much money in it, but it's what I want to do. What do you do? I mean, I know you work with Will and Mason, but I don't know exactly what your job is."

"Marco and I head up things in this area."

"Big boss, huh?"

He smiled. "We're more like middle management in the whole scheme of things. We're both on a little," he paused, "vacation from our duties right now. We have some personal issues to resolve."

"And Marco is your partner?"

Theo's face tightened a little. "Yes."

"Interesting! Yet, you don't seem to like him very much."

Their food arrived. Once they'd settled into eating their delicious meals—Miranda thought she'd have an orgasm right at the table, her salmon was so good—Theo shook his head. "It's not that I don't like him. I do like Marco very much. In fact, he's my best friend. It's just that we're currently having a small disagreement."

"Really? Over what? That is, if you don't mind me asking."

"No, I don't mind. We're having trouble agreeing on how to handle something very, very important to the both of us. Something very personal." He shrugged. "And I guess we're both feeling a little territorial."

Miranda took a sip of her wine. She could feel herself going into counselor mode. "Well, if you're both best friends, and this thing means so much to the both of you, you have to find a way to compromise. To share. You have to find some common ground and learn to respect each other's claim."

Theo lifted a brow. "Did you learn that in kindergarten?"

Miranda laughed. "It is kind of elementary."

Theo nodded. "And yet you're right. You're totally right." He reached across the table and took her hand again. His gaze turned serious and intense. "I like you very much, Miranda."

She squeezed his hand. "I like you too."

"What do you want out of life?"

She smiled. "There's a complicated question."

"If money were no object, what would your life look like?" He released her hand and began eating again.

She paused. "If all my dreams came true? I'd have stability, normality. I'd live in the country, in a big log cabin surrounded by trees and greenery. I'd be able to start my own women's shelter and man it with skilled, caring people." She shrugged and smiled. "I'd have a husky. I love huskies. Maybe some horses."

"Sounds nice."

"I think so. So, tell me a little about yourself. Where are you from?"

"Wales, originally. From a very small village."

"Really. Do you speak Welsh?"

He nodded. "I do. It's the language of my ancestors. It's important for me to be fluent in it, in all the languages of my ancestors. I'm fluent in the old language of the Tylwyth Teg as well."

Miranda suddenly became very interested in her wineglass. "It was a very long time ago that you left Wales, wasn't it?"

"Yes," he replied carefully. "Are you becoming frightened again, love?"

She glanced up at him. "No, of course not."

"Please don't lie to me."

She licked her lips. "Well, can you blame me?"

Theo set down his fork and leaned forward. She felt his warm hand cover hers and she shuddered with pleasure. "Trust me when I say I'm young for my kind, Miranda. I don't have gray hair and the last time I checked, I didn't need Viagra."

Miranda laughed in surprise, looked up and got lost in his warm gaze. God, she really felt the need to test out that statement. Her mirth died in the face of the smoldering look in his eyes.

She cleared her throat and glanced away. "So, you're a five-hundred-year-old fae who has dedicated his life to fighting goblins," she said lightly with a raised eyebrow. "Got any hobbies?"

Theo laughed and leaned back in his chair. "Actually, I do. I'm a hobbyist photographer."

"Really?"

"I started right when the technology was first developing. I was entranced by it. I still am."

She took a sip of her wine. "Why?"

Theo considered her for a moment, deep in thought. The way he looked at her made her stomach do curious flip-flops and warmed her blood. There was emotion in his gaze when he looked at her, deep emotion. She'd always noticed it because it had always been there, ever since the first time she'd met him. It was there every time he looked at her.

"When you live so long and have watched so many lives pass away before you, when you watch history change, governments reach their summits and then fall, you start to see the impermanence of things. You learn to live in the moment, to appreciate beauty, no matter how ordinary it is. Photographs let you capture that and hang on to it for a time. It's comforting."

She was lost in his gaze, totally enraptured. "I see," she replied softly.

"Take that couple to our right, for example," he said.

Miranda looked over to see an older, silver-haired gentleman and an older woman. Rings glittered on their hands and she assumed they were married.

"Look at their body posture. Both of them are leaning toward each other, immersed in the other's smile, words and eyes. How long have they been married, a day, forty years? We don't know any of that. All we know is that they're in love. This restaurant barely even seems to exist for them. All that exists is each other."

Suddenly the scene, which had seemed unremarkable before, seemed incredibly intimate—like she'd just caught the couple with their clothes off. Miranda looked away, back at Theo. He had seen splendor and truth in the most ordinary of things and he'd made her see it too. How remarkable.

Theo held her gaze for several heartbeats before speaking. "You see? *Beautiful.*"

Miranda understood he wasn't talking about just the scene he'd shown her.

"Want to get out of here?" he asked in a low voice that sounded like liquid velvet pouring over her skin.

Miranda barely found herself able to nod.

L ike in some movie, they fell through his front door kissing. She couldn't get enough of the taste of him, the feel of his hands on her. Fumbling, laughing, they undressed each other. No way were they going to make it to an actual bed.

Miranda caught only glimpses of Theo's living room as they made their way toward the couch. Noting the décor in the half-light wasn't her priority at the moment, but it was tasteful and rich looking. She noticed that much.

She finally got the last of Theo's shirt buttons undone and she almost purred as she ran her hands over the hard, warm and leanly muscled expanse of his chest. His fingers fumbled for her bra hook in the front.

"We really shouldn't be doing this," Theo whispered.

"I know," she answered breathlessly as he eased her down onto the couch. "This is crazy. I barely know you."

"There are so many things to consider," said Theo in between kisses. "There are . . . other people to think about. I'm doing this wrong, but, God, I can't stop myself." He finally got the front clasp of her bra undone and covered her nipple with his mouth.

Miranda arched with pleasure at the sensation of his lips around that so sensitive part of her body. He laved over it as he worked her red skirt down over her hips, then shifted and gave the other nipple the same treatment. Suddenly she lost the ability to form coherent thoughts.

They stopped talking.

Somehow they both managed to get most of their clothes off—the important articles, anyway. Miranda's fancy red top was unbuttoned and open, but not off. She was still wearing her heels. Theo's shirt was also unbuttoned and open, but not off.

None of that mattered now. Miranda's whole reality narrowed to the feel of his warm, hard-yet-soft body rubbing against her skin. She ran her hands over him, exploring the way the muscles of his back bunched as he moved, his lean hips and strong thighs.

God, she wanted to lick every inch of him, worship him.

Theo kissed his way down her stomach and eased her thighs apart. She sank her fingers into his long hair, pulling it from the tie at the nape of his neck. Slowly, softly, he ran the tip of his tongue over her inner thigh—right at the tender place where it met her sex. Miranda was already excited, and this just poured fuel on the fire. He tormented her a moment longer, then slid his tongue in to lick her clit. It was swollen and sensitive.

Miranda moaned long and low as Theo teased it with his tongue.

"Miranda, you taste every bit like I thought you would." Theo groaned deep in his throat. He braced her legs open with strong hands and fastened his mouth over her for a longer taste.

Miranda arched her back and hung for dear life as Theo licked her from perineum to clit with long strokes of his tongue. Dear God, he'd had a long time to learn the right way to go down on a woman, and he'd learned well. He spread her labia with his thumbs and laved the very heart of her, easing his tongue into her tight, aroused entrance.

"Theo," Miranda called in a breathless voice as he gently fucked her there, easing in and out of her the way she imagined his cock would. He moved up and pulled her swollen clit between his lips to massage it. His fingers replaced his tongue deep inside her, pushing her and pulling her straight toward a mind-blowing climax. She could feel herself wet between her thighs, drenching his pistoning fingers.

"Ride my fingers, love," came his deep voice from the darkness. He sounded incredibly aroused, his voice deep and thick. "I want to watch you."

She moved her hips, doing as he asked, sliding herself up and down on his fingers as he watched. Their breathing was the only sound in the room, along with the soft sound of her cunt not wanting to give up the penetration on every outward movement.

She'd never been so desperate for a man in her life. Never had she felt this aroused. She'd do anything to have him inside her. Common sense flickered, but was quickly squelched. It flickered again and she grabbed on to it with both hands. And, God, she wanted him *now.*

"Theo . . . condom," she managed to gasp. "Please."

He stopped and looked up at her. Shadows of the room played over his handsome face. "No need, love. Not with my kind."

She licked her lips and nodded. He crawled up her body, threaded his fingers through the hair at the nape of her neck and brought her mouth an inch from his. "I want you," he growled. "More than anything. Nothing can stop this now."

She couldn't even muster the words to agree with him.

He eased his lips over hers softly, teasing. Then he cupped her cheek and took her mouth, parting her lips and easing his tongue inside to glide and rub sensually against hers. She could taste the very faint flavor of herself on his tongue.

He eased his hands down to her hips and pulled her toward him, moving her so her ass was just on the very edge of the couch. It was the perfect height for him, where he knelt on the carpet in front of her.

The smooth head of his cock nudged the opening of her cunt. Miranda rolled her hips forward, wanting him inside her, wanting to be impaled. He entered her in a slow thrust, pushing the head just past her entrance.

She gasped as the width of him stretched her muscles.

"God, you're tight, love," Theo murmured against her lips. "How long has it been?"

His voice felt like silk on her skin, making her shiver. "A-a while. Why . . . is it bad?"

"Oh, no. It's not bad. You're sweet, hot and sweet." He groaned. "You're perfect, tight and excited. Fucking perfect."

Theo pushed in little by little, slowly letting her have an inch of him at a time. Miranda wanted to scream. He filled her so well, stretching her muscles and possessing her utterly. She rolled her hips, wanting all of him in her now, faster and harder, but Theo held on to her. He rocked back out, making sure she was lubricated enough—she was—and then slid in again. Finally he was seated within her to the base of his cock.

Theo stayed that way, completely sunk within her body and staring down at her in the half-light. Miranda thought she'd get lost in his eyes. He reached up and moved a tendril of hair away from her face in such a gesture of love and caring that it made tears prick her eyes. Theo kissed her forehead, then dropped down and kissed her possessively on the lips, taking her mouth with an aggressiveness that made Miranda cream anew, made her whimper in her throat.

Then he cupped her ass and started to move.

Miranda gasped and hit his shoulder with her fist. "Yes," she hissed. "God, that's what I wanted."

Theo groaned and started to thrust harder and faster. Miranda couldn't think, couldn't speak. The feel of his length and width inside her was almost beyond what she could handle.

"I'm coming," she whispered. Her climax skittered through her body, built and threatened to explode. She tipped her head back and moaned. "Oh, don't stop. Don't stop!"

"No way," Theo gritted out.

The climax came up from the very depths of her. It overwhelmed everything. She could feel the muscles of her cunt convulsing around Theo's pistoning length, milking him. The pleasurable waves filled her, took the very breath from her. She couldn't scream, couldn't moan, couldn't do anything but lose herself to it. Miranda had never had a more intense sexual experience in her life.

Theo groaned and threw his head back. She could feel his cock jerk a little inside her as he came. It was erotic, so incredibly erotic watching this man come inside her. She loved knowing she'd given him as much pleasure as he'd given her.

They stayed wrapped around each other, breathing heavily. Miranda could feel herself trembling, not just from the physical exertion but from the pleasure she'd experienced. Her body still hummed and pulsed from it.

Theo found her mouth and kissed her deeply as he stroked her body with his broad skillful hands, making her sigh and shiver. They wallowed in the aftermath of their shared climax, joined at mouth and sex. He still hadn't gone soft inside her and she could feel her muscles rippling around his length.

Without a word, he wrapped her in his arms and pulled her off the couch onto the very soft, plush living room rug. They lay, still half dressed and panting, in the afterglow.

Miranda couldn't remember the last time sex had been this good.

Theo turned over and pulled her against him, scattered kisses over her cheeks and throat. Sated and deeply content, she wrapped her arms around him, seeking his warmth. With care, he removed the rest of her clothing—her shirt, bra and her heels.

She sat up and pushed his shirt over his shoulders, then let her fingers trail down over his very, very lovely chest and wash-board abs. She'd always been a sucker for an accent and a nice chest. Theo had both.

"That was incredible," Theo murmured.

"It was."

He kissed her lingeringly and guided her hand to his cock. It was already getting hard again. "I want you again, love. Stay the night?"

She bit her lip. "Uh, well, I won't leave now, if that's what you're worried about." Staying the night . . . she wasn't sure she could do that. Miranda shivered a little, feeling the cool air touch her bare skin.

Theo took her hand from his chest, kissed her fingers and got to his feet. He pulled a blanket from the back of the couch and laid it over her. It was soft and Theo's scent clung to the material. Sighing, Miranda tucked herself up against the couch.

"Wait here a minute," he said.

Oh, she had a nice view as he walked away. She tipped her head to the side and admired.

He came back with two glasses of champagne and a large pillow. He slipped the pillow behind her back and he settled in beside her under the blanket. There were logs already in the wood-burning fireplace. He looked at them and they ignited.

"Uh, wow," Miranda said. In the face of that, intelligent con-versation failed her.

"One of the nice things about being with you is that I can be myself."

"So, you have . . . magick?"

"I'm a full-blooded Tylwyth Teg, Miranda. We have magick, though different fae have different skills. A lot of it has to do with genetics. Some skills can be learned, as well."

"Olivia said that Will is a part-blood and doesn't have magick. She says Mason isn't Tylwyth Teg at all. He's part shapeshifter . . . dragon breed. It all seems so unreal, and I can almost dismiss it as craziness, then I see one of those things, or you start a fire without even touching it." She paused and smiled a little. "Although I guess you started a fire in me long before you ever touched me."

"I did?"

"It was the way you looked at me." She shivered. "From day one you looked at me like you wanted me." She shook her head. "No, not even that. You looked at me like I was already yours."

Theo remained quiet for a long moment.

"Why do you think that might be?" she pressed.

Theo picked up his glass and took a long sip of champagne. He set the glass down and looked at her. "Because you *are* mine, Miranda. Mine in a very fundamental way. I think maybe I knew that on some level from the moment I first saw you."

Miranda swallowed hard and glanced away. Sometimes commitment felt like a noose tightening around her throat. Even though she knew that her mother's life was not her own, images from her past crowded her mind. Though she'd dealt with what had happened, ghosts still haunted her.

She gave a light laugh that came out sounding forced. "You seem pretty sure of yourself, there, buddy. I mean, the sex was pretty amazing, but—"

"There are things you don't know yet, Miranda."

"More things?" Miranda took a long drink of her champagne. She needed it. It was cold, sweet and a little tart.

"How much did Olivia tell you about her relationship with Will and Mason?"

Miranda took a moment to reflect. "She said they had a lot in common. She said that they shared a lot, the three of them, related to their abilities."

"That's it?"

"Yes. She's not the type to kiss and tell. She doesn't tell me the intimate stuff. That's private."

Theo laughed, and then swore softly under his breath in a

language she didn't understand. "Obviously, she intended for me to do that part," he muttered.

"What? What part?"

He turned and took the glass from her hand and set it on the floor. Miranda looked up at him in confusion. He stared into her eyes with that unsettling, yet lovely way he had. "Miranda, this is all going much faster than I ever intended. There are things I have to tell you and it's better I don't put them off."

"Uh, okay."

"When you first met me, what did you think?"

She smiled and glanced away. *Hot guy, two o'clock,* that's what she'd thought. Yet, there was more than just that superficial attraction. There always had been. "Well, beyond that I was attracted to you physically, I felt in some way that I'd met you before, or that we'd known each other for a very long time. I wanted to be with you, get to know you. But I don't mean just on some shallow level, I mean really grow close to you. I wanted to share things about myself with you that I normally never reveal." She shrugged. "My reaction was strange, but you asked for honesty back in the restaurant. I'm giving it."

"There's a reason you felt that way about me, Miranda. Now I'm asking for complete honesty again. How did you feel when you met Marco earlier this evening?"

Her brow furrowed. She couldn't figure out where all this was going. "Uh, truthfully?"

Theo nodded. "You can say anything. It won't hurt my feelings."

"Okay. At first glance, I thought he was one of the hottest men I'd ever seen, with maybe the exception of you. After that, I felt the same way about him as I felt about you the first time we met. I felt a yearning to know him better, a deep need. When he left us, I was . . . disappointed."

She bit her lip. Had she really said any of that out loud? Miranda watched Theo's face carefully for signs of anger.

Theo only smiled a little and nodded. "Yes. I'm not surprised you felt that way. Thank you for being honest."

"What do you mean?" she asked, irritated. He was hiding something. "Just be straight with me instead of dancing around whatever it is you have to say!"

"Okay." He drew a breath. "You deserve honesty. You're my mate. Not only are you my mate, you're Marco's mate as well."

Miranda fell silent, processing what he'd just said. Then she laughed. "You're joking. Mates? What are we . . . friends somewhere in Australia . . . or animals?"

"Not animals, we're Tylwyth Teg. Can I explain?"

Miranda was busy sucking down the rest of her champagne in big gulps. She waved her hand at him to continue, not really sure how many more revelations she could take. Her reality had already changed so much.

"The Tylwyth Teg and OtherKin who bind themselves to our cause work in groups of three. Initially, the Tylwyth Teg psychics find two individuals who are mystically bonded, for example, Will and Mason or me and Marco. The bonding goes past simple compatibility. It goes much deeper than that. It's an actual compatibility of the patterns of our spirits."

"So, you're like . . . lovers?"

Theo shook his head. "No, not myself and Marco or Will and Mason. Although it has been known to happen with same-sex pairs. Anyway, there is a third. Sometimes the third is found right away and sometimes it takes centuries. The psychics found Olivia for Will and Mason." He paused. "But I found you."

"So it's some kind of mystical dating service?"

Theo laughed. "No, not really."

"So let me get this straight, you found me for you and . . . for Marco?" she said uncertainly, fear tingeing her words.

"United as a triad, we will be stronger and more powerful. This is the way of our kind. Do you know all the meanings of the word triad? It means three people or things that are connected, but it also means three musical notes." He paused. "The three of us together would be harmony."

Miranda realized she was gripping the stem of her champagne glass so hard she might break it. She set it on the carpet beside her. "So what would Marco think of what just happened between us?"

Theo's mouth tightened as he looked away. "He's going to be angry with me, and he's going to be jealous."

Miranda sat for a moment, trying to get a handle on things. With everything that had happened to her in the last couple days, this was the icing on top of the cake of her suddenly changed world.

"So," she began. "This is what Olivia, Will and Mason have?"

"Yes."

"So, I'm meant to be with both you and Marco . . . both of you. Maybe even together? At the same time?"

"That depends on you."

"Will there be . . . love?"

"Usually," he said carefully, "in a pairing or threesome where there's sexual attraction, there is deep, deep love and incredible commitment."

It was too much, way too much for her to handle at that moment.

Not only was the world nothing like she'd grown up believing, she didn't know her place in it. That normality and stability she'd been trying so hard to achieve all her life was slipping through her fingers so fast she couldn't even grab the tail of it.

On top of all that—if that wasn't enough—not only had one man laid a claim to her, but *two*. Miranda shuddered. She wasn't ready to commit to one man, let alone . . .

Miranda pushed the blanket aside, rose and sought her clothes. "I've got to go."

Theo stood. Miranda tried not to look at him in all his naked grace. Even flaccid his cock was beautiful and the lines of his body beckoned to be explored.

Such a pity he was pushing her too hard.

Confusion and pain were clear in his eyes; she tried not to look at them while she dressed.

"Don't go, Miranda," he said.

"Have to."

"You don't have your car. Let me take you home." He stood.

"No!" She turned to him. "No. I'll get the doorman downstairs to call me a cab." Miranda grabbed her purse and, while still buttoning her shirt, walked toward the door.

"Miranda, please wait."

She shook her head. Miranda reached the door and turned to him before she opened it. "You're a great guy, Theo. I like you a lot." Her voice broke. "This is just too much for me right now. Give me some time?"

Theo stood staring at her. He didn't say a word.

She left him like that.

THREE

Theo walked into his dark apartment and set his keys down in the multi-colored ceramic bowl near his answering machine. He had no messages. It had been three days and he'd heard nothing from Miranda.

Damn.

The hair prickled along his arms and at the back of his neck, letting him know he wasn't alone. His head jerked up and his gaze centered on the dark form sitting in a chair in the living room.

"You fucking slept with her," came Marco's low, angry voice.

"Marco—"

Marco was out of the chair and on him before he could utter his next word. Theo slammed back against the phone table under Marco's weight.

Marco grabbed Theo's shirt and dragged him up against his chest. "You fucking slept with her, you bastard," Marco growled and slammed his fist into Theo's face. Blinding white-hot pain blossomed across his cheekbone and over his temple. He tasted coppery blood on his tongue.

Rage erupted in Theo. In a burst of strength, he pushed Marco back and snarled, *"Hie beaucahm!" Stop now!* There was no sense in fighting. They were evenly matched in most every way, magick-ally and physically. It would be a draw. There was no point. Anyway, he didn't want to fight his best friend.

Marco stilled at the use of the old language. He backed away warily, a violent expression on his face. "I can feel the residual emotion in here. I know you did."

Theo put a hand to his aching face. "Yes," he said calmly. "I slept with her. I'm sorry, but I don't regret it."

He watched Marco uneasily. He'd never seen his partner this way. Marco seemed to seethe with rage and frustration. "You need to back the fuck off for a while, my friend," he growled. "You are getting entirely too possessive."

Theo shook his head, gingerly touching his cheek where he was sure a bruise was already showing itself. "She's not ready for us, Marco. Not for either of us, certainly not both of us together."

"Fuck you!"

Theo looked up, half amused, half pissed off. "Excuse me?"

"You're just saying that so I'll ease off you and give you more time alone with her."

Theo sighed. "Look, Marco. I told her about the bonding and she fled my apartment like I'd just told her she was going to die of cancer or something."

"You told her *after* you slept with her."

"Focus, Marco! You're missing the point. Yes, I told her after I slept with her. My tale of OtherKin bonding scared her. The whole of it frightened her to bits, especially the part where I said she was bonded to both of us and likely love and commitment would follow."

"Fuck."

"Yeah." He sighed. "Fuck. She hasn't called me in three days."

Marco walked over and slumped down onto the couch. "So now what?"

Theo flicked the lights on with his mind, bathing his cream and blue living room in a soft glow. "Now, you go to see her. Maybe your charms will be more persuasive than mine were."

Marco shot him a dirty look.

"I'm serious, Marco. I'm backing off, giving you room to woo."
He waved his hand. "So, go . . . woo." The thought of Marco
with Miranda set his teeth on edge, made jealousy rise, but he
needed to tamp it down. They couldn't do this. He sighed and
touched his face. "That's what you want, right?"

"Yeah."

"Go see her tomorrow at work. She's got to be feeling the
bond a little. I know she's attracted to both of us. I don't think
she'll reject you."

Marco grinned arrogantly. "She won't reject me."

Theo smiled in spite of himself. "Well, if you're so sure, go
find out. Just don't push too hard, all right?"

Marco got up and started walking toward the door. He turned
before he left. "Sorry about punching you."

"Hey, believe me, sleeping with Miranda was worth it."

Rage passed over Marco's face briefly, then he turned and
left.

Theo sat for a while in this living room nursing his swelling
face and trying not to think about Marco's hands on Miranda,
her sighs, her moans all for him . . . and failing.

Miranda took her bag from the young kid at the end of
the checkout, mumbled thanks and walked toward the
exit. She walked with her head down, deep in thought.
She was on her break and had several more counseling appointments that afternoon. She didn't feel at her best, however, and
was considering taking the rest of the day off. Her clients de-
served more from her than she felt able to give today, but they
had no one but her. Really, she ought to try and stick it out.

A man stepped in front of her and she raised her head to go
around him. Her eyes widened and she dropped her bag. Cans of
soup and the sundries she'd purchased rolled out onto the floor.

Goblin.

The goblin stared at her in confusion for a moment before realization dawned. He smiled, revealing blackened teeth. "You can see me," he murmured. "The real me."

A clerk hurried over to help her gather her things. "I don't know what you're talking about. You just startled me. I'm sorry," she mumbled at the goblin as she knelt to aid the clerk. She really needed to learn how to quit dropping things whenever she saw a goblin. It was becoming a frequent occurrence these days.

"Riiiight," drawled the goblin.

Miranda paused in the process of gathering cans and stared at the floor as the goblin walked away, laughing softly under its breath.

"What a jerk," the clerk said as he handed her the refilled bag. "He made you drop your bag and then he laughed about it."

She gave the clerk a forced smile. "Yeah, what a jerk," she agreed in a shaky-sounding voice. She took the bag and made a hasty retreat back across the street to the center.

Valerie, the volunteer manning the front counter, buzzed her through the security door. It opened into a large common room with sofas and a television set. In the back of the building there were rooms where the women and their children stayed, a playroom and a cafeteria. Miranda walked toward the offices off the common room. She had time for a quick bite before her next appointment.

She'd just finished washing down her last bit of sandwich with some springwater when she heard a timid knock on her door. Miranda glanced at her watch and frowned. It wasn't time for her next appointment yet. "Come in," she called.

Sarah, one of the women taking refuge at the center, stepped inside. "Hi, Miss Davis."

"Hi, Sarah. What's up?"

Sarah twisted her hands in front of her. "Do you have a minute to talk?"

"Sure. Sit down."

Sarah sat down on the edge of the worn green sofa opposite

Miranda's desk. The woman always looked uneasy, like a wild animal about to bolt. "He's been hanging around, Miss Davis," she said in a quavering voice. Her brown eyes were wide and her hands were white and shaking in her lap. "Hanging around the center, on the street."

Miranda didn't have to ask whom she spoke of. "Okay. How many times have you seen him?" Restraining orders frequently meant little to abusive husbands.

"Yesterday morning. I didn't go to work because I was afraid he was out there . . . watching for me. Then I saw him again today." She inhaled noisily. "He's out there now," she finished with a rush of exhaled air.

"It's okay, Sarah. You're safe here." She reached for the phone. "I'll call Craig. He'll come down and take care of it." Craig was one of the policemen who regularly kept an eye on the center. The police couldn't be here twenty-four seven, but the station was just down the street. They'd have a cop here in no time.

She'd no sooner dialed the number when she heard a crash come from the receiving area.

"*Sarah!*" a man yelled.

Sarah stiffened. "Oh, God. It's Brian."

The intercom on her desk came on. "Miranda," came Valerie's voice. "We've got a problem."

"I'm calling the police now," she answered.

Quickly, Miranda told the policeman they needed someone *right now* and hung up the phone. She turned to Sarah. "You stay here, all right?"

Sarah nodded.

Miranda turned and went quickly for the receiving area. Her pulse raced furiously. This didn't happen often, but when it did . . .

She opened the security door to find Valerie standing at the counter looking supremely pissed off. Miranda sucked in a breath when she caught sight of the man.

Brian was the goblin from the grocery store.

She mastered her reaction as best she could at that terrible surprise. In his fist, Brian held some flowers. He'd probably been at the grocery store to buy them. Behind him Miranda could see he'd tipped over a stand of brochures and education leaflets. That had been the crash she'd heard.

"You?" the goblin said. "You're the damn counselor who's been telling my Sarah not to come home to me?" He took a menacing step toward her.

Crap. All she had to do was hang on until the policemen got here. It wouldn't be long.

"Sarah is making her own choices now," Miranda replied steadily, feeling a rush of anger and fear surge through her body. "You need to leave. *Now.*" The trick was not to engage him in conversation, just persuade him to leave. Firmly.

"No, I'm not leaving until I see Sarah. She needs me. *I love her.*"

Miranda remembered how Sarah had come to them, bruised, with hospital dressings. She'd had quite a history at the local emergency room—lots of accidental falls and mysterious injurious mishaps. Sarah had been afraid Brian would eventually kill her, so she'd come to the center. She expressed fear of Brian, but absolutely no inclination of returning to him. Brian had beaten all the love out of that relationship.

Sarah wanted a new life, a new fear-free life, just like Miranda's mother had wanted but had never achieved. Miranda would do all she could to ensure that Sarah got that.

Brian took another step toward her and Miranda said a little prayer that the cops would show soon. She'd taken self-defense classes, but she didn't want to have to use what she'd learned . . . especially not on a goblin. How strong were they anyway? She had a feeling much stronger than a human.

"Bitch, stop looking at the door and start looking at me!" he growled.

Brian bum-rushed her and Miranda dodged to the side, avoiding him. He came at her again, grabbing her around her middle and pressing her up against his chest.

Everything Miranda had learned came rushing to the fore. She brought her elbow back sharp and hard into his ribs. Brian grunted and released her. She turned and punched him in the Adam's apple before he could react. He gagged and backed away, hand to his throat.

She stood back, breathing hard and shaking. Nice to see the techniques worked on goblins. Her hand hurt like hell, though.

Movement flickered out of the corner of her eye and she saw a man dressed in a long black coat rush into the room. At first she thought it was a cop—but cops didn't dress in long black coats and leather boots. Then she recognized Marco.

Marco grabbed Brian faster than she could blink and strong-armed the goblin out the door. She heard a couple grunts that were quickly drown out by wailing sirens. Miranda glanced at Valerie, who was white and shaking, and then went for the door. By the time Miranda got outside, the police were there, breaking up the fight.

The cops had both men in custody. Brian was fighting two policemen, but Marco wasn't resisting Craig, who held him by the upper arm.

"Wait," Miranda called to Craig as she ran to them. "Let him go. He was just helping me out."

Craig released Marco. "What happened, Miranda?"

"That man, his name is Brian Walker. He was attempting to contact his wife, who is staying with us. He was abusive and belligerent and grabbed me with an intent to harm."

"You want to press charges?"

She glanced at Brain, who was giving her one hell of an evil eye. "Oh, yeah." She answered him. "I do." There was no doubt about that.

Craig rocked back on his heels. "All right. We'll arrest scumbag over there. Come on down to the station as soon as you can."

Miranda nodded shakily and watched Craig walk over to cuff Brian and read him his rights. Brian kept his threatening stare centered on her the whole time.

She felt Marco's warm hand close over her arm. "Come on. I don't like the way he's looking at you." His touch sent shivers through her body and broke the stunned trance she'd slipped into.

Miranda looked up at him. "Thank you." She sucked in a breath as she saw the bleeding cut above his eye.

"You don't need to thank me. I'm just glad the police got there when they did. I had a powerful need to kill that goblin for laying his hands on you."

He led her toward the entrance of the center. Brian started yelling obscenities at them. "You don't even know what you are, bitch!" he yelled.

Miranda shivered and Marco ushered her through the door quickly.

"You saw what he was?" she asked as they entered the center. Valerie was busy picking up all the scattered brochures. Miranda shut up so they didn't say anything to freak Valerie out.

"Yeah," he said, glancing at Valerie and cutting off the rest of his sentence. "Bastard."

Miranda's jaw locked when she glimpsed the crushed bouquet of flowers on the floor. She picked them up and tossed them in the trash can near the counter.

Miranda turned. "Valerie, this is a friend of mine, Marco Collins."

Valerie gave him a once-over and raised a brow. "Nice to meet you, Marco, and hey, thanks for your help."

"Not a problem," he responded. He smiled and it sent butterflies through Miranda's stomach. His smile revealed straight white teeth and made his eyes sparkle. "I have to say it was a pleasure, really."

"I need to go down and press charges against him at the station," Miranda said to Valerie.

"I'll come with you," answered Marco.

She turned to him and looked at his forehead. "You need to have that looked at. It looks like it needs stitches."

"I'm coming with you."

"You need to go to the emergency room. That needs—"

"Miranda. I'm coming with you to the police station." His tone of voice persuaded her not to argue.

Miranda snapped her mouth closed.

Valerie nudged her. "Let the pretty man go with you," she muttered. "What's wrong with you?"

Miranda pressed her lips into a thin line. "Give me a few minutes to go talk with Sarah and cancel my afternoon appointments. Wait here?" she asked Marco.

"Of course."

Miranda was sure Valerie would be eating out of Marco's hand by the time she returned.

After they'd finished at the police station, Miranda hustled Marco off to the emergency room. He sat on a silver table while a doctor stitched up the deep split above his eye. Miranda stood near him.

"I wish we could have met for the second time under different circumstances," said Marco, while the doctor finished up.

"I don't know. I'm pretty glad you showed up when you did."

"You looked like you could handle yourself."

She smiled. "I've never actually had to defend myself before. I hope it's not the start of a trend."

"Me too," he answered. He hesitated, and then added, "Keep me and Theo around and we'll make sure it won't be."

The doctor finished, and gave him some parting instructions. As she did so, Miranda considered him. Physically, he was a little shorter than Theo and a bit more on the muscular side. Theo was leanly muscular, whereas Marco was broader of shoulder and a bit more ripped. Marco's hair was short and dark, about collar-length. His eyes were almond shaped and a lovely, clear blue. Marco's deep, sexy-rough voice was accent-free. He sounded one-hundred-percent American.

He was different from Theo in more than just physical ways. She didn't know either of them well, but she had enough information so far to make that determination. Theo was all cool, controlled power, where Marco seemed to run hotter and faster. Marco reminded her more of a badass James Dean type. Perhaps Marco was a bit more reckless, though it had been Theo, apparently, who'd preempted Marco where she was concerned.

The doctor gathered her things and Marco slid off the counter and came to stand in front of her. "I'd like to talk," he said.

She didn't answer. She just reached up and drew her finger over the thin white scar that marked the skin under his left eye. He closed his eyes at her touch and that now-familiar tingle ran up her arm. "You'll have another scar from today to match this one."

"It will be worth it."

"Worth it? Why?" she asked.

"Since I got it defending you."

Suddenly, she was speechless.

"Theo said he told you about everything. Says you're scared of it." He grabbed her hands and kissed her fingers one by one, while he stared into her eyes.

Miranda shivered. Her body responded to him so fast her knees went weak. She cleared her throat and backed up a pace, needing to put some distance between them. "I have the rest of the afternoon off, and I'm willing to talk." She owed him that much, considering their spirits were compatible or whatever.

"Okay. Where do you want to go?"

She paused. "Don't think this is some kind of come-on, but I'd like to just go to my apartment. I don't want to be around people today." She lowered her voice. "I don't want to risk seeing any more of those things. I've had enough of them for a while."

He nodded. "Let's go settle my bill and get out of here." He started past her.

She held up her hand to stop him in his tracks. "Really. It's not a come-on. Understand?"

"I'll be a perfect gentleman."

She watched the feral way he walked away and wondered if he knew the meaning of the word *gentleman*.

They'd taken Miranda's car to the hospital and then to her apartment. Marco said he'd catch a cab back to his SUV. Soon Miranda was sliding her key into the lock on her apartment door and suddenly the whole process seemed a lot more sexual than she'd ever noticed before. She cleared her throat nervously and opened the door.

Once inside, she threw her purse on the kitchen counter. "Want something to drink? A soda or a beer?"

"Sure. A beer would be great." He wandered into the living room, inspecting her comfy, homey décor. She liked the colors surrounding her to be soothing and her furniture comfortable rather than trendy or classy. She followed after him and watched him sling his long black coat over a chair and sit down on her overstuffed blue couch.

She got two imported beers from her fridge, popped the tops and walked into the living room.

Damn. Why did he look so good there? Why did the sight of him, the scent of him, in her living area please her so much? It really was like she'd known him forever. Like he and Theo were long-lost lovers, men she'd had passionate affairs with sometime in the distant past and a part of her was just thrilled they were back.

It was—like everything else that had happened in the last week and a half—bizarre.

"What's wrong?" he asked her.

She blinked, realizing she'd been staring. "Nothing." Miranda handed him his beer and sat down in a nearby chair. She took a sip from her own bottle and considered him. "Why is that goblin married to a human woman?"

Marco smiled ruefully. "The goblins find humans . . . amusing. They want to exterminate the Tylwyth Teg, but they just play with humans. It's not uncommon to find them intermarrying." He shrugged. "They live among humans, act human for the most part. Not all of them are bad, but the race in general is naturally violent and aggressive. Watch TV much?"

"Almost never."

"Turn it on sometime. You'll be shocked to discover how many goblins hold key places in government and business."

Miranda shivered. Goblins moving themselves into positions of power, like chess pieces. "And if the goblins decide they want to do more than just *play* with humanity?"

Marco smiled. "Well, that's partly why we're here. We hold lots of those positions too. But we have no natural tendencies toward violence, and no agenda regarding the human race. We just want to be left alone, left to live our lives."

"This is all so . . ."

"Mind-blowing?"

She exhaled sharply. "Yes." She paused. "So, Theo told me some interesting things," she said as an opening. "Strange things like you, me and Theo are bonded together in some mystical way."

"Theo told me some things too. He said you weren't sure about the whole thing." His voice was tight, but luckily he knew better than to mention her sleeping with Theo. That was wise of him. Passing judgment on her for sleeping with Theo before she'd known about the bond she apparently shared with Marco would have really made her mad.

"Can you blame me?" she answered with a smile that she knew didn't reach her eyes. "Two weeks ago I was dating whomever I wanted. I was free. Now it turns out I have a spirit-level bond with not only one but two men . . . two men who aren't even *men*, not even human." She sighed. "It'll take me a little time to become accustomed to the idea."

Marco considered her for a moment. He licked his lips and rubbed his palm over his stubbled chin. "Theo told me you have a friend in a similar relationship."

"Yes."

"Is she happy?"

Miranda didn't say anything for a moment, then she stood

and walked toward the kitchen. "Olivia is the happiest I've ever seen her. She's in love with Will and Mason, and they love her." She shrugged, staring past the small bar with stools that divided the kitchen and living room. "It's beautiful. Not traditional at all, but still beautiful. It works for them."

She felt Marco come up to stand behind her. He put his hand on her shoulder and she closed her eyes. It felt good when he touched her, just like when Theo touched her. It felt *right*.

"Then what is it?" he asked. "Do you have a problem with the idea of being with two men at the same time sexually?"

She'd joked about it with Olivia, had said Olivia was lucky. That had been forever ago. So much had happened since then.

She shook her head. "A little. I mean, it's a little intimidating. But, it's not totally that." It wasn't really that she was frightened of being with two men at the same time. Physically, the idea was very intriguing, exciting. The rest of it was simply perplexing. The relationship would be double the work, really, double the commitment. She'd be tying her life to not only one man, but two.

She squeezed her eyes shut, remembering her mother. Her mother had adored her father at first, had met him and fallen deeply in love. She'd thought it would last forever, that nothing would ever part them. Her mother had never dreamed her marriage would end up the way it had.

Yet, not long into their relationship, her father had become very controlling and suspicious. By the time that Miranda had been born, her father had started hitting her mother for imagined affairs and slight infractions—for burning his toast, not ironing his shirt correctly.

Life had been so hard back then. Her mother would leave and drag Miranda with her, only to have her husband sweet-talk her into coming back home. Eventually, he eroded so much of her mother's sense of self-worth, had so effectively brainwashed her, that her mother had begun thinking she couldn't leave him. That she had no options at all and that she was dependant on him for everything.

Growing up, Miranda had walked on eggshells in her house. Her father had never turned his wrath on her directly, but things she did sometimes inadvertently got her mother in trouble. Her home had never been a home; it had been a war zone. Life had become a series of strategies meant to keep her and her mother safe from his anger. It had been no way to live, definitely no way for a girl to come of age. Miranda had grown up hard and fast, feeling as if she mothered her mother instead of the other way around.

Then, when she'd been seventeen, her father had almost killed her mother. That had been when she'd finally convinced her mother to give fleeing one last try. They left the house in the middle of the night, bringing nothing with them but a large sum of cash. They'd traveled across the country, leaving no paper trail, and settled in a new city, started a new life. Her mother had been happy for a while.

But none of it had mattered in the end.

Because the man her mother had loved with all her heart when she'd been young—her supposed soul mate—had tracked her down somehow and murdered her.

Marco exhaled, jerking her from her thoughts. "Just give me a chance. Please. The thought of not being with you is like being denied air to breathe. I know it's frightening, but I care about you, Miranda. Theo cares about you. We would never do anything to hurt you, so if you say leave you alone, we will." He paused. "But please don't ask us to do that," he finished in a heartfelt whisper.

She turned to face him. Miranda was a counselor. She knew better than to nurse such fears about Marco and Theo. For every man like her father, there were lots of good, loving men. Marco and Theo were good and loving. She felt that in her heart.

Your mother felt the same about your father once upon a time.

Miranda closed her eyes for a moment. God, all she'd wanted was stability.

She sighed. "Marco, this is all so . . . so not normal," she said apologetically.

Marco drew her close and kissed her. It was a sweet kiss,

one she wouldn't have expected from a man like him. This was tender, like he was being careful with her . . . or perhaps savoring her. His lips brushed hers softly, and she could feel his hot breath against her mouth.

She grabbed his shoulders as he pressed his mouth down on hers. She parted her lips willingly for him and moaned when his tongue sought and found her tongue. He tasted her, savored her, nipping at her lower lip and made easy love to her mouth. The way the man kissed made her knees turn to butter.

Marco slowly ended the kiss and rested his forehead against hers. He was breathing heavy and so was she. "Sometimes not normal is very, very good, Miranda." He sighed, pulled away from her, took his coat from the back of the couch and walked toward the door.

She hesitated a moment and then walked toward him. "Wait. Please, stay."

He turned toward her with questions in his eyes.

"I want to get to know you better," she explained. "Stay for dinner."

He only stood there. "Are you sure?"

"Please?"

"All right." He put his coat back down.

M arco couldn't even taste the chicken he'd just put in his mouth. Every fiber of his body seemed overwhelmed by the woman sitting next to him. She didn't realize the danger she was in, how bad his control was slipping. He wanted her. Hell, he *needed* her like he needed water or food.

The thought that it had been Theo who'd first touched her breasts, licked her skin and found refuge in her soft body made him tremble with anger. He wanted nothing more than to make love to this woman, hear her sigh in his ear, feel her shatter in the sweet, powerful orgasm he'd unleashed upon her.

It had been so hard to separate himself from her, pick up his coat and move toward the door. Touching her was like heaven. Separation was hell. But Marco needed to be sure that Miranda wanted his company. He'd rather reside in hell than push her too hard.

He knew Miranda needed him too. She needed both him and Theo, but she hadn't been waiting as long, and her need wasn't as pronounced as his. She probably wasn't holding on to the very last shred of her control like he was. Marco could only think of how Theo had touched her, kissed her, and had the ecstasy of sliding his cock inside her and joining with her completely.

Marco shuddered. God, he was jealous.

He reached down and rubbed his hard cock under the table with one hand and gripped his fork with the other. He felt guilty about that since she was telling him about her childhood, spilling her secrets into his lap. Intimate things, things that made him want to take her into his arms and kiss away the hurt of her past. Things that made him want to hold on to her and step with her into the future, create a snug and protective cocoon around her. Marco knew already that Theo wanted the same thing for her.

Her eyes glistened with tears and Marco couldn't take it anymore. He put his fork down, pushed away from the table and took her hand. She came willingly with him to the couch and tucked herself against him.

"God, I feel like I've known you forever," she said as she nestled her head against his chest. A whiff of her tantalizing perfume wafted up and teased him. He closed his eyes and stifled a groan.

Hell. He was in hell.

"It's our bond, the link we share. I feel the same about you." *And so much more.*

She sighed and his mind instantly made it sexual. He heard her sighing while she lay beneath him on the bed, as he slid his cock into her eager, little aroused slit. Marco shook his head, trying to clear the image. All he wanted was to press her down onto the couch, peel off her clothes and bury himself inside her.

Yeah, this was like ice-skating through hell. All his resolve to be a gentleman was melting fast.

"What about you?" she murmured. "I feel like I know you, but I don't."

It took a moment for her question to register. His mind was clouded by the scent of her hair and skin, and the feel of her body cupped so intimately against his. "Me?"

She laughed softly. "Yes."

"Uh . . . well, I came from Italy, but that was so long ago I barely remember it. I came to America when I was young, only a hundred and two. That was the year," he searched his memory, "1806. I was Gaelan from birth. I assumed my father's role. I never went through what you're going through because it was a matter of course that I would grow up and become what I am."

"You say all that so matter-of-factly. But you can't know how weird it sounds to me."

He shrugged. "Reality has many different layers."

She looked up at him and raised a brow. "And women?"

"I've had my fair share."

"Any serious relationships?"

"One, a long time ago. She was another Tylwyth Teg, and a Gaelan to boot. But they found their third and she lost interest in me. There was another, too. A human. I lost her to sickness."

She sat up and cupped his cheek against her palm. "Poor baby."

He grabbed her fingers and kissed them. "Trust me, neither of them could hold a candle to you," he replied sincerely, his voice husky and deep sounding to his own ears. He licked the pad of one of her fingers and heard her breath hitch. Encouraged, he slid her finger between his lips and laved his tongue over it. He sucked it to the second knuckle, then to the base.

Miranda's eyes grew dark as her pupils dilated. Her jaw went a little slack as she watched him take each one of her fingers in turn and slide them into the recesses of his mouth while he held her gaze steadily, putting everything he felt for her and everything he wanted to do to her into his eyes.

Miranda licked her lips, taking her hand from his mouth. She leaned forward and pressed her mouth to his. It was like a firing gun going off in Marco's body. He twined his arms around her, his hand sliding under her hair to the nape of her neck. Marco slanted his mouth over hers with a hungry, feral growl.

She whimpered somewhere low in her throat and parted her lips for him. She tasted hot and sweet against his tongue. He wanted her clothes off, wanted her bare flesh under his hands and rubbing against him. He wanted her legs parted, his cock pistoning deep inside her and her little moans and sighs echoing in his ears.

At the moment, that was all he could think about.

"Miranda," he murmured against her lips. "I want you. I need . . . *more* of you." He slanted his mouth across hers again and she aggressively speared her tongue into his mouth with a little sexy-sounding moan.

Marco slid a hand under the hem of her shirt in the back and slid it up her smooth, soft skin to the clasp on her bra. He had it undone with one move of his fingers and her breasts fell free of the cups. Drawing his hand to the front of her, he held one in his hand and brushed the nipple back and forth until it hardened like a little pebble.

Miranda gasped into his open mouth and pulled away from him. She stood and took a couple staggering steps away from him, like she couldn't see straight.

"Miranda?" he asked, rising. "Are you all right?"

M iranda stood on legs that could barely hold her. She felt wet and achy between her thighs and her whole body hummed with awareness of Marco. "I'm . . . fine," she answered, still making her way toward the hallway. She really didn't have any idea where she thought she was headed.

Three days ago she'd had the best sex of her life on a first date with a man she barely knew. Now here she was, right on the brink of sleeping with another man. A week ago her life had been mundane, normal.

Nice.

Uncomplicated.

It had taken her years to achieve that.

Miranda closed her eyes and reached out, feeling the wall in front of her. And yet, all she wanted right now was Marco. God, she wanted Theo too. She wanted them both at once, kissing her, petting her . . . fucking her.

What's more, she wanted their love.

She squeezed her eyes shut even tighter. Already, even now, she could feel complex emotions for both these men. It was a deep regard, an intimate caring.

It was the leading edge of love, and if she didn't watch herself she'd tip right over the side. She had to remind herself again why that could be a bad thing.

"I barely know you," she gritted out when she felt Marco's body heat at her back.

"That's not true and you know it."

She did know it. On some very deep level, she'd always known Theo and Marco. Miranda licked her lips and swallowed hard. "You know what I mean." Her voice shook.

He put a hand on each of hers, bracketing her face-first against the wall. His breath felt hot on her shoulder. He brushed her hair away and kissed the sensitive place just under her ear-lobe. "We have time to get to know each other, Miranda. You can't deny the instinctive feeling you have for me, can you?"

"No," she breathed. It was so foreign, so frightening. "You're very . . . *compelling* to me."

He chuckled softly—a sexy-rough rasping sound that made her shiver—and kissed her again. "Compelling? Well, that's a good start."

"You could be . . . more than just compelling," she admitted with a sigh. She was losing this battle. Pretty soon she'd be naked and moaning in this man's arms.

His breathing sounded harsh and sweet against her ear. Marco let his hands roam over her waist, and then higher, smoothing up past the bottom hem of her shirt to cup her bared breasts. The feel of his large, warm hands on her, and what she suspected they could do to her, made her breath catch in her throat.

"Do you want me, Miranda? Do you want me to ease your skirt off and take you up against this wall? Because I want to do that," he rasped. "In fact, it's nearly all I can think about right now." He rolled her nipples between his fingers and Miranda felt her cunt grow even warmer. A trickle of cream slid slowly down her inner thigh.

"Yes," she said shakily. "God help me, that's exactly what I want."

"I want to fuck you, Miranda. Long and hard, until we both come. I want to make love to you, slow and easy, and draw pleasure from your body over and over."

Her pussy responded to his words as though he'd been arousing her with his hand. Her clit grew swollen and sensitive. "Yes," she hissed. "God, yes."

He reached down and gathered her skirt in a hand, drawing it upward toward her waist. The slow drag of the material over her flesh made her shiver.

His fingertips grazed her stomach, dipped lower to brush over her mound through her undergarment. He groaned low in his throat. "I can't wait to touch you." Marco slipped his hand down the front of her panties. He rubbed over her clit and slid his middle finger into her heat.

Miranda grasped the edge of the window with one hand and splayed the other out flat against the wall. A hard, fast breath hissed out between her lips as Marco gently fucked her. He thrust his finger in and out of her very slowly, over and over and over. He drew her moisture out as she soaked his hand in her desire. Her pussy was sensitive, hot and slippery with her cream.

He pushed her panties down to her knees and eased a finger of his other hand over her anus, awakening all the little nerves there, then carefully pressed into her. Miranda gasped, then groaned. She wanted to tell him to stop . . . she really *should* tell him to stop, but the invasion was like nothing she'd ever felt before. Soon he was fucking her in both places, in a delicious rhythmic penetration that wiped all thought from her mind and brought her close to a climax.

"W-what are you doing to me?" she gasped.

"Ah, baby," Marco whispered as he fucked her slow and easy in both places at the same time. "Is this your first time?"

"Y-yes," she whispered.

He kept up the easy double penetration, pressing her body against the wall with every inward thrust. He groaned when her cunt muscles rippled around his fingers. She was teetering on the razor's edge of a powerful climax. "You've been neglected in your sex life, but you have a lot to look forward to. Do you like what I'm doing to you right now?"

"Yes," she gasped. She couldn't help but bend her head down a little, offering her rear to him. The feeling of having both her cunt and her anus stimulated at the same time was incredible. The sensations seemed to blend together until she couldn't separate them. She could feel how wet she was and for the life of her—as much as she should've been shocked—nothing in the world could have forced her to tell Marco to stop.

"Is it going to make you come?"

"God, yes," she panted. "Don't stop. Please don't stop."

"Oh, honey, I won't. I love to see you like this, with your skirt up around your waist and your panties down around your ankles, up against the wall and moaning for me. I hope to see you like this very often in the future."

Those words sent her spiraling right off the edge. He kept up the slow, easy glide of his fingers in and out of her body as she came hard. She felt herself soak his hand as she cried out.

Her muscles pulsed around his fingers, still pistoning in her cunt.

"Turn around," he said roughly.

She turned.

"Damn, that was the prettiest thing I ever saw," he growled. He kissed her hard while the very tail end of her climax still rippled through her body. At the same time, he lifted her and kicked her panties away, leaving her clad from the waist down in only her shoes and her skirt up around her waist.

Her hands went to the waistband of his pants. She fumbled, trying to undo them and finally freed his cock. It was rigid and ready, wide and long. Just the feel of it in her hand made her even wetter between the thighs.

She hooked one leg around his waist as he guided his cock into her and pushed in. "Marco, yes," she moaned in relief at the feel of him filling and stretching her to the maximum limit. It was like she'd been missing a part of herself she'd forgotten about. It had been that way with Theo too.

Marco closed his eyes, splayed a hand flat against the wall beside her head and exhaled sharply. "God, you feel good."

He opened his eyes and kept his gaze locked with hers as he started to thrust up into her. Her hands sought and found fist-fuls of his shirt and she moved her hips downward, matching his thrusts and trying to get him ever deeper within her body.

Marco kept the pace slow, so slow and easy that it sent little shivers of pleasure through her. Her back was up against the wall and every thrust pushed her against it, though it didn't hurt.

Of course, she wasn't feeling any pain.

She closed her eyes, breaking their gaze. Her body moved with his, meeting each thrust. It was like a dance they'd danced a million times. His cock fit her perfectly. The head rubbed her sensitive place way deep inside her with every inward thrust and his body rubbed her clit just perfectly.

"Marco," she whispered, staring into his eyes. "I'm coming again." She closed her eyes and felt her muscles clench and release around his length and her cream make the slide of him into her body even easier. She bit her lower lip as the waves of it crashed over her.

When the last spasm had racked her, Marco cupped her bottom in his hands and quickened the pace. He pushed up and in, thrusting faster and harder into the depths of her. At the same time, he let one hand, the same one he'd used before, stray back and play with her anus. This time she didn't jerk in surprise.

"You like it when I touch you here?" he growled into her ear.

"Yes," she moaned. She ought to have been shocked and appalled, but instead she found it very pleasurable.

He slipped a finger into the small, tight opening and thrust it in and out. Miranda's hips bucked forward as another climax flirted hard with her body. She dug her fingers into his upper arms for support.

"One of us will take you here, lovely Miranda," he murmured. "While the other fucks this sweet, tight little cunt of yours."

"Uhn," was all she could say in response. She was lost in a haze of pleasure.

He leaned down and caught her earlobe between his teeth, gently pulling at it. She relaxed. "I think you'd like two men at once. I can just imagine how excited you'd be. Tell me. Would you like that?"

"Y-yes, maybe," she breathed.

He added one more finger to the first and thrust gently in and out. It was just a little . . . *just enough.*

Miranda screamed as her climax hit her full force, this one stronger than the other two. This time her orgasm forced his. Marco thrust deeply within her and she felt his cock jump. He groaned low near her ear as he shot his come into her.

"Ah, hell," he gasped. "You feel so good."

He held on to her tightly after both their climaxes had abated, each of them breathing heavy. Finally, Marco pulled out of her and hugged her to him, kissing over her forehead, face and mouth and tangling his hand through her hair.

"Stay with me tonight," she murmured into the curve of his

throat. The words were out of her mouth before she'd even thought to say them.

Marco stilled against her. He tipped her face to his. "Really?"

She licked her lips and glanced away, hardly believing she'd asked him. "I want to sleep beside you tonight and wake up next to you in the morning."

"Theo will be jealous," he said with a note of amusement in his voice.

She smiled, trying hard to ignore the feeling that she actually wanted to be sleeping between the two men.

They took a shower together, each soaping the other's body until they were ready for each other again. They collapsed onto the bed, their hair and skin still damp, kissing and exploring each other with eager, busy hands and mouths.

Miranda couldn't believe how beautiful Marco was. He was muscular, but not *too* muscular. His chest was lovely and powerful, but not *too* ripped, like a weight lifter's. His waist tapered narrowly and his ass was the cutest thing she'd ever seen. She couldn't seem to keep her hands off it.

She licked and kissed the excess water off his shoulder as he rolled her beneath him and parted her thighs with his knee. He made her feel drugged with desire, like the whole world could blow up around them and she wouldn't even care. Miranda felt completely immersed in him and she loved it.

Beyond her window came the first pattering of rain and a clap of thunder. It made what she now shared with Marco seem even more cozy and intimate.

She let him settle into the cradle of her pelvis, his cock resting against the entrance of her cunt. They stayed that way for several heartbeats, Marco staring down at her with something like amazement in his eyes. His damp hair shadowed his face, swept across his brow. Outside the rain increased along with the lightning and thunder. It felt comfortable, nice to be in Marco's arms while outside a thunderstorm raged.

Marco took her wrists and pinned them to the mattress above

her head, forcing her body to arch into his. Comfortable and nice suddenly became passionate and urgent as she felt her body respond to his sexual dominance. Her breathing hitched and her cunt grew hotter and wetter. He held her that way for a moment, staring into her face, then kissed her. His tongue slid past her lips and he took her mouth possessively while he shifted his hips a little and slid the head of his cock inside her. Miranda gasped, feeling the length and width of it stretching the muscles of her sex as he tunneled farther and deeper.

He kept her wrists pinned to the bed and his tongue in her mouth as he took her hard and deep and steady. It didn't take long for her to come. The muscles of her pussy pulsed around his cock as she orgasmed. Marco caught all her cries and moans on his tongue.

Finally he also came, shooting deep into the heart of her.

As they curled up together under the blankets and sheets of Miranda's bed, the storm still rattled the windows of her bedroom. She snuggled into Marco's arms, laid her head against his chest and fell into one of the best sleeps she'd ever had in her life.

M iranda woke to the scent of coffee brewing. Rubbing her eyes, she threw back the covers and found herself nude. Shivering, she grabbed her bathrobe and headed to the kitchen, where Marco stood in all his shirtless glory. He wore only his jeans, nothing else, and Miranda had to take a moment to admire the view.

He turned toward her and smiled. "Morning."

"Morning."

He walked to her and dragged her up against his chest for a kiss. Apparently he didn't care very much about morning breath. His stubble scraped her cheek, but she hardly cared. "God, you look gorgeous in the morning," he murmured against her lips before releasing her.

She touched her pillow-styled hair and smiled. "Liar."

"I'm not lying." His eyes darkened. "If I didn't think you were sore, I'd want you again right now."

She felt a sexual flush envelop her hard and fast. Arousal filled her up so quickly it took her breath away. "I won't say I'm not a little sore, but it's a good kind of sore." She bit her bottom lip before smiling and dropping her voice suggestively lower. "If you want me again I think I could—"

His mouth closed over hers, stealing the rest of her sentence along with her breath. Marco walked her back a few steps, until the kitchen counter was behind her. She felt light-headed—almost faint—from wanting him again. He was some kind of drug she'd had a taste of and now couldn't get enough of.

Marco ripped her bathrobe open and slid his hand within to find her bare waist. She lifted her leg, sliding it up over his hip. The rasp of his jeans against her bare cunt made her shiver and sigh. Just as he slid his hand down to cup her behind, someone knocked on the door—hard.

He stilled, his mouth on hers. Then he swore softly. "It's Theo."

For a moment, Miranda felt guilty. She felt as though she'd been unfaithful. But that was silly. Of course she hadn't been unfaithful at all. She wasn't even with Theo . . . or Marco, not officially. Even if she had been, they were trying to get her into a three-way relationship; therefore she had a perfect right to sleep with either of them.

The realization was jarring and not unpleasant.

She let herself relax. "Do you want to get it?" she asked.

He smiled. "I'd rather ravish you against the kitchen counter, but yes." Marco released her and she did up her bathrobe as he answered the door.

Theo walked in with a tight look on his face. He took in the cozy domestic scene, seeing clearly that Marco had spent the night. In his hand he held a bouquet of daisies. Even though Miranda knew that she'd done nothing wrong, she still felt a

pang of unease and could sense the flare of jealousy that emanated from Theo. He obviously was trying to be okay with the
fact that Marco had spent the night with her, but he wasn't handling it very well.

She stepped forward and took the flowers. "Thank you. Did
you know that daisies are my favorite flower?"

Theo caught her up against him and kissed her lightly on the
mouth. "I only suspected, love."

"Want to have breakfast with us?" asked Marco. "I was just
going to make omelets."

"Omelets?" Miranda asked in surprise. "I don't think I have
enough ingredients for those."

Marco smiled. "You have everything I need," he said, then
sobered. There was a notable double meaning to what he'd said.

Both men stood staring at her and Miranda felt the pressure
of their regard.

Two men. God, *two of them*. She didn't think she could handle
a serious relationship with one man, let alone two, and the way
they stared at her . . . They both had expectations and those expectations felt very heavy at the moment.

Suddenly nervous, she needed to be anywhere but near them
both. "Uh. I'm going to go get dressed. I have to leave for work
soon." She rushed off to the bathroom.

FOUR

Miranda thrashed in her bed, caught in the grip of a powerful nightmare. Consciousness flickered, making her aware she dreamed, but she couldn't pull herself away from the powerful memories that assaulted her mind.

Seven-year-old Miranda heard her father scream something at her mother in the living room. Wincing, she clapped her hands over her ears as something crashed to the floor and her mother's thin, high voice filled the apartment. Miranda bolted off the chair she'd been sitting in surrounded by her dolls. She grabbed Mr. Teddy and crawled under her bed, where it was safe. Clutching Mr. Teddy against her with one arm, she lay on her side and pressed her palms against her ears, trying her best not to hear what went on in the rest of the house.

The scene flashed to the small apartment she and her mother had rented when they'd arrived in the city from California. Miranda put clean dishes into the cabinet while her mother sat drinking tea at the kitchen table. A darkness tinged the scene, growing darker. Her mother laughed at something Miranda said . . . and the front door burst open. Standing in the frame was her father, looking angrier than she'd ever seen him.

A plate slipped from Miranda's fingers and crashed to the linoleum.

• • •

Miranda sat bolt upright in bed, screaming. The memories that followed the plate crashing to the floor were ones she still couldn't bring into her conscious mind. They were simply too painful. She closed her eyes, willing them away.

Maybe one day she could deal with those images, but not yet . . . maybe never.

Breathing heavily, she flipped the blankets away and stood up. She was alone in her bedroom. The ticktock of the clock on her nightstand was the only sound in her apartment. Part of her was happy she was alone, but another part wished for Marco or Theo to be here to hold her and tell her everything was all right.

Funny how she instantly thought of them for comfort.

Shivering, she grabbed her bathrobe and went into the kitchen for a glass of water.

She'd had counseling, lots of it. All counselors were required to undergo therapy, and she had especially sensitive issues. Miranda knew she did a good job keeping her personal issues separate from her work. If anything, her personal issues made her a better counselor, a better servant to the women who sought her out. That didn't change the fact that Miranda would likely never fully recover from the violent events of her past.

There were some hurts time could never erase.

She took down a glass from the cabinet and went still, staring at the stack of plates. Grief twisted in her stomach.

The phone rang. The shrill sound made Miranda jump about three feet in the air. She set the glass down and picked up the phone. "Hello?"

"Miranda?"

Theo's voice. Relief rushed through her faster than she had time to process her reaction. "Yes."

"Are you all right?" he asked.

She stilled. "It's the middle of the night, Theo. Why are you calling to ask such a strange question?"

Theo drew a breath. "I can feel you, Miranda. Your emotions, I mean. I can feel the ebb and flow of them. Marco is able to do that too, but I'm a little more sensitive in that area. You woke me."

Miranda bit her lower lip, fighting tears. Something in her didn't like that Theo was so connected to her. It scared her. She shivered.

"Miranda?" he asked after a moment when she didn't respond. "Are you there?"

"I-I had a bad dream," she answered in a low, breathy voice, on the verge of crying and trying not to succumb.

"A really bad one, huh, Miranda?"

She could only nod, even though she knew that Theo couldn't see that. The caring and emotion in his voice broke her apart. She might have been able to suppress her feelings about the nightmare if he hadn't called, but he seemed to be drawing all of it out of her.

She hated that too, because it frightened her so much.

"Let me come over, Miranda." He paused. "All I want is to hold you, feel you breathe. That's all. Understand? No demands."

Miranda sighed into the receiver. Her emotions where Theo and Marco were concerned were such a jumbled mess. A part of her wanted to just hang up the phone and not let him into her life the way he seemed to want. Another part knew that in Theo's arms she could find comfort for the night.

The latter part of her won.

She glanced into the kitchen, seeing the stack of plates there. "Uh," she answered shakily. "Can I come over there instead?"

Silence. Then, "Of course. You can come here whenever you like, love," he answered in his low, rich voice. "Do you want me to come get you?"

"No. Thank you. I'll be there in about twenty minutes."

"I can't wait."

Miranda hung up the phone and stared into the kitchen for

a long moment, realizing she wanted nothing more than Theo's comfort tonight, wanted his strong arms around her to protect her from the past. She wiped her cheeks and went to get dressed. She couldn't get to Theo's fast enough. Miranda didn't want to examine why.

She dressed quickly and drove to Theo's apartment building in the wealthiest part of the city, where all the bankers, lawyers . . . and Tylwyth Teg Gaelan warriors lived. The doorman of the historic, classy building had been instructed to allow her in. He escorted her to the elevator and punched the floor for Theo's place.

Theo opened the door to allow Miranda in and lost his breath for a moment. Even with a tear-streaked face and tousled hair she was lovely. Perhaps because of her tear-streaked face and sleep-tousled hair. All Theo wanted in that moment was to hold, protect and soothe her.

And he wanted to do it forever.

He wanted to trace every part of her body with his fingers and cherish it all. He wanted to treasure and adore her very spirit, her breath, her dreams and her nightmares. He wanted to love every part of this woman unconditionally. The force of that desire clogged his throat, making him almost choke from the force of it.

But he saw the uncertainty in her eyes when she stepped over the threshold. He saw wariness and fear. It did not bode well for his cause, or Marco's cause.

He led her in and closed the door. Without a word, he pulled her into his arms. Miranda let her purse drop to the floor of the foyer and returned his embrace. He felt her shudder against him, probably crying. She allowed him to gather her into his arms and carry her into his bedroom. He sat her on the edge of his bed and pulled her coat off, then her shoes and the rest of her clothes.

She glanced at the bed, noting the size.

"It's custom made," he explained. "I'm tall, so my bed is long and it's a bit bigger than a king-size in width." He didn't say he'd recently ordered it, in the hopes of working this out between the three of them.

Miranda seemed to accept his explanation and helped him remove her clothes, murmuring that she wanted to feel his bare skin against hers. Theo was more than happy to grant that wish.

With every creamy bit of skin that was exposed, he only wanted her more, but now was not the time to make demands like that on her. She needed his support and he would give it. Once she was beautifully bare, he tucked her into his bed, slipped off his robe and got in with her.

She molded herself to his body almost the moment he covered them with the blankets and nestled her head under his chin with a deep sigh. Her hands roved his side, back and his chest curiously and Theo grit his teeth, resisting the urge to do anything but hold her.

No demands, he'd told her, and he'd meant it.

"It was a nightmare about my mom," she whispered.

His arms tightened around her. "I figured as much." He paused, not wishing to push her. "You can tell me about it if you want. If not, that's all right, too."

Miranda remained silent for several moments before answering. "It left a fracture in my heart, Theo. I'm damaged. What my father did injured my ability to have relationships. Do you understand?"

"Let Marco and me fill the fracture, Miranda. Let us in and we'll do our best to salve that pain as much as we can." He kissed the top of her head. "You can trust us, you know. With your body, your heart and your mind."

She said nothing in response. She only clung to him like she was drowning in the middle of the ocean and only he could keep her afloat.

Finally, her breathing deepened to sleep, although Theo couldn't find any rest until the early morning hours. Not with the feel of her body pressed against him and the scent of her hair infusing his senses. He eventually fell asleep with a raging hard-on.

He awoke to the heavenly sensation of Miranda's soft mouth around that hard-on.

A groan of pleasure that started somewhere near his toes ripped from his throat as he woke. He tangled his fingers through her hair as she slipped her lips down his length, sucking him into the recesses of her throat.

"Miranda," he groaned again. "You're going to kill me, woman."

She flicked a playful glance up at him, and then slid her mouth down again. Theo closed his eyes and arched in pleasure. Her tongue danced shyly along the length of his shaft. The interior of her mouth felt warm, silken. The sight of her head at his pelvis and the feel of her hair brushing his thighs was enough to bring him to the brink of coming. His body jerked as he fought it.

He sat up a little and took her by the shoulders. "I want to be inside you when I go, Miranda," he rasped in need. "I want to feel your muscles rippling along my cock as I come."

Miranda gave up her mouth's hold on his cock and let him ease her back onto the mattress. "I have no particular objections to that," she sighed.

In awe, he watched the beautiful woman before him, her blonde curls tangled around her face and over the sheets. She arched her back, stabbing her breasts into the air and spread her thighs, revealing her pink, glistening sex.

He hovered over her, one hand flat on the mattress beside her head, and let his other hand trace up her inner thigh to her cunt. Her breath hissed out of her as he explored her folds, slicking the pad of his finger through her dampness to stroke her aroused clit.

"Does that feel good?" he asked, watching her face. She'd closed her eyes and bitten her bottom lip. She did that, he was coming to find, when she was really excited. It was an endearing habit.

She nodded.

He ran his finger over her labia, caressing her until she shuddered and he could feel the damp heat of her cunt intensify. "How about that?" he murmured.

"Yes," she moaned.

He leaned down and caught one of her nipples in his mouth as he slid a finger up inside her, widening her, then quickly added another. Her muscles clamped down around his fingers. It was so hot, so tight. He licked her nipple and gently, ever-so gently, rasped his teeth across it.

Miranda responded by moaning and digging her heels into the mattress. She moved her hips, helping him drive his fingers in and out of her.

He couldn't take it anymore.

Theo removed his hand from her cunt, forced her thighs apart as wide as they could go and placed the head of his cock to her slick opening. He could feel her heat radiate out, tempting him.

"Please," Miranda whimpered and pushed her hips up against him. The head of his cock slid inside and he closed his eyes from the pleasure of it. He thrust in slowly, feeding her his shaft inch by inch, until he was balls-deep inside her.

"Yes, Theo, please," Miranda said. "I want to feel you."

She shifted her hips and he felt all her tight, silken muscles ripple around his length. He drew almost all the way out and thrust back in, making them both gasp. Together, they set up a natural, easy rhythm.

Theo rocked back, watching the thrust and withdrawal of his cock into her soft heat, the shaft glistening wetly with her juices. Watched how the head of his cock tunneled past her labia and speared into her cunt over and over.

Wetting his thumb, he reached down between their bodies and stroked her clit. Miranda thrashed under him at the contact, a needful look on her face.

He held her gaze as he stroked into her faster and faster, feeling his climax rise as hers did as well. Miranda shuddered and then almost screamed as her orgasm ripped through her. The muscles of her cunt milked him as she came long and hard, dragging him to the edge of his own climax, then pushing him over.

Theo sank himself deep into her sweet cunt and felt the unbe-lievable tremors of pleasure racking his body as he came.

When they'd passed, he lowered himself on top of her, wrapped his arms around her and kissed her deeply. He watched her glance around and notice the eyebolts set into the bed's headboard.

"What are those for?" she asked.

He brushed her curls away from her face. "All the better to tie you up with, my dear," he purred into her ear and felt her shiver. He kissed his way across her cheeks to her mouth. "You're feeling better then, I take it?" he asked against her lips.

He felt her smile. "A night spent in your arms cures all ills, I guess. Plus, I couldn't let that luscious erection I felt pressing against me this morning go to waste."

"You're incredible."

"That was incredible. I'm still tingling. I like waking up to that."

"You could wake up to that every morning."

Something dark flashed through her eyes and she glanced away.

Theo ignored it, though it troubled him. He rolled over, tak-ing her with him. She ended up sprawled across his chest. He smoothed the hair back away from her face, hooking it behind her ear. "Are you okay? Really?"

She sobered a little. "I am. I mean, I'm as well as can be ex-pected for a person who watched her mother be murdered by her father."

Theo didn't say anything for a moment, then murmured, "Must be hard for someone with your past. You have not only one man wanting you, but two." He paused. "I imagine you have a hard time trusting any man."

He regretted the observation because she sat up and moved away from him. "Consciously," she replied slowly, "I know you and Marco are nothing like my father. Subconsciously . . . I have fears."

"That's understandable."

She glanced at him. "Is it?"

He smiled. "Of course. Only time spent in the company of myself and Marco would banish those fears." He paused. "It's Saturday," he observed.

A trace of a smile flickered over her mouth. "So it is."

"Would you be willing to grant Marco and me the weekend? Today and tomorrow, here in my apartment. I know it won't be enough to ease all those insidious fears of yours, but it might go a little way toward helping. Plus, it would be fun." He'd been planning to ask her this before, but seeing exactly how afraid she was of commitment to him and Marco, he knew it was more important than ever. They needed to prove to her that they cared about her and they could be trusted.

She grinned. "You're evil to tempt me that way. How can I resist the offer of unbelievable sex with two of the hottest men I've ever seen?" She fell silent for a moment. "Two men I really like a lot . . . on every level."

"There's one catch." He paused. "I want you to agree to be submissive to me and Marco. Trust us . . . just for this one weekend. Let us do whatever we want to you."

She chewed her lip. "Trust . . . today and tomorrow. Two days in sexual thrall to two gorgeous men. Sounds . . . intriguing."

Hope flickered in Theo's chest. "Is that a yes, then?"

"Make me some coffee and I'll mull it over."

"Deal." Theo got up, feeling her gaze on him as he sought his discarded robe. He turned to her. "Are you going to shower?"

She nodded.

"In the hopes that you would say yes to my proposition, I placed something in the shower for you to use. It's fairly self-explanatory." He walked to her and cupped her chin, raising her gaze to his. "Use it, all right? It's for your health and to prepare you for things Marco and I will want to do to your sweet body this weekend."

"Uh, okay," she answered, frowning.

He bent his head, kissed her and then headed for the kitchen.

He and Marco needed to work together to seduce Miranda. He realized that now. It was time they both put their jealousies aside and presented a united front, because Theo sensed if they didn't work together, they both might end up losing her to her past and to her deep-seated fears.

In his living room, he picked up the phone and called Marco.

B rian sat in his sedan outside the dark Gaelan warrior's apartment. He'd recognized him that day at the shelter and had tracked him down, figuring he could lead him to the little bitch who was keeping him away from his Sarah.

He wasn't no servant hobgoblin, working his ass off for a little extra blooded flesh on the side. Wasn't no stinking kingpin goblin, either. He was just a workaday goblin, trying to make his way in the human world. His hands gripped the steering wheel until they were white. A workaday goblin who'd done nothing wrong, only fallen in love with a human woman. He loved Sarah so damn much . . . too much, maybe.

It was true that he was so passionate about her that sometimes he lost his temper. It was her fault, though. She always pushed him into it, was always tempting him to hit her. It was as though she liked it.

He couldn't live without his Sarah, and he felt bad about putting her in the hospital those few times. He wished she didn't bait him the way she did, then he wouldn't lose his temper so often. All he needed was to talk to her, tell her that he loved her and apologize. Then she'd come back to him and everything would be like it was.

Perfect.

But that stupid bitch wouldn't allow him to see Sarah. Then she'd gone and had him arrested. That just couldn't stand. Brian couldn't let her get away with that shit, especially because of what she was.

His lips curled back in a semblance of a smile. She didn't even know.

She thought she was like her two men, the fae Gaelans, the bright and shining Tylwyth Teg. How little she knew about her heritage. He had a hankering to teach her all about it.

But he had to find her first.

Brian's buddies had bailed him out of jail after the bitch had pressed charges. Right after he'd gotten out, he'd tracked down Marco Collins. He knew he'd recognized that bastard from somewhere. Recognition had come right before Marco's fucking fist had connected with his face. Brian gently touched his black eye. He had a score to settle with the Gaelan too.

But not yet.

Marco would lead him to the bitch. He just knew it.

About an hour later, Brian was rewarded for his patience. Marco left his building, wearing the long, black leather duster and black boots he seemed to favor, and got into his SUV.

He started up his car and followed the Gaelan a ways back, trying his best to stay off the fae's visual and mental radars. He followed him through downtown to the swanky east side.

Marco pulled into the parking lot of a historical building. It looked expensive, classy. Brian watched Marco park and enter the building while he remained in the parking lot, staring up at the building with a scowl on his face. This couldn't be where she lived, could it? Counselors at women's shelters didn't make that much money. Maybe Marco hadn't led him to her after all.

As Brian stared up at the building, he caught a flash of white at one of the windows. A blonde woman, her arms clasped over her chest in a protective gesture, stared out over the manicured landscape.

It was her.

Brian smiled. He'd found her.

Now he just had to find the right time to take her.

• • •

Miranda felt Marco before he even rang the doorbell. Theo let him in and she turned from her place at the window. He wore black from head to toe and a hot expression on his face that seemed all for her. Miranda's stomach did a little flip-flop, watching the two men standing side by side, knowing they both wanted her . . . and cared for her.

God, she was so lucky. Why couldn't she just surrender to this? She closed her eyes for a moment. This weekend she would attempt her best to do just that. She owed it to both of them to try. She owed it to herself.

"Come here, baby," Marco said in his low husky voice.

She walked to him and he kissed her softly. One wouldn't think a bear of a man like Marco could ever be gentle, but he was . . . well, unless he wasn't. Miranda shivered, remembering. Not-so-gentle Marco was awfully nice too.

"Theo tells me you're ours for this weekend. Submissive to us," Marco said, running his fingers through her hair. "You think you're ready for the two of us, then?"

She let out a breath slowly. "I guess we'll see, won't we?"

He smiled in a friendly way, but there was an unmistakable heat in his eyes. "You want us to be gentle with you?"

She remembered what she'd done that morning in the shower to prepare her body for the erotic games that they had planned for her this weekend. It had made her ready for anal sex. Her cunt pulsed at what lay ahead of her, remembering the things Marco said they would do to her. She licked her lips and swallowed hard. "No."

His smile widened and he lifted a brow. "Have you ever been with two men at the same time?"

She tipped her chin at him. "Why? You think I can't handle it?"

Marco laughed and glanced at Theo. "You know, even if we weren't bound by soul and spirit to her, I'd still be head over heels for her."

"I would be too," answered Theo solemnly. "Without a doubt."

Miranda retreated from them, feeling uncomfortable. She sat

down on the couch, folding her legs underneath her. "That begs a question. How many women have you been with in your very long lives and how many of them were you *head over heels* for?"

"Me?" Marco rubbed his chin, considering her question. "Besides you? Two. We talked about this before." He eased his long coat off and laid it over a nearby chair. "I cared for two women before you, but I didn't feel as intensely for either of them as I feel for you, Miranda."

Miranda stilled, watching him, her heart pounding. She didn't want words like that from him. He might feel their . . . *bond*, but she didn't. She was far from ready to hear words like that. "Tell me about the human woman," she said tightly.

"I can do better than that. I can show her to you." Marco lifted his hand and she felt the hair at the nape of her neck rise. The air in the center of the room shimmered and a hazy image of a woman appeared. Miranda gasped and put a hand to her mouth.

Magick.

She stared at the shimmering, flickering image in the center of the room. The woman had long brown hair and was dressed in a long calico dress. The lady smiled and laughed, making her green eyes twinkle in her mirth.

"This image comes from my memories." He paused. "Her name was Emily," Marco finished.

"She was beautiful."

Marco nodded and closed his hand. The image blinked out of existence. "She was the only human I've ever shared my secrets with. We were together for thirty years, until she took ill and died."

There was an unmistakable note of regret and sorrow in his voice. "I'm sorry," she answered sincerely.

Marco shrugged, but his face still wore an expression of painful remembering. "It was a long time ago. I've been in other relationships, but I haven't been with a woman that I wanted to commit to since Emily." He paused and looked at her meaningfully. "Until now."

Ignoring that last comment, she looked at Theo. "What about you?"

Theo came and sat on the leather sofa opposite her. He wore a pair of blue jeans—no underwear, she knew that because she'd watched him dress that morning—a gray T-shirt and no shoes or socks. The man looked good enough to eat no matter what he wore, and especially if he wore nothing at all.

He drew a breath. "There have been three women in my life that were more than a casual relationship." He held her gaze. "What I felt for them didn't come close to what I feel for you, Miranda. I'm sorry if that frightens you, but I can do nothing but tell the truth."

Miranda fell silent, considering her words carefully before responding. "You both feel that way about me because of some intangible, metaphysical bond thing between us. You don't really know me. You don't know if you can stand to spend the rest of your lives with me." She blew out a frustrated sigh. "This is . . . crazy."

Theo shook his head. "You don't understand, love."

"Well, then *explain* it to me."

Marco walked into the living room and raised his hand again. The air in the center of the room shimmered in a glowing pattern of different, pulsing tendrils of light. It was beautiful. "This is the essential pattern of Theo's spirit, Miranda."

She gaped. "It's . . . lovely."

"We can't access the patterns of just anyone, only those closest to us," Marco explained. The picture changed, the pattern became different but no less gorgeous. It was like looking at a real-life kaleidoscope. "This is mine."

"Okay."

The pattern shifted a little again, the patterns changed and the colors shifted. "This is yours." Marco sucked in a breath. "Theo?"

Theo got up and walked toward it. He glanced at Marco and then at Miranda. "It's fine," he said tightly.

"What's wrong?" Miranda asked.

Theo shook his head. "Nothing's wrong. Come take a look."

Something quivered deep inside her. "That's really mine?" She got up and went closer. It was like a holograph, this magick that Marco used. She had no real reason to believe what he was saying except for the undeniable sense she had that he wasn't lying.

"Do you notice anything interesting in the three patterns?" Theo asked.

She'd noticed it right away. "Yes," she answered warily.

"Your pattern is a synthesis of mine and Marco's, isn't it, love?" said Theo said softly. "You see that, don't you?"

"I did notice that, yes," she admitted.

"Here's your pattern overlaid with mine and Theo's," said Marco. "Prepare yourself."

She scowled at him, wondering what he meant, and a flash of white light flared in the center of the room. Miranda fell backward, onto the couch. "Oh, my God!"

"That's what happens when two of us find our third," said Marco. He closed his hand and the light disappeared.

"Do you understand now, Miranda?" Theo asked.

"Not really," she answered shakily.

"Your elemental makeup suits ours, love." Theo paused. "You are the heart of Theo and me. With your introduction, the three of us are whole."

Marco took a couple steps toward her. "We care about you regardless of this, Miranda. I think I can speak for Theo when I say that we admire you, like you, are drawn to your personality regardless of this connection we share, but the connection makes it all undeniably strong."

"Why don't I feel it?"

"Your human blood," Theo answered quickly. "You're much more human than you are anything else. Give it some time and you'll feel it like we feel it."

She licked her lips. "Let's say—just as a hypothetical—that we all bond and decide to spend the rest of our lives together.

Won't I die much earlier than you two?" She frowned. "How does it work for Olivia, Mason and Will?"

"There are ways to bring your other blood to the surface, Miranda. You probably won't have a lot of powers other than a very long life and your seer's vision, but you won't wither and die before our eyes."

She didn't want to ask how. Not right now. She didn't even want to know. Miranda got up, crossed to the window and gazed out of it, over the lawns of the luxury high-rise, over the city.

Near immortality and two gorgeous men.

It sounded too excellent to be true. But would it always be good with them? Would she end up like her mother—happy and in love at first and then scared and hunted sometime down the road?

Marco came to stand behind her. She could feel the heat of him radiating out and warming her back, could smell a trace of the sexy cologne he normally wore. "You're thinking way too much, Miranda. That's a nasty habit you have."

She gave a short laugh.

"You said you'd give us the weekend. Do you still want to do that?"

She turned around and stared up into his handsome face. "Wouldn't I be an idiot to say no to you, either of you? Of course, I'm prepared to stay here for the weekend."

He stared down at her with his dark, hooded eyes. She noted uneasily that she barely topped the man's chest. Knew without a doubt that if he ever wanted to hurt her, she would have nothing to say about it. Marco or Theo could snap her like so much kindling. She shook her head, clearing the thought. They would never hurt her. She sensed that.

"What are you thinking about, Miranda?" he asked in a low voice. "I wish I could read your mind." His eyes seemed full of things he wanted to do to her, sweaty, carnal things, up against the glass behind her.

Miranda licked her lips, feeling her body respond to the

sound of his voice and the look in his eyes. "I'm thinking about you and Theo . . . having both of you." She swallowed hard, staring up at him, wondering what he'd do. "Being submissive to both of you."

"Oh, you'll have us both before the weekend is through, baby. No doubt about that. You'll be submissive to us and you'll like it too." He reached out and cupped her cheek in his palm. "I'm glad you're staying," he murmured in his deep, velvet voice. She felt it . . . everywhere. She closed her eyes and nuzzled his palm, feeling his calluses and wanting them to rasp over her breasts, expecting him to touch her . . .

He turned and said, "Well, should we go to a movie then? I've been dying to see *The Eliminator.*"

Her eyes opened and she blinked rapidly in surprise. A movie? He wanted to see a movie?

On the couch, Theo shrugged. "Sure, I'm up for a movie. How about you, Miranda?"

"A movie?" she asked stupidly, forcing herself to recover quickly. They were going to start their weekend by seeing a movie? "Uh, okay." She blinked.

"Great," answered Marco. "I haven't seen a movie in a long time."

Miranda wondered if she'd get lucky and there would be necking during the movie or, better yet, *groping.*

They took a few minutes to get ready and then they all piled into Marco's black SUV and went the short distance to the theater. Once inside they bought popcorn and an assortment of candy.

Gaelan warriors, Miranda was quickly discovering, ate a lot.

She noticed uneasily how the other women in the theater noticed her escorts in a very female, predatory fashion. Beautiful women, long-legged, big-breasted women. The kind of women who should be with men like Theo and Marco. The kind of women who looked like they fit with such gorgeous men. She was short, small-breasted and would be called *cute,* rather than beautiful.

Miranda gave them all the evil back-off-bitch eye, but they seemed to not even notice her. Maybe the women thought she was their little sister or their cousin, clearly not hot enough to be with either of them . . . let alone *both* of them.

The nice thing was that Marco and Theo did not seem to notice the attention they garnered. They seemed to have eyes for no woman but her and were extremely solicitous of her, making sure she had everything she wanted at the snack stand, which was a bottled water and a box of chocolates.

Annoyed by the fawning of the females in the lobby, Miranda followed Marco and Theo into the theater. They made sure she sat between them. As the lights went down, Miranda had to admit to feeling quite happy. The warmth of the men on either side of her was comforting. She felt so safe in their presence—even content.

There, alone with them in the dark of the theater, watching the action film flicker on the screen, Miranda understood how maybe—just maybe—she might find happiness with these two men.

That evening, after dinner, neither man had yet to touch her. They both looked at her with hungry expressions on their faces, dark looks in their beautiful eyes, but neither had touched her in any way that was unlike a brother's contact.

Miranda was getting frustrated.

They sat in Theo's gorgeous living room, candles flickering on the end tables and on the kitchen counter. A fire had been started in the hearth and it lit the room with a romantic glow. She sat curled up on the couch, talking with them about everything. About their childhoods, about how they'd watched all those time periods pass by. She'd always been interested in history and seeing it through their eyes was better than any college course she could have taken.

They spoke long into the night. It was fascinating and she felt like she knew them better because of it.

She shifted in the seat. Still, she had to admit that she wanted them, craved their touch. Just being in their presence made her horny. She wondered how they felt.

Were they restraining themselves?

Did they hesitate to touch her because they feared it would scare her away?

Did they think she wasn't ready for them? Didn't want them?

Did they think she was made of glass? That she was so fragile she would shriek and run away if confronted with two dicks at one time? Miranda wanted to show them what she'd do if confronted that way. She wouldn't be running away, she knew that much.

It was time to push a little.

She unbuttoned the top few buttons of her shirt as she listened to Marco talk about his father, who'd also been a Gaelan warrior. He'd been expected to assume his father's place and he had, though not without some doubts. Idly, sincerely concentrating on Marco, she reached in and rubbed her skin. Marco stuttered over a word and his gaze centered itself on her hand that was plunged into her shirt.

Theo looked ready to spill his glass of whiskey on the floor.

Yes, they were holding themselves back.

Miranda yawned when there was a pause in the conversation. "I'm tired," she said, stretching. "It's been a wonderful day, but I think I'm almost ready for bed."

They both looked kind of disappointed, she noted with an inward smile.

She rose and walked to the fireplace. As she went, she unbuttoned her shirt and the top button of her skirt. "I guess I need to find some pajamas," she said in a faux coy and demure tone. She favored them with a sultry backward glance. "I didn't bring any with me."

Smiling, and filled with mischievous playfulness, Miranda

shrugged off her shirt and let her skirt fall to the floor. Beneath she wore only a black lace demi bra, matching black silk panties and her black pumps. She stood with her back to them, one hand on the mantel and one of her knees bent. The fire warmed her bare skin, bathed her in its light.

Everything went silent.

"I think that's an invitation," Theo said finally in a strained voice.

"I guess so," answered Marco.

She turned toward them. "Am I breakable, guys? I did say I didn't want you to be gentle."

"We didn't want to frighten you, love," said Theo. "You've had a lot to digest over the last couple of days. We wanted to take it slow."

She took a few steps toward them. They both look so needy in the half light. Feral. They wanted her and Miranda reveled in that power. These two gorgeous men . . . they burned for her. She felt her panties get wet from the very thought.

She took a few more steps toward them and then stopped in the center of the room. Miranda met both their gazes in turn. "I'm not frightened."

FIVE

Miranda watched Theo set his glass down and rise. Marco leaned back against the cushions of the couch and simply watched, his dark gaze heated and roving her body. Theo walked to her, around her, but didn't touch her. She could feel the heat of his body radiate out and warm her flesh, could feel the whisper of his breath along her skin. His nearness made her heart beat faster, made her body temperature rise faster than standing near the fire.

Theo cupped her shoulder in one of his huge hands and Miranda shivered. He leaned down and put his mouth close to her ear. "We both want you badly, love. I hope you know what you're getting yourself into."

Miranda shivered.

"You agreed to submissiveness this weekend. Your sweet body is ours to do with as we please." He paused, his breath warm against her throat. "Sure you're ready?"

"Yes," she whispered.

He eased his hands down her arms, moved to her waist and glided slowly up her stomach to her breasts. The drag of his fingers over her body raised gooseflesh, made a whimper of need curl up from the back of her throat.

Marco watched raptly from the couch as Theo cupped

her breasts, warming them in his palms. The lace of her front-clasping demi bra scraped her rigid nipples with every breath she took, which seemed to be coming faster and harder with every moment he touched her. Theo traced her collarbone with his index finger, and then trailed over the plump of one breast to the clasp.

"Want me to take her bra off, Marco?" he asked in a low voice. His hand rested on the rise of her breast.

"Take everything off her," Marco growled, leaning forward a little.

With a skillful twist of his fingers, he undid it. Her breasts fell free of her bra and Theo eased it over her shoulders and off. From the couch, Marco watched, his dark eyes hooded. His erection strained against his pants.

Miranda knew she'd agreed to submissiveness this weekend, but she also knew exactly how much power she wielded, how much these two men yearned for her.

She stood in only her silk panties and her pumps. The cool air of the room kissed her skin and her breasts felt full, her nipples hard as diamonds. Theo remained motionless behind her, letting Marco drink his fill of her unbound breasts.

Finally, Theo eased a hand up and rubbed one of her nipples, drawing her back against his chest. She sucked in a breath at the welcome contact and closed her eyes against the pleasurable rub of his index finger back and forth over the peak of her breast. Her cunt grew hot and wet.

"Do you like it when I touch you this way?" Theo purred in her ear.

"Yes."

"Your nipples are very hard for me. So lovely. Such a beautiful, responsive body you have, Miranda. Where else would you like me to touch you?"

"Uh."

"You can say it. Tell me, Miranda. Where else do you want my hands?"

"Between my legs," she breathed.

"You want me to touch your cunt, love? Is it excited for me?"

She nodded.

He gently cupped her breast in his hand and continued to stroke her nipple with the pad of his thumb. At the same time, he smoothed his hand down her abdomen and slowly, ever-so mind-numbingly slowly, past the waistband of her panties to tangle in her pubic hair.

"Spread your legs, love. Shoulder-width apart."

She complied, giving him better access to her aroused pussy.

Miranda watched Marco shift on the coach as he watched Theo's hand cup her mound in her panties, then dip between her thighs. She shivered with pleasure as he stroked her folds and clit.

"You're so wet," Theo murmured in her ear. "So hot and wet." He nipped her earlobe and made her knees go weak. "I think you want us as much as we want you."

Yes. With a force that was damn near crippling.

Marco watched Theo's hand work her between her legs, his gaze becoming more heated, his body becoming visibly tense. Miranda knew that her panties concealed most of what Theo was doing to her there. Theo slipped one, then two, fingers inside her and began to thrust, and Marco leaned forward on the couch, a hungry expression on his face.

Her cunt muscles rippled around Theo's gently pistoning fingers and she creamed against his hand. She felt him shiver at the feel of her, but it was the only indication that Theo was not in complete and utter control of his lust for her.

Working her breast and her cunt skillfully, Theo had her moaning in no time. Her body felt tense, on edge, and she wanted a cock . . . wanted one of them so bad she found herself grinding herself down on Theo's fingers. Found herself trying to stop begging for his cock.

Before she could draw another breath, Marco was there kneeling at her feet. He gripped her panties, eased them down and off. Theo removed his hand from her sex and, with a growl, Marco buried his face between her thighs.

Miranda cried out at the abrupt sensation of Marco's long, wide tongue slipping through her folds and lapping her sensitive clit. Theo lowered her to the floor and eased her back against his chest as Marco parted her thighs and pushed her knees up, blatantly exposing her pussy for his lips and tongue. He kept her that way forcefully. If Miranda had wanted to close her legs— which she didn't—she wouldn't have been able to.

And he feasted.

Theo raised her arms. She hooked them behind Theo's head at his guidance. The position arched her body and thrust her breasts out. She felt like she was on display, spread for their satisfaction. Theo slid his hands slowly down to cup her breasts and tease the nipples with skillful fingers. He rolled and stroked and gently pinched them until Miranda was panting.

Theo put his mouth to her ear as he toyed with her nipples and murmured, "Is he doing it right, love?" in her ear. "Is Marco licking your cunt well?"

"Uh, huh," she answered, feeling drugged.

Marco had his hands on the inside of her thighs, holding her legs apart, while his tongue explored her labia and licked her clit. The sight of his dark head moving between her spread thighs and the feel of Theo's hard body bracing her from behind was almost more than she could take.

"Damn, you taste good," Marco growled. "Hot and sweet." He eased back onto his heels and stared into her eyes. His blue eyes were heavy-lidded with arousal and she could see his erection pressing against the zipper of his pants. "I want to make you come this way."

She had no real objections to that.

He licked his fingers to wet them and stroked her swollen, sensitive clit. Her hips jerked and she almost closed her knees. "No," Marco said. "Close your legs and I'll tie you up, princess. You saw the eyebolts on Theo's bed. There's rope and I'm not afraid to use it. I want you submissive, baby. Understand? We do whatever we want to you this weekend. Keep your legs spread, or I'll bind you that way."

She licked her lips, feeling excitement coursing through her at his words.

Theo eased his hands down and pulled her thighs apart so she couldn't close them. "Make her scream, Marco."

Marco continued the slow, torturous stroke of his finger against her clit. She watched his hand between her thighs as he teased her. Her clit had pulled from its hood and his caress of it was so intensely pleasurable that it made her squirm and moan against Theo. "Yes," she murmured. "Right there, like that."

"Is it good?" asked Marco. "Are you going to come for us?"

"Let me," she moaned. She knew Marco was teasing her, making her climax build and grow more and more intense.

"When I decide, baby. I like to see you like this, naked and moaning from the stroke of my hand on your gorgeous cunt."

His blunt words made her shiver. She never would've pegged herself for a woman who was turned on by rough sex talk, but it appeared she was.

He slipped down and caressed her labia, rubbing his fingers through her folds. "Your pussy is so pink and pretty. So eager to be fucked. You want to be fucked, baby?"

"Yes."

He eased a finger into her cunt and she felt her muscles react, pulling at his long, thick digit. Theo spread her thighs a little more, making her totally open to Marco. Marco added a second finger and watched her face intently as he slid them in.

"Oh, God," she moaned.

Theo held her fast as Marco pulled them out and pushed back in again. "Mmmm . . . so hot and tight. I can't wait until I get my cock in here." He leaned down and latched his mouth over her clit, while he finger-fucked her harder and faster. His hot tongue skated over her clit and his lips massaged as he found that sweet spot deep inside her and rubbed . . .

"Marco!" she cried as her climax overwhelmed her. "Oh God, yes!" She felt her cunt muscles ripple as she came hard. The pleasure enveloped her body, stealing her breath and even her scream. Marco kept thrusting his fingers in and out of her, kept sucking her clit, riding her through her climax.

As the waves receded, Marco buried his face deep between her thighs and licked her, making sounds of deep, masculine satisfaction. Then he climbed up her body, threaded his fingers through her hair and kissed her roughly.

Heart pounding and breathing heavy in the aftermath of her orgasm, Miranda let Marco pull her away from Theo as he kissed her. She could taste herself on his tongue as it stabbed between her lips in coarse, exciting domination.

They fumbled at each other, Miranda trying to get Marco's clothes off. She pushed him back onto the floor. Behind her, she heard Theo also shedding his clothes.

She ripped Marco's shirt, hearing the buttons pop and fly. Working at his pants, they finally got them down and off and his luscious erection sprang free.

Miranda turned to find Theo behind her. He drew her into his arms, fisting his hand in the hair at the nape of her neck and forcing her head back, exposing the line of her throat. She was on her knees on the floor, between the two of them. Marco ran his hands over her back and ass while she faced Theo.

Theo ran his lips lightly down her throat, trailing his tongue across her skin. When he reached the place where her shoulder met her neck, he bit her. Miranda shuddered at the gesture of possession, the slightest bit of pain. Her cunt grew even warmer and wetter. Theo eased his hands over her ass, delved between her cheeks, touching her everywhere, sometimes bumping into Marco.

Theo released her throat. "I want to watch you suck his cock, Miranda." With heavy-lidded eyes, he rubbed his thumb over her mouth. "Do it."

Marco pulled her back away from Theo and she pushed him

to the floor, straddling him on all fours. He sunk his fingers into her hair as she kissed, licked and nipped her way from his lips, down his chest. She dragged her tongue through the tangle of dark hair at the juncture of his thighs, then up the length of his gorgeous, hard cock.

"Ah, hell," he groaned when she lowered her mouth over him, taking every inch of his cock into her mouth that she possibly could. His hands fisted in her hair. The hardness of his cock against her tongue felt like pure heaven. She groaned in the back of her throat and closed her eyes for a moment, enjoying the taste and feel of him.

She felt someone push her curls to the side and saw that Theo was indeed watching her suck Marco's cock in and out of her mouth. He studied her lips moving over Marco's rigid flesh. The thick, veined shaft glistened with her saliva on every outward mouth stroke. She glanced at him, giving him a heated look, knowing it turned him on.

After a moment, Theo got up, got something from another room and returned. He caressed her ass with his hand and eased her thighs apart. She moaned around Marco's cock when Theo spread her labia with his thumbs and licked her. He speared his tongue into her, fucking her with it, and her hips jerked involuntarily. His hands on her waist kept her steady.

Marco thrust his hips up, spearing his cock into her mouth. She had a man at each end of her, possessing her, dominating her. Marco's cock down her throat and Theo's tongue deep inside her. She felt drugged with need and passion, yet felt completely at ease with these men. She'd let them do anything to her . . . wanted them to do anything to her.

Theo backed away and she heard the sound of a bottle being opened. Then she felt the press of two of Theo's fingers at her cunt. They were slick with something wet and a little cold. "Spread your thighs for me, love," Theo demanded.

She did so and felt him push inside her. Miranda pounded her closed fist on the floor as she feverishly worked Marco's cock in and out of her mouth. Theo eased his fingers in and out of her slowly.

Then she felt pressure at her anus. She jerked a little, startled, and Theo shushed her. "Relax. You'll like this, Miranda. Marco told me he's already done this to you."

Trust.

Miranda closed her eyes and let Theo have his way with her. She felt pressure in her ass, something being pressed inside her. It felt graduated in size. The object started small and gained in width as he pressed it farther within.

She gasped around Marco's cock, feeling pain and pleasure and the burn of her muscles being stretched all rolled into one. She closed her eyes, letting Theo work it into her ass, letting the pleasure override the pain until the pain only played a sweet counterpoint to the pleasure.

Miranda lost her hold on Marco's cock and moaned. "What is that?"

"It's a plug, love. To ready you to take a cock into your pretty little ass." He pulled it out and she could feel it was ridged. He pushed the well-lubricated plug in again, all the while, gently finger-fucking her.

She almost came on his hand.

"Oh, Theo. It's good," she moaned.

"Your body was made for this, love," Theo purred. "You're open for me, taking the plug really well." He pulled it out again and pushed back in, making Miranda moan again.

Marco played with her breasts, which hung over him, fingering her nipples. "Wait until one of us takes that lovely ass of yours with our cock, while the other is in your cunt. Baby, you'll come hard, so damn hard you'll see stars."

She bit her lower lip as the plug hilted within her. She felt so possessed, so filled.

Marco pulled himself out from under her and rested on his knees in front of her. He guided his cock to her mouth as Miranda felt Theo remove his fingers and place his cock to her cunt. Both entered her simultaneously.

Marco gently fisted his hands in her hair and thrust between her lips as Theo eased himself in and out of her slit, bumping the plug in her ass with every inward thrust. It sent foreign, indescribable pleasure coursing through her every time. Her lower body, where Theo fed her his cock, was pleasure blurring into ecstasy. She couldn't separate what was happening to her cunt or her ass. It just all blended together, making her eyes practically roll back in her head from the intensity.

Theo's hips moved rhythmically, his muscles flexing as he thrust in and out of her body, his hands steady on her hips. Her cunt rippled and pulsed around his width and length, stretched deliciously. He rocked her into Marco's cock every time, pushing it down her throat. She had to make a conscious effort to relax her throat muscles so she wouldn't gag.

Marco tipped his head back, his hands buried in her hair, and groaned her name. She could tell he was close to coming, and so was she. Miranda closed her eyes and reveled in the feeling of being totally overcome and overwhelmed by these two men. The whole world had fallen away. All that existed now was Theo, Marco and what they did to her.

Behind her, Theo dipped his hand between her thighs and stroked her clit. "Come for us, Miranda. I want to feel you come around my cock." He stroked her and increased the pace and depth of his thrusts.

Miranda came.

Hard.

She fought to retain her hold on Marco's cock as her cunt convulsed with pleasure and her orgasm crashed over her. Marco sank his shaft deep into her mouth and it jerked twice. He groaned and she tasted him on her tongue, swallowed him down even as her body shuddered under the intense waves of pleasure.

Once her climax had just begun to ease, Marco pulled her forward. She looked up at him confused, but he only kissed her, his tongue spearing into her mouth. Theo pulled his cock from her and then the plug. She heard the sound of the bottle of lube being opened again.

Confused, she broke her kiss with Marco. "What's—"

"He's taking your sweet ass, baby." He brushed her hair away from her face. "You need to be conditioned to this with two men in your life."

Pleasure skittered up her spine. It seemed incredible that she'd come very hard twice and she still ached for more. The thought of Theo entering her where she'd never had a man before was incredibly exciting to her.

Marco reached down between her spread legs and stroked her clit. "You'll like it," he purred. Miranda closed her eyes as he caressed her. She was sensitive from coming twice, yet under Marco's expert touch she felt the edge of another climax slowly begin to rise.

"You-you just want to see how many times I can come in one night, I think," she said in a breathy voice.

Marco grinned wolfishly. He kissed her as he eased his middle finger up inside her cunt and dragged her lower lip between his teeth. "Mmmm," he growled. "Sounds like a good game to me. I love to see you come, *hear* you come."

Theo pushed her down gently. She ended up across Marco's lap. Marco could still touch her pussy in this position and he rubbed her clit continuously; keeping up a light, perfect pressure on the aroused bundle of nerves. Warm, liquid pleasure filled her even as Theo set the head of his cock to her anus.

"Theo," she said, suddenly unsure.

"You're open, love," he answered in a strangled voice. "So open. The plug did its job and you're aroused beyond belief."

She felt the head of his cock breach the tight rim of nerves. It burned, the ring taut around his width, but it eased for him and the burning turned to pleasure. She moaned and clawed the floor, feeling him pin her down with his big body as he slowly and carefully slid inside her.

"Mmm," Theo murmured. "Perfect. So good."

Marco pressed her down on his lap and kept rubbing her clit with his fingers, making pleasure tingle and pulse through her cunt, as Theo worked his cock into her ass inch by inch.

The erotic, forbidden nature of the scenario, the utter and total dominance of having a man enter her this way, wiped all thought from her mind. Miranda bucked as Theo gently, so very gently, began to thrust. Nerves that had never known stimulation flared to life, pulsed and rippled. Her body was soon awash in incredible ecstasy.

Theo groaned. "Oh, God, Miranda. I'm not going to last long." He said something in some language she didn't understand, gripped her hips and shafted her slow and easy.

Marco caressed her clit and labia. "Is it good, baby? Do you like that?"

"Yes," she hissed. The feel of having him in her ass was just on the edge of too much. She was going to climax very quickly.

"Come for him. That's what he wants. He wants you to scream for us," Marco said as he slipped his fingers inside her.

Miranda's third orgasm hit her so hard, she really did scream. She screamed and came all over Marco's caressing hand. He stroked her through it, riding it out and prolonging it.

Theo groaned and she felt his cock jump inside her, fill her with his come.

"Oh," Miranda said as Theo pulled out of her. "Oh." She felt stunned and sated both. Happy. Well pleased.

"God, you're pretty," Marco said. He drew her against him. He pushed her hair out of her face. "I think we wore her out, Theo."

"She wore me out," groaned Theo.

Marco lifted her and she snuggled into him. "Bath and bed, baby. There will be more games tomorrow."

They bore her into Theo's shower, which was big enough to fit about five people, washed, and then all snuggled into Theo's huge custom-made bed—Miranda between them. She fell asleep feeling totally safe and protected.

And with a smile of ultimate sexual satisfaction on her lips.

But the games didn't end that night. They were serious about getting her used to sex with two men. Miranda awoke in the middle of the night, draped facedown over Theo's lap.

"What?" she said drowsily. Her cunt felt aroused, her nipples achy. "Oh," she moaned. "What are you doing to me?"

Theo's strong hand caressed her back and shoulders, at the same time holding her down. Marco fingered her cunt between her spread legs, making her cream hard and her clit throb.

"You looked so pretty lying between us, we couldn't resist," answered Theo. "You did sign up to be totally submissive to us this weekend, remember?"

"Mmm," she answered, rubbing her pussy against his caressing hand. She remembered and definitely didn't regret it.

Theo grabbed a pillow and put it under her hips, and then he moved to her head and held her wrists straight out in front of her, pressing them to the mattress so she couldn't get away—not that she wanted to. His hands were like cuffs, holding her down and in place while Marco guided the head of his cock into her cunt and fucked her in long, easy, relentless strokes until the room was filled with her moans and his groans and she came hard enough to raise the roof.

M iranda awoke the next morning, naked, sprawled across the bed and with two gorgeous, equally naked men stroking their hands over her body.

"Oh, my God," was all she could say at the sight. "Every time I wake up you're doing something to me that should be against the law," she sighed.

"We're enthralling you sexually and making you see the benefits of having two men please you," answered Theo. His fingers grazed her hardened nipples and she felt her cunt pulse. "It's all part of our nefarious plan to have you addicted to us by this evening before my bed turns back into a pumpkin."

Miranda sighed. "This is so decadent. Really, there must be . . . *oh* . . . rules against this much pleasure," she moaned as Marco delved between her thighs and gently teased her clit.

"Are you sore?" Marco asked.

She bit her lower lip, trying to sort the pain from the pleasure. "Not enough to make me want you to stop."

He grinned. "That's good. Very good." He stroked her labia, drawing her thighs apart. "Ah, perfect," he purred. "Sticky sweet, like hot sugar."

Theo moved between her thighs and stroked her clit. The feel of both their fingers on her at once nearly made her lose her mind. She watched the flex of their biceps and forearms as they explored her. Their heads—one light and one dark—bent together as they examined her pussy.

"It's pretty, pink and swollen," said Theo.

"It's gorgeous." She felt Marco's finger enter her slowly. "Wet and ready, wanting to be fucked again, wouldn't you say, Theo?"

"Mmm hmm." He inserted a finger inside her next to Marco's.

Miranda's back arched and she spread her thighs for them, moaning. The sensation of both their fingers buried deep inside her was nearly more than she could handle.

Theo removed his hand and traced her nipple, leaving a wet mark. Marco stroked her clit. "We've plans for you today, love," said Theo. His pupils were dark with arousal. She glanced at his hard cock.

Suddenly, she wanted to touch them both.

Miranda got up and knelt between them, taking each of their cocks in a hand and stroking them. They both groaned. "Maybe I have plans for *you*," she answered.

"Uhn," said Marco as she stroked his thick, wide shaft. "You're the submissive this weekend, baby, although I don't mind what you're doing right now."

She gave him a wicked grin, lowered her head and sucked Marco's cock into her mouth. With her other hand, she stroked Theo's shaft. When Marco's body seemed tense and his groans ricocheted off the walls, she switched, sinking Theo's cock deep into her mouth.

Miranda switched off again and again, wondering who would come in her mouth and who would come in her hand.

Theo got her mouth in the end. Marco groaned and came all over her hand a few moments later.

Satisfied with herself, she rose and stared down at them both. Maybe she could handle two men after all. "I'm hungry," she announced, "what's for breakfast?"

She sat naked on Marco's lap as he fed her pieces of sliced apple. His hands roved her body territorially while she nipped bits of it from where he held it between his teeth. His impressive erection poked into her hip. Once she'd chewed and swallowed the last of it, he tangled his fingers through her hair and slanted his mouth over hers with a growl in the back of his throat.

That familiar, slow warmth in her cunt ignited under his hands and lips. It was incredible how much these men excited her and kept her that way. She'd never had any idea her body was capable of this—so many climaxes in such a short amount of time.

God help her, she wanted more.

She whimpered under his sliding, nipping lips and he lifted her onto the edge of the table, pushing away the breakfast dishes. Miranda didn't know where Theo had gone. He'd disappeared into the bedroom several minutes ago.

Marco plunged his fingers into her curls on either side of her face and slanted her face up toward his. His eyes were dark, serious and filled with emotion. "Damn, Miranda, I want to eat you up, devour you. Make you mine in every way. Fuck," he swore under his breath. "*I love you.* Understand?"

She found herself touched by his admission, rather than afraid. Marco wasn't a man who spoke eloquently and she could tell it was hard for him to find the words. She reached up and touched his cheek. She couldn't use the word *love*, but . . . "I care very deeply for you too, Marco. You and Theo both." Emotion swelled in her chest as she stared up into his eyes.

They remained that way for a pregnant moment before Marco kissed her again, urgent and tender. His lips slid over hers, nipping and licking until Miranda felt powerless, limp and breathless.

"Put your hands behind you," he commanded. "Flat on the table."

She did it. The position arched her spine.

Holding her gaze with his heavy-lidded eyes, he yanked her hips forward and spread her thighs. Marco stood between them, his erection nudging her clit and brushing her pubic hair. "Better. Don't move, baby. Not a bit." He stepped back and let his gaze rove over her where she sat on the edge of the table with her thighs spread and her breasts prominently displayed.

He licked his lips, stepped forward and threaded his fingers through the hair at her nape. Gently, he forced her head back, exposing the line of her throat, and then let his gaze slide down her body once more. She felt her nipples go hard in the cool air under his slow perusal of her body.

Marco lowered his head to the sensitive spot just under her ear and breathed. The feel of his hot breath and his lips on her skin made goose bumps erupt all over her. He licked and kissed his way down the long exposed arch of her neck, gently biting her from time to time. Where his mouth touched he left a trail of heat. Her cunt felt heavy in its arousal, thick and damp and swollen, wanting to be penetrated and taken hard and fast. She felt insatiable for both these men.

He nibbled his way over her collarbone, over her breasts and paid such exquisite, special attention to her nipples that Miranda thought she'd come from that alone. She stared down as his sensual lips worked each in turn, causing things to happen to her much farther down her body. Instead, he continued on, bracing one hand at the small of her back while he kissed his way over her abdomen and dragged his tongue through her pubic hair.

Marco's tongue flicked her clit and she jerked, not out of surprise, but raw enthusiasm. "Don't move," he growled. He groped on the table, found a bear-shaped bottle of honey and knelt between her thighs.

She heard the *snick* of the bottle being opened and felt a thin trail of thick, slightly cold honey drop on her clit and run between her labia. Miranda gasped and fought not to squirm backward.

Marco made a low sound of approval in the back of his throat and spread the honey over her sex with his index finger, massaging it into the opening of her cunt and over her labia. He worked it into her clit patiently until she was moaning and tipping her head back with her eyes closed.

Then he licked it all away.

Her breath hissed out of her as his hot mouth closed over her pussy and began to work. The man seemed to really enjoy going down on her and—wow—he was good at it. His skillful tongue delved through her labia and teased her clit, pushing her closer and closer to climax.

Miranda's elbows gave and she had to lower herself onto the table. Marco pushed her back a little, placing her feet on the table and spreading her thighs wide. Her head hit a plate and she was pretty sure she had some jelly in her hair, not that she really cared at this point.

Marco slid his hands beneath her ass and cupped her cunt to his mouth, like water to a parched man. He nibbled and licked her into a sexual frenzy. She tried to resist the urge to mash her pussy up against his lips in her excitement. God, he was going to bring her by using his tongue . . . again. He latched on to her clit and concentrated on it.

This morning he seemed to want to take no prisoners. This was no tease like last night. This was flat-out pussy eating at its best and it pushed her right over the edge.

Miranda shuddered, shivered and orgasmed against his quest-
ing tongue. Her soft, passionate cries filled the room, along with
Marco's noises of satisfaction.

Once the waves of pleasure had passed and her heartbeat had
more or less returned to normal, she looked up to find Theo standing in the hallway, his cock hard as rock. He held it in one strong
hand and slowly pumped while he watched them. "Looks like
Marco enjoyed his breakfast," he commented, staring at Miranda.

Marco pulled her up and kissed her forehead. "Come, Theo's
ready for us."

She frowned. What did they have planned for her now? She
took Marco's hand and followed Theo down the hallway toward
the bedroom. "Why is it that I seem to never be sated with you
two this weekend?" she asked. "I just keep coming and coming and
I'm still excited." She paused, considering. "It's like I'm in heat."

Theo turned to her in the hallway and pressed her against the
wall. His hand found her pussy and stroked while he kissed her
deep and hard, slanting his mouth over hers. When he'd finished
and she was panting and weak-kneed again, he murmured, "It's
the bond between us you're feeling, Miranda. You yearn to tie
yourself to us physically and emotionally. Therefore your libido
is running extra hard this weekend, just as ours have been ever
since we first laid eyes on you."

"What's the cure?" she breathed against his lips as his fingers
gently caressed her between her thighs. Not that she minded the
disease.

A wicked smile curved his lips. "Lots and lots of sex."

"Oh."

He grabbed her hand and pulled her through the doorway of
the bedroom.

"Oh!" she said again, seeing what Theo had been doing while
Marco had been busy with her on the dining room table. "Is that
for me?"

"Oh, yeah," said Marco, muscling her toward the contraption
set up at the end of Theo's bed.

He helped her onto a small platform several inches high. Above her head swung ropes with soft-lined cuffs. Miranda understood the concept. The platform made her tall enough to match them in height more or less—cunt to cocks.

Theo stared into her eyes as he gathered her wrists and pulled them up, securing them in the lambskin-lined cuffs. The locks closed with a snick and she was stretched upward, bound and helpless to them.

"How do you feel?" Theo purred as he kissed her face, his hands rubbing over her back.

She grasped the ropes and let them take her weight. The ropes were strong enough that she could probably swing from them if she wanted. "Exposed," she breathed.

"Yes." He eased a hand to her cunt, spreading her thighs, and stroked her with sureness and experience.

"Helpless . . . uhn," she murmured, feeling herself cream against the slow drag of his fingers over her sex.

"Mmm, you like that a little bit, don't you, love?"

She felt drugged. Something had happened when they'd bound her, she'd relaxed and gone limp. She'd given up to them, everything up to them. Miranda trusted them both enough to do that. She knew somewhere deep within her, past all her fears, that they would never hurt her. "Uhn," she moaned again.

"Do you trust us?" Theo asked as he gently worked her clit between his thumb and forefinger. "You know if you want us to stop you just say the word."

"I trust you," she sighed, knowing it was the truth.

She did trust them.

"I don't think you'll want us to stop, Miranda," Theo finished. He closed his mouth over her breast, still working her clit.

Her head hung back and she let the ropes take her weight. Groaning, she decided she really probably wouldn't.

Behind her, she felt Marco slick lubricant over her anus. She jerked in surprise and he held her hip, holding her in place as he eased his fingers into her tight rear opening, relaxing the muscles and widening her. A long groan came from Miranda as he gently thrust in and out, murmuring sweetly to her in a language she didn't understand.

Theo guided the head of his cock to her cunt and wrapped his arms around her, gently taking her weight against him and kissing her mouth as he thrust slowly and surely into her heat even as Marco worked his fingers in and out of her from behind.

It was almost too much.

It was like sensory overload to the point where she could barely find the beginning and the end to what Theo and Marco did to her. It was just all pleasure, intense and overwhelming. It stole her breath, her thought, her ability to reason at all. At this point she was completely at their mercy and she loved it.

She did trust them. Totally and perfectly in this one moment. She wanted nothing more than to please them, to let them use her body to find their release. The thought excited her.

Theo thrust his hips up, hilting deep inside her. Miranda gasped at the sensation of having him fill her so suddenly. Her cunt muscles pulsed and rippled around his shaft. Theo groaned and nuzzled her throat, holding her against his chest as he gently and slowly fucked her until she was whimpering and moaning his name.

"I love you," he murmured into her ear. He fisted his fingers through her curls and kissed her earlobe. "I love you, Miranda. Do you understand?" His voice was filled with emotion. "I would do anything for you, do anything to have you in my life." Over and over he told her he loved her as his cock glided in and out of her body.

She couldn't respond. "Oh, Theo," she whispered. She felt tears fill her eyes, emotion for him well in her chest.

Marco braced her back, ran his hands over her. His hands slipped between her body and Theo's to cup her breasts and roll her nipples. All the while Theo eased in and out of her.

"Easy, baby," Marco said as he set the lubed head of his cock to her ass. He pressed up into her, widening her and tunneling deeper within. "Mmmm, relax, okay?"

Miranda clenched her hands on the rope above her head at the erotic onslaught. It was incredible. She'd never felt so dominated and utterly possessed as she did now.

"Okay baby?" Marco whispered into her other ear. "Are you all right?"

She nodded slightly, her eyes closed, and panted. "Don't stop," she pushed out.

Marco chuckled and pushed within her another inch. "It would be hard to stop now, Miranda. You feel so damn perfect around my cock." Another slow inch, another . . . "Awww, honey," he groaned. "Hell, you feel good."

Finally they were both balls deep inside her and motionless. There was a little pain from having Marco in her ass, but it was nearly swallowed up by the sensation of pleasure.

Oh, God, could someone die of sexual ecstasy? she wondered through the fog in her brain.

In tandem, Marco and Theo began to gently thrust. The feeling was indescribable. She couldn't tell where Theo started and Marco began. It was just rapture, pure and intense. Each of them thrust into her, synchronizing their movements.

Miranda glanced to the side and caught their reflection in Theo's full-length mirror. She stood in the center of these two powerfully muscled men, her arms straight above her head and cuffed. Both men held her waist, their powerful legs and buttocks flexing as they both thrust up into her body on either side of her.

Her face was slack with lust and her eyes were dark and hooded under the heavy sexual fog she felt. She watched their pelvises thrust in the mirror's reflection as they took her slow and steadily, watched the expressions on their faces and recognized they felt this ecstasy too.

Their groans and sighs filled the air of the room, growing louder and more intense as they all found completion in each other.

Pleasure tingled through her, growing more and more intense until it exploded. Miranda tipped her head back and sagged in the ropes as she climaxed . . . and climaxed and climaxed. She heard both Theo and Marco groan as they, too, both came.

The orgasm stole parts of her vision, she felt defenseless under the power of it. Her cunt rippled and convulsed around Theo's pistoning cock until he gradually ceased his movements and the two men pulled out from her body.

Theo reached up and undid her cuffs. She let herself collapse on him and they laid her on the bed, one on each side of her. Miranda drowsed in a twilight zone of satisfaction, mostly unable to move or form words. She felt their hands moving over her flesh and their lips kissing over her. She heard them both murmur how much they loved her.

"Fireworks," Miranda murmured and then fell asleep.

F ireworks," murmured Marco as he snuggled in on one side of her.

Miranda drowsily opened her eyes. They'd slept on and off throughout the day, piled like puppies in the middle of Theo's enormous bed. She couldn't get enough of them. Periodically, they'd stroke her body into a frenzy of need and one of them would slide between her thighs and ease that need, while the other caressed her clit, kissed her mouth and petted her breasts.

Theo kissed her brow and stroked his strong hand down her arm. "Do you see how you fit with us, Miranda?" he whispered. "You're a puzzle piece. The one that makes the three of us a picture."

But what kind of picture? she wondered, nuzzling Marco's throat. A strong one, she suspected. A beautiful one. But only time would reveal that.

She felt like she wanted to give them that time. She wanted to see what they would be as a unit, a partnership . . . a family.

Outside, evening fell. It signaled the end of an amazing weekend. She had no clothes at Theo's apartment and she had to get up early for work, but she seemed unable to get out of his bed. She wanted to stay in their arms, receiving their kisses and caresses.

Theo must've seen her glance out of the window. "Thinking of leaving us?"

She smiled and kissed Marco's throat. "I want to stay," she answered simply.

SIX

"Bye, Valerie!" Miranda called as she pushed open the doors of the center and stepped outside into the late afternoon. She stopped and inhaled the fresh air and smiled. God, had she ever been this happy?

For the two last weeks, she'd seen either Theo or Marco almost every night, sometimes both of them together. Sometimes there was just rocking hot sex, other times they took her out to eat, or to an art gallery. Theo had taken her on a midnight cruise down the river once.

Every night she'd gotten to know them each better.

And could say she'd fallen in love with both of them.

Fallen in love with handsome, powerful and sophisticated Theo. What woman wouldn't fall prey to a man with the charms he possessed? He could make her orgasm hard enough to see stars and discuss Goethe with her afterward while he stroked her with his strong hands.

Fallen in love with Marco, who was far more bark than he was bite . . . with her anyway. Really, the man was a teddy bear who liked to cuddle after he'd blown her mind—several times—in bed. He was sensitive, passionate and loyal to a fault.

Fishing her keys out of her purse, she walked toward her car. It was clear she cared for both men, and they cared for her. Her doubts and fears still lingered. In truth, they were so deep-seated she wasn't sure they could ever be completely vanquished. However, she trusted both Marco and Theo, trusted and loved them.

It was time she demonstrated that.

Theo had once broached the subject of all three of them moving in together, as Olivia, Mason and Will had done. Theo said that all three of them could sell their condos and buy a house that would suit them all, maybe somewhere a little ways away from the city on a pretty piece of land with trees.

It would be a huge move for Miranda, a large investment in her love for them and a rejection of her lingering fears. It was a bold move, and an impulsive one, but this was far from a regular relationship and more and more every day she felt that incredible bond Theo and Marco spoke of.

Tonight she intended to tell both Marco and Theo that she wanted to do it.

She had invited them to dinner at Seventh Heaven, a wonderful restaurant downtown. There, she'd tell them everything she was feeling—how she'd come to love them both and how strange it was that her caring for them seemed so deep and so strong. She'd tell them that, despite her fears, she wanted to bind her life to theirs. Miranda wanted to tell them that so intertwining her existence with theirs felt natural, normal and oh-so very right.

Smiling at how she expected her men to react, she opened her car door and sat down behind the wheel.

The sound of creaking leather from the backseat had her freezing in the act of starting her car. She glanced into the rearview mirror and saw the goblin, the abusive husband Brian, leaning toward her.

Miranda gasped and went to open the door to get out, but Brian pressed the muzzle of a gun to her temple.

"No," he snarled. "You will close that door, start this car and drive."

She paused, breathing heavy through her nose and trying not

to panic. Miranda pulled the door closed, leaned back in her seat and started the engine. Then reached over and buckled her seat belt. She did it all smoothly and easily. Out of habit. Her mind had gone strangely clear.

"Pull out and head down the street. At the corner take a left."

"Where are we—"

The muzzle pressed so hard against her temple it made her yelp. "No questions. No words from you, understand? I do all the talking."

Miranda guided the car out into the street, glancing from side to side for anyone she might know and could signal for help. Unfortunately, only stranger after stranger met her gaze.

Her hands shaking and her heart thumping wildly in her chest, she rolled past Seventh Heaven . . . and down the street. A sob caught in her throat as she pictured Marco and Theo there waiting for her. They might get a sense of her alarm and stress, but they wouldn't know what happened to her, where she was or how to help her.

Brian caressed the side of her face with the cold muzzle of the gun. "I can't wait to get you alone, honey. Teach you to have proper respect for your betters. I'm gonna beat it into you . . . respect." He motioned with the gun. "Turn left at the next light."

Turning left at the next light would put them on the road that would take them out of the city, out into the country. It was the road to the large lake about ten miles from the city. She glanced around out of the corners of her eyes, hoping someone would notice that she was being held captive, that the man in the backseat of her car was holding a gun on her. However no one in any of the cars around her seemed to see. They were all concentrating on the road, talking amongst themselves or rocking out to their car stereos and in their own little world.

They traveled out of town, the buildings gradually giving

way to trees and the two-lane highway eventually becoming one.

"I'm taking you to my friend's cabin out on Capawin Lake. It'll be nice and quiet out there." He paused. "Nobody to hear you scream while I teach you. Tell you what you *really* are."

A shiver ran down Miranda's spine. She realized that if she didn't get the upper hand she wouldn't make it out of this alive. "What I really am?"

The muzzle of the gun smacked her head. Pain lanced through her temple. "I said no words from you!" He made a low growling sound and Miranda watched in the rearview mirror as his green gums pulled away to reveal blackened teeth.

Oh, if Sarah only knew what she'd married.

"You want to know what you are, bitch? You're so eager, can't wait until we get to the cabin." Brian let out a strangled laugh. "Your shining fae boyfriends think you're like them . . . Tylwyth Teg. I knew the truth the first moment I touched you." He paused. "You've got goblin blood, not fae."

Miranda's hands shook so hard on the wheel the car jerked. "That's not true."

The muzzle dug into her temple. "Oh, it's true. Whether or not you believe it, it's true. Goblins never mistake one of their own. If your boyfriends pulled up your spirit pattern, they would have seen it. It's subtle, but noticeable. You probably come by it on your father's side," he finished with a cruel snicker.

She went cold, remembering the exchange in Theo's living room when Marco had pulled the pattern up. They'd both been surprised by something, but had masked it, brushed it off. She'd noticed it, but had been far too enamored of the image shimmering before her to pursue it very far.

God. What if it was true?

Her father had been like Brian in many ways. He'd laid claim to her mother like she was his property to do with as he pleased. Was that a goblin trait as well as a trait of an abusive human man?

But how could she have a bond with Marco and Theo if she was part goblin and not part fae?

"Don't worry, honey," Brian said silkily. Every word he spoke dripped with undisguised hatred. "I'm going to teach you what being with a goblin is like. It'll be fun." He laughed. "'Course then I'm going to sink you to the bottom of the lake so you can't stand between me and my Sarah anymore."

Miranda clutched the steering wheel so hard she swore it would break. She needed to get away from him, but that gun muzzle to her temple precluded any of the plans riffling through her mind.

She glanced out at the pastures and four-board fences of the country that zipped past—at the trees and telephone poles. She did a double take. A telephone pole. She could . . . *Oh, God.* She could crash the car. She was wearing her seat belt. She'd buckled up purely out of a force of habit.

Brian wasn't belted in at all.

"Once you're out of the picture, I'll find a way in to see my Sarah. I'll convince her to come back with me. If she doesn't . . . " he trailed off. "If she doesn't want to, I'll make sure we spend eternity together."

Cold, metallic fear spread over her tongue as memories rose up in her mind. *I'll make sure we spend eternity together.* He would kill Sarah and then himself. Just like her father killed her mother and then himself. Miranda felt tears clog her throat as the memories she always tried to suppress flooded her mind.

She'd been standing in the kitchen, putting away the plates, while her mother sat drinking coffee at the kitchen table. A loud crash met their ears and they looked to the door, seeing who stood there. Shocked and horrified, a plate slipped through Miranda's fingers and broke on the linoleum at her feet.

"I love you!" her father screamed at her mother. "I love you more than anything! Why can't you understand?"

Her mother rose to her feet and backed away from him, toward the windows behind her.

Her father raised his hand and Miranda saw he held a gun. "No!" she screamed. But it was too late. Everything was happening so fast.

Her mother, face white and eyes wide, looked at Miranda and Miranda saw resignation in her eyes. As though her mother had expected this would happen from the very beginning.

"I love you," her father said again softly, and then pulled the trigger.

The gunshot was ear-splittingly loud in the small apartment, but Miranda was too shocked and numb to react to the sound. She only watched her mother crumple to the floor, red already beginning to stain her cream-colored house-dress.

As if in slow motion, Miranda looked from her mother to her father and saw that he'd placed the muzzle of the gun under his chin.

He held her gaze, murmured, "Miranda," with a shiny, crazed look in his eyes, and pulled the trigger for the second time. He also crumpled.

It took a few seconds for help to arrive. People from the building rushed in to gawk, some to help. By that time, Miranda was sitting on the ground, cradling her mother's head in her lap.

She was already dead. Her open eyes looked glassy, her life cut off way too soon.

Right when it had begun again.

She couldn't let that happen to Sarah.

"No," Miranda said softly.

She spotted the pole on the right side of the road and veered violently toward it. The action took hardly any conscious thought on her part at all.

This was her only option.

"Marco, Theo," she whispered. "I love you."

"No! You stupid bitch!" Brian yelled.

The pole loomed in their vision. Brian cried out and lunged for the wheel, but it was too late. The gun discharged, blowing a hole through the driver's-side window.

It all happened in a split second.

The impact brought a terrible mind-numbing crash and the sound of twisted metal. The impact sent her straight into the steeling wheel. The air bag inflated and smacked her with a white-hot blossom of pain that echoed through her entire body. She hit her head against the remaining part of the driver's-side window. Incredible, unbelievable pain left her vision black. Hot liquid poured down her face and she knew without a doubt it was her own blood.

Her last thoughts were of Marco and Theo before she knew nothing else.

SEVEN

The gray jeweler's box containing the gorgeous diamond and sapphire ring Theo and Marco had purchased for Miranda sat on the center of the table. Candlelight flickered over the white linen tablecloth, the highly polished silver and the fine china plates. Expensive champagne chilled in an ice bucket at their side.

While they waited for their mate to show up, Marco and Theo drank single malt scotch from short chunky crystal glasses. Miranda had invited them to dinner tonight under a mysterious pretense, but Marco and Theo had been sensing her moods of late. She'd been growing increasingly fond of them, could even come close to saying *love*.

I love you were the words they both coveted to hear from her lips.

Marco glanced at the box and opened it, letting the candlelight reflect on the insanely beautiful—and expensive—ring. Miranda had never said she loved them, but both he and Theo knew she did. They both felt those words were forthcoming tonight. They'd bought her a ring as a symbol of their love. It was an engagement ring of sorts, Marco supposed, though their kind had no rituals for such a thing. There was just the natural bonding, a much stronger thing than the human's concept of matrimony.

Abruptly, emotions filled his mind that were so harsh, sudden and bitter that it made parts of his vision go black. Marco dropped the ring box on the table and gripped his glass so hard he thought he'd break it.

Miranda was in distress.

He looked at Theo who sat still at the table, his face pale. "Come on," he said tersely. They both could sense that it was bad, really bad.

They got up. Marco stuck the ring box in his pocket while Theo left enough money on the table to pay for their drinks and the bottle of champagne and then they headed out of the restaurant. Once they were on the street Theo looked up and down, rubbing a hand over his chin the way he did when he was frustrated.

"Where?" Theo growled.

That was the problem, they could feel Miranda's tumultuous emotions, but they had no idea where to find her.

Marco's fists clenched. "I don't know."

"Can you remote view?" Theo asked tightly.

Remote viewing was one of Marco's abilities, but it was unreliable and difficult to do. It might bring them a little information, but not much. He closed his eyes and honed in on his mate's feelings, focusing every bit of his power on them.

"I see the interior of a car. It's driving down . . . a country road." The vision went black. That's all he was going to get. "Fuck," he swore violently. "That's all I got."

Miranda's emotions spiked and then . . . nothing.

"What the hell just happened?" asked Theo. "I can't feel her anymore. I can't feel anything coming from her at all."

"Been knocked unconscious, maybe."

"You saw a car? She was driving?"

Marco shook his head. "I don't know if she was driving or not. She could've been a passenger. I don't even know if what I saw has anything to do with Miranda."

"We have to assume it does. Did you recognize anything? Landmarks?"

"It was the country . . . pasture, black four-board fences."

Theo swore under his breath. "Come on, we'll take my car. Fastest way out of town is Capawin Trail. Logic says that in the time it took her to leave work and for us to feel her distress, that's the most likely route."

They got into Theo's silver BMW and headed off as fast as they could in that direction. There still wasn't the slightest flicker of emotion coming from Miranda and that was a bad sign.

Both men were stoic as they raced through the city and down the two-lane country road that led out into the more rural part of the state. They didn't say a word as they passed pasture after pasture.

Marco was more and more sure that this was the direction he'd seen the car going in, but they were flying blind. If whoever had Miranda had rendered her unconscious, Marco had no chance to remote view through her eyes any more than he had.

Marco was staring out the window, trying to get a fix on Miranda when Theo sucked in a breath next to him. "What the hell is that ahead?"

His head snapped up to see a line of cars backed up and the flashing lights of fire trucks, police and ambulances. "An accident." He paused as the realization hit him. "Fuck. Do you think that Miranda could have been in that crash?"

A muscle worked in Theo's jaw. It made sense. It would explain the abrupt cessation of Miranda's emotions. "Hold on." He guided the car onto the shoulder to bypass the line of the cars that were backed up as a result of the accident. It was at a standstill and people had parked and were walking around. "We're going to find out."

Dread grew in Marco's stomach as they reached the scene. It was Miranda's blue sedan all right . . . wrapped around an electricity pole. Theo's expression was grim. He found a place to park and they got out of the car, heading toward the wreck. Marco could barely look—hot, twisted metal, broken glass. Power lines had come down from the broken pole and lay like dangerous snakes on the ground around the accident scene.

Where was Miranda?

Both Theo and Marco began to walk toward the car, but a uniformed policeman walked out in front of them, his hand raised. "Stop where you are and go back to your vehicle. Can't you see the downed power lines? Professionals only past this point."

Theo began to raise his hand, to cast a charm over him. Marco slapped his hand down. They were both upset and not thinking straight.

Marco knew how Theo felt. He had to restrain himself from punching the cop out. "We know the person who owns that car," Marco explained through gritted teeth. "A woman. Is she okay?"

He couldn't tear his gaze away from the wreck. It looked like no one could've come out of there alive. Something tightened in his throat and stole his breath. A strange calm had stolen over him. Somewhere in the back of his mind, disbelief reigned. He refused to fully accept the scene in front of him.

The cop jerked his head toward the ambulance that was just pulling away from the scene. "They're taking her to Mercy Medical. Sorry, guys, I don't know her status. I know they worked a long time to get her free of the car."

Marco exhaled in relief. She was alive. That was something, at least.

"Did you know the man who was with her?" the cop asked.

"Man?" Theo asked.

"I'm sorry if you did because he didn't survive. About five eight, two hundred and fifty pounds, brown hair. ID in his wallet said Brian Simpson."

Marco sucked in a breath. All the pieces were starting to fall into place. "No, we didn't know him."

"Well, head on down to Mercy Medical if you want. That's where we took the girl."

Theo thanked the cop and Marco looked over at a second ambulance where they were loading a body bag. Brian Simpson, the bastard who'd accosted Miranda at the shelter. The goblin who'd married a human woman and regularly used her as a punching bag.

Good riddance.

Bastard had fixated on Miranda for some reason. "Fuck," Marco swore as he got into the car and Theo started to pull away. "I should've seen it coming, should've suspected."

"Marco, don't beat yourself up. You couldn't have known that guy would come after her."

"He was probably pissed that Miranda pressed charges against him."

"Let's just get to the hospital. This isn't over yet."

Theo drove like the wind back into the city and to Mercy Medical.

She looked so pale and fragile in the bed.

Theo stood nearby and looked down at the woman he loved more than life itself. Tubes and hoses connected her to beeping, humming machines. Her face and body were a mass of bruises and bandages. Her arm and one of her legs were broken, plus several of her ribs.

Worse, she hadn't woken up.

The doctors said she'd been badly traumatized in the accident and might *never* wake up.

He wanted to get into the bed with her, pull her close to him so he could feel the beat of her heart, her body's warmth and the gentle rise and fall of her chest, just to assure himself that she lived.

Marco stood at the end of the bed. Theo knew he still had the ring box in his pocket. Theo also knew that Marco was blaming himself for Miranda's abduction and accident and would probably never forgive himself.

Theo glanced around to make sure that no one could hear what he was about to say. They'd been able to flirt their way into Miranda's room via the nurses at the nursing station. They'd told them that they were Miranda's close friends and her only real family. It hadn't even been a lie. The fact that they'd moved her into a private room and were paying for all her medical bills had swayed them somewhat as well.

"We need to give her our blood," said Theo softly.

"If she never wakes up . . . it's a risk. She could lay in a coma for a very, very long time." He paused. "And we'd be binding her to us without her permission."

"I know. She's part goblin." He paused. "You saw that as clearly as I did. If she were part fae, she would need goblin blood and that would be more complicated. But being part goblin, she needs the pure blood of the fae to bind and activate her goblin DNA. It will make her stronger." He paused. "She might survive this with our blood."

Marco stared down at her for several moments. "I'll be back," he said quietly and slipped from the room with a whisper of his black duster.

Theo stared down at Miranda, wondering what had happened. They were pretty sure that Brian had abducted her. They now knew the cops had found a gun at the scene of the accident. Miranda's policeman friend, Craig, had told them that.

After that, they had several theories about what might have occurred. According to the paramedics, she'd been driving. Theo and Marco thought either she'd been battling with the goblin and had crashed the car, something happened on the road to cause the accident, or . . . she'd crashed the car on purpose.

He rubbed a hand over his face wearily, feeling a heavy weight in his chest. God, he just wanted her back, whole and safe in his arms. He'd give anything for that. Theo felt helpless and he knew Marco felt the same way. The goblin had died in the car crash, so there wasn't even any way for them to take vengeance for Miranda.

Of course, if Miranda had crashed the car on purpose, she'd already taken her own vengeance.

A feminine gasp of dismay made Theo turn.

"Mira," Olivia said softly, putting her hand to her mouth and slowly approaching Miranda's bedside. "Oh, no." She shook her head, looking at Theo. "This can't be. It isn't possible."

"I wish we were all just having a nightmare," replied Theo wearily.

Olivia's eyes were filled with tears. "So . . . they don't know if she'll . . . ever wake up?"

Theo said nothing, but he knew the answer lay plainly in his eyes.

Olivia looked back at Miranda and sniffled. "I don't have to ask if you're in love with her," she said softly. "Or Marco. I know the process. Have you bonded her yet?"

A muscle moved in his jaw. "Marco went to find a syringe."

She frowned. "You have a vial of goblin blood with you?"

He paused. "Olivia, there's something you should know."

Olivia looked at him with dread in her eyes. "No more bad news please."

"It's not bad or good. It's just a fact. A surprising fact." He licked his lips. "Miranda is actually part goblin, not part fae as we assumed."

"Really?" She frowned and looked at her friend. "How odd."

"They're just rare. Rarer than fae and human crossbreeds. I'd make a guess Miranda only has a little blood, passed down somewhere from within her family tree. We saw it clearly, however, when we pulled her spirit pattern up."

Olivia chewed her lower lip. "So you're injecting your blood into her to make the bond."

"Yes, well, I'll blend Marco's blood with mine and inject the mix."

"It should make her stronger. Maybe she'll heal herself."

"That's the gamble we're taking. The thing is . . . she never gave us permission to do this. I-I don't know how she'll feel, linking her life to ours," he finished miserably.

Olivia smiled and walked toward him. She reached up and cupped his cheek in her palm. Her voice was warm when she spoke. "She loves you back, Theo, you and Marco both. Believe me, I'm her best friend. She is a sister to me. I see it all the time when she talks about you or looks at you." She sighed. "Believe me when I say that her caring for you goes every bit as deeply as mine for my men."

The sound of Marco's duster came from the doorway. He walked to them both and opened his palm. In it, lay a syringe in a plastic package. He ripped the package open with his teeth and took the syringe out.

Olivia watched as Marco and Theo went to stand at Miranda's bedside. Marco rolled up his sleeve and Theo took some blood from his arm. Then Theo rolled up his sleeve and Marco did the same.

Theo held the syringe up to the light, seeing their blood mixing.

A nurse rolled a cart toward the door and Theo put the syringe down quickly.

Olivia moved fast. "Excuse me," she called to the nurse as she blocked her entrance to the room. "I have a few questions about my friend's condition . . ."

Their voices seemed to fade away. Theo looked at Marco and then injected their blood into Miranda's frail looking arm.

Marco took the ring box from his pocket and slipped the sapphire and diamond ring onto her thin finger.

Together, they stared down at her.

It was a question of time.

Three weeks.

Marco sat in the hospital chair by Miranda's bed and hung his head. Either he or Theo were here every moment, listening to the gentle hiss and beeping of the machines that surrounded Miranda.

She never woke.

She'd healed, though, much faster than normal. It perplexed the doctors. They told them she'd always been a fast healer, but of course that thin explanation only went so far.

Marco raised his head and ran his hand over his face. He hadn't shaved in a while and stubble pricked his skin. For several moments, he watched the gentle rise and fall of her chest. A nurse came in and asked him if he wanted something. He shook his head. She smiled sadly at him and left him alone.

God, the time just seemed to inch by. Would she never wake up? Would she sleep out her whole, now very long life? Marco shuddered as grief clenched somewhere near his heart. He couldn't live without her. Not now. Not after he'd met her, gotten to know her and fallen in love with her.

He missed the warmth of her body, the sound of her voice, her gentle smile. He missed the way the sun glinted in her curls. He missed her laughter and even her tears.

The universe couldn't be so cruel. It *had* to give her back.

Anger surged through him. Clenching his fists, he looked skyward. There was no one to direct his rage at. The goblin was dead and fate was too vast and intangible to fight.

Marco got up and for the fiftieth time that day, went to Miranda's bedside. He reached out and smoothed her lank hair away from her pale face. He could trace the fine blue veins under her skin. All her bruises and cuts had healed and faded. Her broken bones had mended. All as a result of infusing her with their blood and activating her goblin DNA. It hadn't healed whatever had happened in her brain, however. It was possible that nothing could mend that.

Sorrow caught in Marco's throat.

Someone moved in the doorway and Marco looked up to see Theo standing there. Theo looked about as bad as he felt. He walked over to stand on the other side of Miranda's bed to look down on her.

"No change," said Marco unnecessarily.

Theo nodded and picked up Miranda's small hand in his own. "Come back to us, Miranda," he said. *"Tae onae su tae maelavicti."*

It meant *we need you or we'll die* in the old language.

Marco picked up her other hand and rubbed his thumb across her chilled flesh. *"Tae onae amouraei."* We love you. He lowered his head to her lips and kissed her.

Maybe he thought the words, the kiss and the emotions coursing between himself and Theo might wake her.

He was wrong.

She didn't stir and after a few moments, he and Theo stepped back away from the bed. They both sat down in chairs and settled in for the long, long night.

At some point, Marco drifted off to sleep and dreamed about the time before Miranda's accident. Of how he and Theo were jealous of each other at first, but now they were one—united in both love and sorrow.

Something woke him and Marco groaned, finding himself in an uncomfortable position in the stiff backed chair he sat in. The room was dark, save for the glow that spilled in from the hallway. Beside him, in another chair, Theo also slept.

The sound came again, a rustling near Miranda's bed.

Suddenly alert, Marco rose to his feet and inched closer. The rustling sound, like blankets being moved, came again. He reached her bedside and saw the most beautiful thing he'd ever seen—

Miranda's wide blue-green eyes open.

"Miranda," he breathed, smiling.

She smiled back at him and took his hand, squeezing with weak fingers. The ring glinted on her finger. She tried to remove the tube from her mouth, but seemed unable to manage it. Marco pulled it gently from her lips.

"Marco," she croaked. It was the most gorgeous sound ever to his ears. Music.

"Theo!" Marco called. "Theo, she's awake."

Theo came awake as if someone had shot a gun in the room. He rushed to her bedside. "Miranda." His voice broke. "We were afraid we'd never see your pretty smile again, love. You've been sleeping on us."

"How long?" she asked.

"Over three weeks," Marco answered.

Her eyes widened. She seemed unable to talk or move very well, undoubtedly a result of being immobile for so long.

Theo sought the nurse's call button and pushed it.

Marco smoothed her hair away from her brow and she closed her eyes and sighed at his touch. "God, I'm so happy you've come back to us," he said with emotion thick in his voice. He felt anger tighten his body. "Did you have to fight that bastard in the car, Miranda? Is that how it crashed?"

She shook her head.

"You crashed it on purpose, didn't you, love?" asked Theo.

She nodded, her eyes filling with tears. "He was going after his wife, Sarah," she rasped softly. A tear rolled down her cheek. "Like . . . my mom." She began sobbing quietly.

The nurse came into the room, saw that Miranda was awake and rushed back out again. In moments she returned with a doctor and a couple of nurses and soon Miranda was swallowed up in them.

Soon, though, she would be all theirs again.

EIGHT

On the other end of town was another road, this one also leading out into the country. It was this road that Miranda took with Theo and Marco the day she got out of the hospital.

They got into Marco's SUV and drove through the city.

They'd kept her in the hospital for another week, running tests to make sure she'd be okay once she was released. Her healing, of course, had verged on the miraculous because Theo and Marco had bonded her. She glanced down at her ring and smiled, bonded her in more ways than one. In any case, she'd wanted to get out of the hospital quickly before government agents whisked her away to be "studied" or something.

The bright sunlight of the afternoon had nearly blinded her when she'd exited the hospital. Theo had bundled her into the passenger seat of the SUV—belted her in tightly—and handed her a pair of shades. Now she had the window open and was practically hanging her head out of it, enjoying the fresh air. She thought maybe she'd be afraid to get into another car, but no . . . she was enjoying life.

"So, where are we going?" she asked for the hundredth time. They wouldn't tell her.

"It's a surprise," answered Marco. "We're almost there." He

turned down a small lane, lined on each side with tall, mature trees. They traveled over a small hill and a house came into view.

Miranda frowned, taking in the scene before her. It was a huge log cabin. Gorgeous. With a wraparound porch and gabled windows. The land it sat on was fenced—perfect for a dog—with rough-hewn logs and dotted throughout with trees, bushes and flowering plants. A short distance away stood an outbuilding—a horse stable by the looks of it—that matched the house. It was beautiful, her dream home. It was the kind of home she'd told Theo she'd wanted on their first date.

It couldn't be . . . could it?

Marco parked his SUV in front of the garage door and the three of them got out.

Silence.

The road was far away and the only sound was of the birds and wind in the trees. It was her idea of paradise. "Where are we?" she asked, confused.

Theo walked to her with a set of keys in his hand. He held them out to her. "You're home."

"Home?" Her mind stuttered. "I'm home? What do you mean, you bought this place . . . for me?"

"That's not all," said Marco. "On that key ring is a key to an empty building downtown. We bought it for you so you can start a women's shelter, if that's still what you want to do. You'll have funding. Theo and I will finance you. We've both been able to build up nice amounts of money over the years and we're always looking for good ways to spend it."

She looked from Theo to Marco, speechless. They'd made her dreams come true. "But-I" she started. "But—" And then she burst into tears.

Marco and Theo drew her into their arms and she sobbed, feeling stupid. So much had happened. The accident, now this.

The accident had—ironically—healed something inside her. Knowing she'd prevented Sarah from being harmed by Brian had helped her come to terms with her mother's murder. Nothing would ever make it okay, but she felt like she'd at least saved another woman from suffering the same fate.

Sarah would get what her mother never had—a fresh start.

She felt Theo lift her like she weighed nothing. She curled her arms around his throat and nuzzled the place where his shoulder and neck met and inhaled the scent of his skin. It comforted her.

Marco opened the front door of her new house and Theo bore her over the threshold. He set her on an overstuffed red velvet couch and the two men sat down on either side of her.

"Don't you like it?" Marco asked.

She wiped her eyes and looked around her. There was a huge creek stone fireplace, red velvet chairs and couches, strewn with pillows, hardwood floors and matching end tables. The open kitchen was to her left, clearly state-of-the-art. A spiral staircase near the kitchen led to the loft above her with a hallway that led to other rooms.

"I love it. It's gorgeous," she sniffled. She shook her head. "I can't accept this—"

"You must," answered Theo. "It's a gift because we love you."

"We watched you fight for your life in the hospital for over three weeks," Marco cut in. "Buying this house and getting it ready for you was the only thing that kept us going. You have to accept it. We hired people to decorate it, if you don't like it—"

She put her hand over Marco's mouth. "I was going to say that I can't accept this house unless you both live here with me." She replaced her hand with her mouth. Marco twined his arms around her and dragged her up against his chest with a groan.

"Don't crush her, Marco," said Theo. "She just got out of the hospital."

Marco let her go reluctantly and grinned. "Sorry, couldn't help it."

"I'm fine, you guys. Really. The doctors kept me for far longer than I had to be there, I think." She shrugged. "I feel up to anything you might have in mind, actually," she finished suggestively.

Theo raised an eyebrow. "Really? Well, that's good news."

Actually, she was dying for them to touch her, hold her, kiss her. It had been all she could think of since she'd started to feel better. God, she'd missed them so much. Though they'd visited her every day in the hospital, she still longed for the feel of their hard, naked bodies against her and their hot breath on her skin.

Being with them both was like being wrapped safe in a cocoon and Miranda had realized that that was the only place she ever wanted to be.

"We were hoping you might say that," Marco said, grinning. "We made sure we ordered extra-large beds."

Miranda laughed. "That shows incredible foresight."

Marco stood. "Well, we've got our priorities in order."

Theo stood as well and held out his hand. "Come on, take the tour."

She rose and took his hand. The three of them toured room after room of the house, which was decorated much the way she'd always dreamed—comfortably, big overstuffed couches and chairs, lots of throw pillows and soft blankets. The colors were blues, greens and creams. They'd gathered her things from her apartment and scattered them throughout the place.

She tried to muster up some anger at their presumption that she would want to live here, but she couldn't manage to command any. After all, the night of her accident she'd actually been on her way to tell them she wanted to take up Theo's offer to do just this—move to the country and in with the two men she loved.

The house was beyond her dreams and any expectations she'd ever had. In the time she'd known Theo and Marco, they'd managed to get to know her so well that she didn't think she could've selected and decorated the house any better than they had. Tears clogged her throat again and she stopped in front of a doorway to control herself.

It was that more than anything, more than the house itself, that choked her up and made love swell in her chest for Marco and Theo.

She really was coming home.

Theo guided her into a room.

"We meant this bedroom to be yours. We thought we'd each take one to be our private digs," said Theo. "Though I hope we can work out a way where you spend some nights with me, some with Marco and maybe some on your own, if that's what you want."

The room had a cherry sleigh bed, piled high with pillows. Matching furniture dotted the room. A door leading to a private bathroom stood to her left and a patio door with a deck that overlooked a grove of trees was directly in front of her. "It's lovely," she sniffled. "Everything's perfect."

"Miranda, what's wrong?" asked Marco.

She turned and hugged him. "I love you," she said. She looked at Theo. "I love you both so much I think something might break in my chest."

Theo drew her from Marco and pulled her against him. "We know, Miranda."

"But I never said it out loud."

Marco touched her back. "The words are sweet to hear and we hope to hear them often, but we already knew you loved us. You loved us from the first time you met us, you were just too stubborn to admit it to yourself."

She gasped and turned toward him. "Oh, really? That's a pretty arrogant assumption—"

He drew her against him. "Well, I'm an arrogant guy, baby," he murmured right before his mouth came down on hers and stole her words and all her thoughts.

Arousal flared through her body, hot and heavy. It had been so long since she'd had sex, over a month now since her automobile accident. She yanked Marco's duster off. It dropped in a pile at their feet.

Marco raised an eyebrow. "Theo, I think she's asking for something."

She turned to Theo, grabbed his shirtfront and yanked him toward her.

"Miranda—" he started

"I'm fine," she murmured as she started unbuttoning his shirt. "I've had a week of bed rest when I was already completely healed. I'm fine and I'm," she got the last of his buttons undone, "incredibly horny." She ran her hands over his hard, muscled chest and couldn't stop her groan of pleasure. "I want you both . . . *now.*"

"Well, milady gets what she wants," Theo answered with a grin.

Marco reached over and switched off the light.

EDIBLE DELIGHTS

Jan Springer

ONE

Several days earlier . . .

Max Rivers couldn't stop inhaling the succulent scent wafting off the lavender-colored letter that accompanied the large sample of edible underwear his elderly assistant had placed on his desk early this morning.

The sweet smell intrigued him. Made his cock stone-hard while memories of a certain sexy redhead bombarded him. After all these years apart he still remembered her sparkling blue eyes, her slender waist, the curve of her wide hips as she bucked against him and oh those alley-cat screams that made him all hot and bothered when his partner Nick and he double penetrated her.

At first he was surprised to discover the sample of her edible underwear on his desk. It wasn't normal for uptight, irritated, seventy-five-year-old Maybell to bother him with such an intimate arrangement unless they belonged to an extremely famous designer.

Why the sudden change?

His design and distribution company Impulse only dealt with veterans in the design industry and Allie Masters had a long way to go before she was a veteran. Small companies owned by sexy redheads who unexpectedly dumped Nick and him in their ménage a trois relationship several years earlier didn't come into the equation.

Come to think of it, why was Allie, owner of Edible Delights, sending him her erotic wear? What was the sexy bitch up to?

He inhaled deeper, allowing the sensual smell to seep farther into his lungs. Those same wild feelings he experienced every time he'd been around Allie surfaced immediately.

It was *her* scent. Intoxicating. Delicious. Fucking addictive.

The throbbing way his cock's blood vessels pumped wicked jolts of hot blood into his shaft could attest to the fact he hadn't lost a smidgen of interest in her. No woman could make him swell this quickly, this painfully.

Only Allie.

Alluring. Sexy. Evasive Allie. The woman who provoked all his carnal senses just by her scent.

She had been his and Nick's assistant. So damned elusive and seemingly businesslike. Until the night the three of them became trapped in the elevator together. The sexual tension sparking between the three of them over the past couple of years exploded that night.

Nick and he took her there. Took turns fucking her hot, curvy body. In the end they double penetrated her.

Fuck! She was so tight with both of them inside her.

So hot. So wild as she stood trapped between them.

He blew out an excited breath and glanced at the address on the package. He did a double take. It was a California address. Allie's company's name was on it but in the care of Allie's older sister Sindie.

Hmm . . . interesting. Obviously Sindie was up to her matchmaking playtime now that Allie had returned from her stay in Europe. Sindie had a knack for matching up lovers at the right time and it was odd that she wasn't attached.

Max found himself smiling despite the uncomfortable way his cock throbbed. Okay, he would play along with Sindie. It was high time Nick and he got Allie back. Then they could all move back in together again and continue the hottest, most satisfying relationship he'd ever been in.

Slamming a finger onto a speakerphone button, he waited anxiously for his elderly assistant to answer.

"Yes, sir?" came Maybell's nasally bored tone.

He hired Maybell shortly after Allie had left her position and moved to Europe. Maybell was a snobby, prim and proper elderly grandmother and totally not his cup of tea. But she once worked for the competition and quit mere months before her forced retirement. He heard rumors she had done it to spite her former boss' son. He had recently taken over the company where she worked for almost fifty years. The new boss had told her she was being "put out to pasture" and she was too old to know anything about the new fashions.

She proved them wrong by making the jump to Impulse with ease. She brought with her many trade secrets that quickly pushed Impulse to the top in fashionable erotic wear. She also used her contacts to acquire famous, beautiful models to show off Impulse's designs as well as securing choice spots in fashion shows all over the world. With her help they opened their own successful clothing distribution company.

Maybell ran their company with damned accurate efficiency. He knew without a doubt she had brought Impulse to the top of the fashion industry just to spite her old employer. But that didn't matter. Nick and he would be forever grateful for her help.

"Maybell, get ahold of the owner of Edible Delights."

"Edible Delights, sir?"

"The samples you brought in this morning."

"Samples, sir? I didn't—Oh! You mean *those* samples. I noticed they are quite different than what we're used to. Although I'm sure she has her edibles patented, I have contacts who can go around this small-time company. I thought you might want to copy them. Send them to one of our own top designers to duplicate."

Like hell!

"I want a meeting with the owner . . . Allie Masters . . . at

Club Rendezvous." Club Rendezvous was a swingers club in Alberta, Canada. A friend of theirs owned it. Allie wouldn't suspect Nick and he were behind the meeting if it took place way up in Canada—that is, she wouldn't suspect until it was too late.

"I want Impulse to try out her European Fling line." That's what Allie was calling her latest line of edibles. "Make it this weekend. Saturday night. Tell her to bring enough sexy edibles to outfit at least two hundred people. She'll be generously compensated."

There was a momentary silence on the other end and he could almost picture Maybell pursing her lips in disappointment. Up until now he always followed her ideas and suggestions because he knew her fifty years of experience was a hell of a lot better than his ten.

"But, sir, I thought it would be better for one of our own experienced designers—"

"Maybell?" he cut her off, suddenly feeling very impatient with her.

"Yes, sir?"

"Don't tell her who Nick and I are. Or the company we represent. Give us a couple of famous names from a top competition company."

"Sir?"

He could hear the utter surprise in her voice. Her curiosity about his steering away from the norm. Maybell had never seen his impulsive side so it was understandable she'd be knocked off kilter and question him.

Allie had always brought out his wild ways. Ways he never even knew he had until the sexy redhead had applied for the assistant position.

The way he reacted to her was another reason he loved her so much. Up until meeting her, he had planned everything in his life around Impulse. Since she left, he returned to that boring routine. Even sex with the handful of casual dates over the years was planned. Planned and boring.

It was time he and his good friend and business partner Nick

Edwards showed Allie exactly how much they still missed her and how much they wanted her back.

"Make her an offer she can't refuse. And, Maybell?"

"Yes, sir?"

"Thanks." He cut her off and returned his attention to the elite arrangement of edibles he'd strewn across his desk. The first one that caught his eye was a rose-colored thong with an elegant sparkling of edible pale blue crystal beads that edged the waistband. There were several other items including a skimpy champagne-colored panty and bra set. It was made for a woman who wanted to give the impression she was angelic, a virgin.

Definitely not Allie.

He picked up a red-hot bra and instantly smelled juicy strawberries. Exquisite, delicate red lace edged the sheer see-through cups.

It had been designed for a sexy, daring woman by a sexy daring woman.

Allie.

He let out a tense breath and leaned closer. Stroking his tongue along the middle of the right cup where a tight, hard nipple would have been, he enjoyed the smooth way the material melted onto his tongue. He groaned at the deliciously sweet explosion of strawberry bursting against his taste buds. His eyes widened with surprise as he noted another flavor. Damned if the material didn't have a hint of Italian sweet port wine in it too. Real wine, if he wasn't mistaken.

Fuck.

She really learned something working over there in those European fashion companies, hadn't she? She really had known what she wanted when she left their company and headed overseas to be a red-hot designer.

Nick and he had not supported her efforts. Didn't encourage her to pursue her dreams. They were selfish. Wanted her all to themselves. Wanted her to remain their assistant and warming their beds.

Max shook his head and shoved aside the feelings of regret and guilt. There was no time for regret. No room for guilt. No time to waste.

He wanted Allie back. Knew Nick had never gotten over the ménage a trois relationship they shared either. Truthfully, it had been a bit awkward for all three of them at first, after that night in the elevator. Having sex with Allie and having Nick there watching them and vice versa. But Nick and he admitted to each other they were in love with Allie. They decided the best way to save their close friendship as well as get the woman they both wanted would be a ménage relationship. Thankfully she agreed. Deep down in his gut he knew she was the only woman they would ever share with each other because she was *the one.*

He gave the bra another lick, loving the way the silky material disintegrated in his mouth. He had never tasted anything so good in edible underwear. Hell, it didn't even taste like edible material. It tasted like strawberries and port wine, and not a hint of an aftertaste.

Nope, he had never tasted anything so perfect. Except Allie's hot, pink pussy.

At the memory of how juicy and sweet she tasted, his cock swelled to yet another painful level. This time the sensations felt sharper. Fiercer. He found himself shifting uncomfortably in his chair. Maybe this weekend was going to be too long a wait for him. He looked down and watched the harsh way his pants tented beneath his erection. He'd waited a long time to react this way to a woman again. Too damned long. Nick and he would make Allie cat's pussy purr and rest assured, they'd make her think twice about leaving them again.

TWO

Several days later . . .

Allie Masters nervously inspected the crisp bouquet of edible undergarments she laid out on the long table. Everything looked perfect. Just like a buffet. From the tasty panties and matching bras flavored to taste like ice wine in a bright watermelon-color to the brown-and-green-colored striped thongs for men tasting of Irish mint chocolate alcohol.

She brought along every savory piece of erotic clothing she had available in the factory on such short notice including her most popular side dishes—Austrian raspberry brandy nipple shields and Swiss chocolate edible condoms.

To tell the truth, she still couldn't believe her luck. The assistant to one of the United States' most popular adult clothing designers had called and asked if she would be interested in presenting a demo of her opening European Fling line.

Hell! Who wouldn't be interested? She said "yes" before she realized she hadn't even targeted that particular company or known the full details of supplying a club full of swingers in Alberta, Canada, as a test for her clothing line.

Later that same day she received a hefty certified check via courier sealing the deal.

Her first instinct had been to decline the offer. She knew the swinging scene would bring up too many memories of her time with Max and Nick. Even now as she thought about her two former bosses and what she experienced with them, she felt so hot she literally had to fan herself with one of the panties she held in her hand.

Sex with Nick and Max had been awesome. She would have stayed with them for the fantastic sex alone but she discovered she wanted more from the three-way relationship. She knew she had their love but she also wanted their support. She hadn't found that support. When she decided to spread her wings and pursue fashion design, Nick and Max had seemed more concerned in keeping her as their assistant and in bed with them rather than helping her achieve her goals. It had been a blow to her self-esteem and to her confidence. Realizing her need for independence, she left Impulse and her two well-hung lovers, accepting a job at a prestigious erotic wear company in Italy. She moved up the ranks, getting jobs in Portugal then ending up in Paris, France, before gleaning enough experience to return home and launch Edible Delights.

Business was brisk following her round of fashion shows and now she could barely keep up with supplying her customers with her unique designs and erotic-flavored edible fashions. All her hard work and sacrifices had paid off. But now it was time to jump into the big time and she needed a distributor to help.

With her dreams fulfilled she was happy careerwise but unhappy personally. Not to mention she was awfully horny without Max and Nick. Lately she craved them as never before. She wanted to pick up their relationship but pride kept her in California near her sister Sindie and away from New York City where her two ex-lovers lived and ran their lucrative fashion design and distribution company. The last thing she wanted to do was to go begging for some red-hot sex from the two men she abandoned.

She hadn't even realized what she left behind until she'd been in Europe. She hadn't realized how much she loved the untraditional setup of their ménage a trois relationship either. Two men who adored her so much they willingly shared her. She knew too if they ever forced her to decide between them, she wouldn't be able to. She loved them both dearly.

Max hid his sensuality behind a stern, rigid routine she finally managed to collapse. A man who made her heart skip a beat every time she thought of him.

And Nick whose easygoing attitude and dreamy brown eyes turned her hotter than hell with just one bold "I'm going to fuck you" look.

They were absolutely the perfect combination for her. They were straight men, boyhood friends, who happened to have the same ideas of designing and distributing erotic wear. Men who just happened to fall in love with the same woman.

Her.

She let out a tight breath as she caught her reflection in a nearby mirror. Her shoulder-length wavy red hair glowed brilliantly beneath the overhead lights. She wore little makeup. Just a dusting of gold eye shadow and a zip of pink lipstick.

Tonight she dressed herself in a sexy curve-hugging, gold-colored Gianni Versace viscose-jersey dress with soft fuchsia panty hose and snappy high-heeled shoes. She wore blue sapphire drop clip-on earrings that highlighted the blue in her eyes and diamond line bracelets that clinked gently every time she moved her arms.

Allowing the zipper of her dress to remain open to mid breast, she gave everyone a curvy glimpse. She also allowed several necklaces to scatter prettily along her chest area. Necklaces that included a diamond sun medallion pendant and an imitation diamond sautoir necklace. She hadn't wanted to look like the perfect businesswoman but instead opted for a fresh, alive appearance. Someone of confidence. A carefree woman comfortable with her own sexuality.

"Why so glum?" her older sister Sindie asked as she entered the room with the last box full of edible wear. "You should be ecstatic, woman. Free rein of a swingers club and two top designers who want to sample your stuff. I'd be over the moon, Al. How come you're not?"

"Oh I am happy," Allie replied as she pounded the nervous but-terflies back down her throat. She grabbed a handful of clothing. Laying them out on the table, she made sure to put the appropri-ate note in front of each pile to let the swingers know the name of each item and a warning to beware of alcoholic content in the clothing.

"You don't sound it, sweetie." Sindie frowned as she lifted a bundle of Spanish mango champagne-striped panties. She settled them between the almond-colored Italian Assassin-flavored and the buttery yellow-colored Italian Limoncilla drink flavored outfits.

"Okay, so I'm nervous as hell," Allie admitted. "This is prob-ably a once-in-a-lifetime chance. If these Nico and Leo guys don't like my designs and decide not to distribute my lines, that's it, game over. I may as well just stay small-time."

"First of all, you aren't even small-time. You can barely keep up with the orders. Second, you already have a second factory waiting to prepare upcoming orders and third—trust me—these guys will love you and they'll love your designs. No one can deny Edible Delights erotic wear."

"I wish I had your confidence, sis."

"That's why you asked me to come along." Sindie wiggled her eyebrows. "Because I inject confidence. What else are sisters for? And it's perfectly normal for you to be nervous. This is some-thing big and exciting."

"I just don't understand why you went behind my back and sent that company my samples. They're one of the top distribu-tors. They shouldn't be giving me the time of day."

"Because you are one of the top, that's why."

"They could easily have had someone duplicate my designs. I would have been knocked out of business."

Sindie laughed. "That's what they have patents for. And yours are all up to date. Besides, you should have an agent to represent your stuff. I've told you that so many times. But just don't worry. The big guys want to look at your wear in action. That says some-thing." Her sister winked. "And you can do a little swinging on the side just like I'm going to do tonight. No-strings sex is right up my alley. And I'm going to have fun showing off your French Stinger lingerie and have even more fun when my catch of the night nibbles it off my body."

Allie felt herself flush. "Like I said, I wish I had your confidence."

Sindie had loads of confidence. She was a beautiful woman, five years Allie's senior. Tonight she wore a gorgeous baby blue slinky tube dress with a cutout front area that showed off her gold belly ring. With mid-back-length auburn hair and glittering hazel eyes, not to mention a gorgeous body that most women would die for, her sister looked like a top fashion model and Allie had used her quite often for her fashion shows.

With an extremely profitable wedding planner business, several employees working for her and lots of friends who adored her, Sindie appeared to have it made. But her sister was also one of those women who played matchmaker to everyone and ended up the bridesmaid and never the bride at those friends' weddings. Allie hoped her sister's luck would change. She hoped her own luck would change too. Since leaving Max and Nick she was spoiled from ever having a normal relationship with just one man. In Europe she went out with several men and dabbled in sex. She always compared them to Nick and Max. Those European men had always come up short, in more ways than one.

Dammit! Would she ever get over Max and Nick?

She would have to try. Tonight after her business meeting. She would play with the swingers. Have some wild, hot, no-strings sex. It would be her "coming out" party. Or if she were lucky, it would be a sex party to celebrate a business venture with the two designers who were so interested in distributing her European Fling line.

"There, that's better," Sindie giggled. "It looks as if you're starting to be happy. Hold that thought and that smile, little sister. It's time to party!" She grabbed Allie's hand, pulling her away from the buffet of clothing and toward the door.

The minute they erupted into the stairwell, Allie's heart began a frantic pound. The music sounded wild and loud as it drifted from below. Several men and women were already heading up the narrow staircase. The men's eyes glittered with lust as they eyed Sindie and Allie.

Allie's pulse pounded erratically as one of the men, a very Italian-looking hottie of maybe ten years her junior, rubbed his thick erection against her thigh as he squeezed past.

As the swollen flesh pushed against her, she found herself shivering with both nerves and excitement.

"You two. Upstairs. I'm hot tonight," he said softly, and stopped on a stair above them.

"She's taken, stallion," Sindie laughed, and pulled Allie along farther down the stairs.

"Maybe later, gorgeous ladies?" the man purred after them.

"Sure, later. It's a date," Allie called out to him, and couldn't believe what she just said.

"Wowsa, woman. You're getting into this fast. But first you need to meet these distributors. Remember? The business meeting? Come on. The private dining areas are back here."

She was pulled through an almost dark room jam-packed with dancers. The hordes of men and women danced erotically to a pounding beat of wild ear-splitting music. It was hot in the room. Hot and wild. She could literally feel the music sift into her body. Could feel herself begin to gyrate and hum.

The magic was broken as a moment later they pushed past a thick set of doors and entered another hallway.

At least it was a little quieter. Quiet and totally deserted.

"Here, Dining Room Number Seven. This is your room. Go on in. I'll see if I can't find them."

Before Allie could stop Sindie and remind her that the distributors might already be inside, she had swept down the hallway leaving her alone. The rush of nerves hit her again as she stared at the closed door.

She thought about taking off. Of pretending these two men weren't going to show. She could melt back into her little business. Back to the status quo. But she didn't want the status quo.

She wanted full distribution like the big guys. She wanted to be with the big guys. She wanted recognition for her hard work. Recognition and a good sexual release.

The last thought made her flush. Then reality bit into her again. Business first. Playtime later.

Taking a deep breath she summoned the nerve to knock, waited a moment and then opened the door.

She stepped inside. And froze.

Two men sat at the table reading menus. When they looked up and saw her, lust shone brightly in a pair of glittering blue eyes and a pair of breathtaking brown eyes.

Fuck! Her knees almost melted at the intoxicating way they gazed at her.

"Hello, Allie cat." Max's deep voice sparkled along her nerve endings bringing a long forgotten warmth shooting into her body. Max was the spitting image of Richard Gere. With gorgeous white teeth as he smiled at her, a light dusting of silver stranding through his black hair, he looked absolutely stunning wearing a black tuxedo and crisp vanilla-colored shirt with a sprig of white freesia peeking out from the breast pocket.

"Long time no see, kitten," Nick, the younger of the two partners, added. He also wore a black tuxedo with a shimmering white shirt. A striking red rose was stuck in the breast pocket.

As he placed the menu back on the table, he studied her boldly. Nick wasn't as shy as Max and he looked as gorgeous as ever. He wore his golden brown hair shoulder-length and always had a sexy five o'clock shadow. Her pussy creamed as she remembered how erotic that beard felt brushing against her sensitive inner legs all those times he went down on her.

"What are you two doing here?" She could barely talk, her voice coming out in a breathy, sexy whisper.

"Having a meeting," Max replied casually.

"Oh I must have the wrong room."

She felt flustered. Too stunned to move. Too surprised to even formulate a thought.

She should leave but all she could do was stare at the two men who captured her heart several years ago.

"Since you appear to be staying, let's have a drink for old time's sake," Max said as he grabbed a bottle of wine chilling in a nearby crystal bucket.

"Yes, come on, kitten. Join us," Nick drawled.

Shit. She needed to leave. Needed to think.

"I . . . have a meeting." Yeah, that's it. She had a meeting. A very important meeting. "I must have made a mistake about the room."

"Oh there's no mistake, kitten." Nick smiled. "If you're looking for Nico and Leo, you've found us."

What?

Max poured the wine into three goblets and held one up to her. "Cheers to your sister for bringing us together again."

Disappointment rolled through Allie in one horrible wave. "My sister?"

"She set it up for us to meet," Nick said smoothly.

Her stomach plummeted in disappointment. God! How cruel of them to get her hopes up like this. What in the world had Sindie been thinking?

A sudden burst of tears bit the back of her eyes and damned if they were going to see her cry.

"I'm outta here," she said quickly. Turning on her heel, she headed for the door.

God! She worked so hard to get tonight together. Had her hopes pinned on this meeting. Until now she had no idea how high those hopes had been. Sparing no expense, she had persuaded her workers into overtime to produce more garments at such short notice. Some of them had given up valuable family time during the evenings to help her out. Obviously it had been all for nothing.

"It was my idea for you not to know. I was afraid you wouldn't come." Max's soft voice stopped her at the door.

THREE

Nick broke in quickly, obviously noting her distress. "There really is a business meeting. We wanted to talk to you about your . . . edibles."

The strangled way he said "edibles" made her think he was talking about more than just her clothing line. Despite the devastation, she felt her face heat as she remembered exactly how good his tongue felt when he tongue-fucked her.

"Don't look so disappointed, Allie," Nick soothed. "We're extremely interested in seeing what you have to offer after your European Fling."

She stiffened at his remark and turned to face the bastards.

"Fling?" The familiar anger burst from inside her. The sons of bitches had never taken her seriously when she informed them she wanted to become a designer instead of just their assistant. Why in the world did she still care what they thought anyway? She knew she shouldn't give a rat's ass about their opinions, but she did.

"Isn't that what you're calling your new line?" Nick said coolly. "European Fling. Edible underwear with a European taste. Love the hint of alcohol in the material by the way."

"There is no business meeting between us. I can make Edible Delights big on my own. I don't need your help."

"Ah yes, the ever independent woman. It's one of the reasons we were so attracted to you, kitten," Nick answered softly.

Were? As in past tense. A painful spear of hurt ripped through her. They considered her their past, just as she should be considering them her past.

"We've upset you. Please, sit down, cat." Max lifted one of the wine goblets and held it out to her while taking a sip from his own then smacking his luscious lips, groaning his appreciation. "We truly want to talk about your edibles. What have you got to lose?"

My heart, dammit! she wanted to say. Even though they didn't support her dreams, she still wanted to have them in her life. Other than not being behind her career choice, they had been so attentive to her emotional needs and sexual cravings. She always felt loved by them and never regretted living with the two of them.

Although they may consider her a part of their past, Max's blue eyes glittered with the same intense interest he always looked at her with. And she could read the same amusing glint in Nick's brown eyes that had always been there for her. She found herself marveling again at how these two men were a perfect combination. Max, ever-so serious, planned his every minute of the day, while Nick his total opposite, had no schedule and just simply flew by the seat of his pants. But together they made the perfect team, owning an extremely successful distribution line of erotic wear as well as designing men's and women's erotic clothing with such intricate care they were the envy of competing designers.

And she fell into the envy trap too. Wanted to be just like them. Wanted to be their equal in every way. Was that such a bad thing to strive for?

"Don't let our rift screw your future for Edible Delights. You've got a winner on your hands," Nick said coolly as Max continued to hold out the wine goblet for her.

She snatched the goblet away and sat down on the empty chair. Holding Nick's gaze, she felt a burst of boldness and immense pride at her accomplishments as she stared him down. Sure, she knew she shouldn't base her self-worth on what other people thought of her, but this was Nick. He was a man she lived with for several years. A man who fucked her daily. He loved to tease her and please her. He was a weakness of hers and it felt good to be acknowledged by him.

She took a big swig of the sweet wine, marveling at the sweet explosion against her taste buds. Max always had damned good taste in wine and by the soft way he was smiling at her, she knew he was just as proud of her as Nick.

Her earlier disappointment at being duped was disintegrating fast. If it were a business meeting they wanted, they'd soon realize she wasn't so easily pushed around.

"You're damn right I have a winner, Nick," she said firmly.

She watched with smug satisfaction as a look of surprise washed over his face. She wasn't one for accepting compliments easily and it was obvious he hadn't expected her to agree. In the past she would have fluttered and gushed like a teenager but now she was prepared to fight to expand her company.

"Looks like our kitten has grown claws," Nick teased, and guzzled back some wine.

Allie found herself gazing around at her environment for the first time. The tablecloth looked exquisite in a solid coral shade with a cream-colored embroidered overlay. An arrangement of gorgeous white flowers—dahlias, tulips, snapdragons and clustered hydrangeas sat in a clear glass container in the middle of the table. A pang of nostalgia hit as she remembered receiving a similar bouquet of flowers the morning after the fantastic night they'd spent fucking her in the elevator when it had stalled between floors.

She inhaled quickly as she remembered their guttural grunts, the sharp slap of flesh against flesh. Could still remember how hot it felt to be sandwiched between their hard masculine bodies. Her yowls during climaxes and mews while being aroused had earned her the nickname of "cat" from Max and "kitten" from Nick.

"No, this is no business meeting," she found herself whispering. It was a setup to take her down memory lane.

"Your face is starting to flush," Max said in a hoarse voice.

Despite the heat enveloping her, Allie forced herself to meet Max's eyes. "I'm sorry, but it won't work, gentlemen. I won't be seduced by either of you tonight or any night." Hell, the last thing she wanted to do was play easy. Oh she wanted them all right, but she wanted them on her terms.

"We've missed you, kitten. We want you back in our lives. Back in our bed. You're the only woman who makes us feel alive and loved." Nick's admission had her blinking in surprise. He usually made a point in a teasing way, not at all serious as he was suddenly being now. And the way he was looking at her with deliberate seriousness had her breath catching.

"You've taught us a valuable lesson, cat," Max said. "We won't forget it. We realize we can't live without you. Obviously we didn't appreciate you as a whole woman. A woman with dreams and goals. We were selfish. Infatuated with the fantastic sex and not willing to realize you had other needs as well."

"You've got that right," she said coolly. Inside however, she was burning up with excitement. Her two men still wanted her, even after all this time apart.

"We should have come after you, Allie," Nick said. "But we were stubborn. Later we realized you needed your space to grow into the independent woman you wanted to be. We would just have been in the way."

"Hmm, that's nice of you two to admit, gentlemen." She managed to continue to keep her voice calm and businesslike, although inside she was crying with a giddy immature happiness. They missed her just as much as she missed them.

Suddenly both men were standing.

Mercy! She'd forgotten how tall they both were and—

"Oh my God," she found herself whispering as a wave of erotic shock rolled over her.

Neither man wore pants! Nor underwear. Just their tuxedo jackets, white shirts and impressive solid erections.

A split second later her surprise wore off and she shifted uncomfortably as the familiar hot flush of sexual awareness raced through her.

"Um," she found herself saying as she nervously licked her suddenly dry lips, quite unable to keep her eyes from going from one luscious cock to the other.

"Wh-what's gotten into you two?" Like, duh! As if she didn't know.

They'd shared many a business meeting having sex. She shouldn't be so surprised. But she was.

At her question, Nick's lips pursed into an amused pout. Max's eyes blazed with a rush of intense need. Both men watched her as they began stroking their long, thick cocks.

She became all too aware of how wet and pleading her pussy had suddenly become. How intensely hard her breasts were pushing against the tight restraints of her business suit.

As they touched themselves, both men came toward her from her right. She could literally see the web of veins throbbing in Max's huge, flushed penis. His plum-shaped cock head had already burst free from its sheath. Her fingers clenched as she remembered how heavy and silky his two swollen balls would feel in the palms of her hands. And Nick's cock, her heart fluttered wildly, his cock was just a little thicker and longer than Max's. One lone blue vein ran along his entire shaft topped perfectly with a huge mushroom-shaped head shaded purple.

She blew out a slow breath remembering both men were well over eight inches long and three inches thick.

"As you can see, we've missed you, cat," Max said. His voice sounded strangled and aroused.

"Missed you is quite the understatement," Nick hissed. "Get down on your knees, kitten."

His commanding voice intoxicated her.

Ah shit, she thought as her self-control disintegrated and she found herself going down on her knees before the two.

Reaching out, she grabbed Max's swollen balls and opened her mouth for Nick.

Nick's thick cock head came quickly inside. Hard, needy and hot, it pulsed against her lips.

Both Max and Nick groaned at the same time. The guttural sounds were like music to her ears.

Oh she missed this so much. Missed touching them. Tasting them. Fucking them.

The heat of Max's scrotum laced her palms and she began a hard, sensual massage just the way she knew he liked it. Tightening her lips around Nick's shaft, she felt the lone vein pulse against her tongue. The long, thick shaft sunk into her, his mushroom-shaped cock head tickled the back of her throat. He quickly withdrew and then came into her again.

"We want to hire you to run Impulse's edible line," Nick growled. "You'll have full control over the division. Full creative access. Full hiring capabilities. The works. You'll be the boss of Edible Delights as well. But we want exclusive rights to your edibles and to have the trade secrets you've acquired under the protection of our company."

"In other words," Max growled as she continued her massage, not quite believing what she was hearing.

"We want you as a full partner in the business," Max finished.

Allie was stunned. Both at the way her body responded so brilliantly to their moans of arousal and at their proposition. She would be their equal. Their partner. It was something she had only hoped for in her wildest dreams. Not to mention having full access to her two lovers again.

It would be a perfect union. Something she wanted. She would have an even wider access to suppliers.

She stopped massaging Max's cock and let go of Nick's penis with a pop.

"I'm already the boss of Edible Delights," she whispered hoarsely. "I won't deny my current clients. You can't have exclusive rights but you can have subsidiary rights."

She opened her mouth and Nick slipped in again. She restarted her massaging of Max's hot flesh.

"Fuck," Max moaned.

"Jesus," Nick whispered as she raked her teeth along his rigid shaft.

She loved the way it jerked in her mouth. Loved the hot brand of Max's swollen spheres in her palms, but she had another delicate area to tend to. She let go and grabbed the base of Max's shaft with both hands. Velvety heat licked her fingers as she began a gentle twisting motion she knew he loved.

"You're a shrewd . . . business . . . woman," Max gasped.

In answer she gave his cock an extra hard twist.

"Ouch," he hissed, grabbing her wrists, stopping her cold. "I think I understand. We better be good to you."

She winked at him, signaling he understood her point perfectly. She devoured Nick's cock, taking it deeper into her mouth, allowing his hard velvety flesh to come down into her throat. He slid his fingers through her hair, holding her head, forcing her to look up and meet his intense gaze.

Max let go of her wrists and she could hear the zipper on the front of her dress lowering past her breasts. He pulled aside the cloth and warm air brushed against her flesh. Although Nick's cock impaled her mouth and she couldn't see what Max could see, she noticed his eyes glaze over and knew immediately he liked the bra she wore beneath.

She had picked the cream-colored, strawberry-champagne-flavored one. One of her latest creations using her softest material to date. She watched him lick his full lips. Nice and slow as he studied her heaving breasts. She knew what he wanted to do and she could feel the sexual haze begin to intoxicate her business smarts.

Bastards. They weren't going to seduce her into getting anything less than what she wanted.

"What are your demands, Allie cat?" Max asked.

Nick slid out of her mouth allowing her to answer.

"Edible Delights remains as is. Under my full control," she said, sucking in some needed breaths during the break.

Edible Delights was her baby. Hers alone. Was it wrong not to share it with the two men she loved? *No,* an inner voice answered. *It isn't wrong. It's a sweet deal but the company is your dream. Hold on tight to her. You made her.*

"As I said, I'll grant Impulse subsidiary rights. But for certain future lines that I decide to design for Impulse. And of course I want Edible Delights to get full distribution with Impulse's lines."

"We deal only with exclusive rights, Allie cat. You know that," Max growled. Despite the serious way he spoke, he licked his lips again and lowered his mouth over her right nipple. Heat and moisture seared through her tender flesh and she could literally feel the cloth disintegrate. Pleasure-pain burst through her nipple as his sharp teeth began a rough nibble.

In answer, she grabbed ahold of Max's balls and ran her sharp fingernails along the bottom of his sac.

"You're a fucking tease," he mumbled, and let go of her aching nipple. But she knew he enjoyed the pleasure-pain she inflicted. He looked up at Nick who nodded and traced his swollen cock head as if it were lipstick along the contours of her lips.

"Okay, you win," Max grumbled. "We'll have the lawyers draw up the details and they'll contact you. I'll have our purchasing department contact you first thing when we're finished. We'll send a hefty advance so you can prepare for the order."

Fuck! She'd done it! Woo hoo!

"It's been nice doing business with you, gentlemen."

She opened her mouth and allowed Nick's hot cock back inside her mouth. In turn Max began a wild suckle at her breast, making her gasp at the wicked intensity.

Nick couldn't believe how the vixen kitten had been able to get what she wanted so easily. He promised himself he would tease her for as long as possible, but one look at the disappointment crushing her face at having been duped and one second of having her lush mouth latch around his cock, she literally sucked all business sense out of him.

He loved Allie.

She made him hot. Made him feel protective of her, teasingly loving and just plain happy. She had him from the moment Max and he interviewed her for the job as their personal assistant.

A young woman. Full of ambition and so sensual. He found himself masturbating to her resume photo right there in his office. He'd masturbated since she left for Europe too.

Sweet shit! All the years they lost. But the three of them needed the separation. He knew that now. She needed to grow and Max and he needed to grow up.

It had been hard to move out of Max's place after she'd left and try to move on without her. Fucking hard not to go to Europe and yank her on to the first plane back to New York. But now she was back. She would run her own company within Impulse's protection and she would be their partner in every sense of the word.

His erection throbbed as he looked down at her. Necklaces glittered across her perfectly shaped chest, pretty pink lips were stretched around his cock and she stopped her ministrations. Her blue eyes were glazed and she mewed those cute kitty sounds as Max's mouth sucked on her full breast.

"Jesus," he found himself muttering at the erotic sight of another man at her breast. He knew a normal man might be jealous. He wasn't. Not where Max and Allie were concerned. He trusted the two of them so implicitly that sometimes it hurt.

He watched Allie's cheeks flush a deeper red as she caught his gaze. Her blue eyes grew darker and her chest heaved harder.

Oh yes, she missed this too.

He pulled his cock from her tight mouth and pushed into her again, loving the sensual way her smooth lips moved over every sparking nerve ending.

She mewed sweetly again and he lost himself. Circling his fingers around the area of his shaft to where he knew she could take his penis into her, he began a barely controlled thrust in and out of her voluptuous mouth. He closed his eyes and shuddered as an orgasm quickly snowballed.

He thrust once. Twice. Three times. Then his entire body tightened into an erotic ball of pleasure. White-hot blades of arousal licked his scrotum and seared straight up into his shaft.

He exploded on a strangled shout, spurting into her throat and loving the way her muscles contracted as she eagerly swallowed his seed.

Ah, yes. She hadn't lost her sensual touch. Not by a long shot.

Fuck! You're so damned beautiful," Nick said a few minutes later as he reached down and with a linen napkin dabbed at the semen drooling from Allie's mouth. Having her on her knees before him made him feel fantastic. Having her pink lips wrapped tightly around his shaft, her warm tongue sliding along his sensitive flesh once again was unbelievably great. Even watching Max sucking on her nipples created an erotic sight that aroused him to new heights.

He had dreamed of this day for so long. Now it was finally happening. He could see the lust glowing bright in her eyes. The need for pleasure. The craving to be fucked again by her two lovers.

"Get dressed, kitten," he said.

"Where are we going?" she asked breathlessly.

"Phase two of our business meeting."

And he could barely wait.

FOUR

Allie watched with growing excitement as women giggled and men grinned while they browsed the edible underwear her sister and she had laid out on the table earlier.

As she watched, she tried to ignore the strong, demanding masculine scents of the two men who flanked her. Not to mention she found it hard to overlook the throbbing of her aching breasts where Max had suckled. As well as the intense way her weeping pussy demanded to be filled.

Not even half an hour had gone by since she left this second-floor room. Most of the garments were gone and there was still a lineup of swingers eagerly waiting to get something edible to wear. She noted all her business cards were gone too.

A shot of nervousness coursed through her.

"I didn't bring enough for everyone. I'm so sorry," she whispered anxiously.

"You're a hit, cat. We knew you would be," Max said softly against her right ear where he began a bold nibble on her neck behind her earlobe, which sent wickedly delicious shivers racing through her.

"I can go back to my hotel suite and get more," she said in a rush. There were no more edibles back at their hotel. Sindie and she had brought everything with them in their rental van, but it would be a good excuse to leave and gather her bearings. To try to establish some semblance of self-control. She knew they were in the process of successfully seducing her. Knew it was a matter of time before she fell completely under their spell. She always felt so sexually helpless around the two men. Had managed to be elusive for a long time, until that night they'd been trapped in the elevator.

That night she acknowledged what she wanted from them. A need to be fucked by her two bosses. They obliged. Tonight they gave her what she wanted again. Equal partnership. The need to be fucked was just as bad as that first time in the elevator.

Maybe she should get out of there before she caved totally. Before it was too late and she lost her heart all over again.

She made a move.

Nick grabbed her hand stopping her cold. "Uh-uh, you're staying here with us. Our meeting is far from over, kitten."

Max leaned in close to her right ear. "Yeah, cat. We haven't even gotten to the main course yet—you."

Allie shivered as Max once again drew her earlobe into his mouth and nibbled saucily. Nick's hand slid over the curve of her ass making her moan softly as he started a slow massage against one of her cheeks. His fingers dug into her flesh so perfectly that she could barely concentrate on watching the rest of the men and women quickly pick through the remaining underwear before vanishing through a nearby doorway.

When all but a handful of people stood around the tables looking dejected, Max intertwined his hand with hers and Nick took her other hand.

"Let's go find the changing rooms," Max whispered as they brought her to those mysterious doors where the swingers had disappeared. Her heart crashed a mile a minute as both men silently led her down a long hallway. Doors lined each side of the hall and sexual tension wrapped all around her despite the relative quietness.

The silence was a big contrast to the wild music from the floor below. Instead, there were soft giggles from behind closed doors. She swore she could even hear the rustling of clothing as people undressed.

A nearby door opened and several men and women dressed in her sexy edibles pranced proudly down the hallway toward them.

One of them was her sister!

And she was with the man who hit on them earlier. The Italian stallion.

He wore a skimpy red, strawberry and sherry-flavored thong that enhanced a most impressive package. Allie shivered wonderfully as she spied the vivid outline of his long, thick cock pressing boldly against the material and the two perfectly shaped balls begging to be fondled by a woman's hands.

"Remind me to kill you tomorrow, sis," Allie said when she sufficiently recovered from ogling the stallion.

Sindie smiled prettily, cocked an eyebrow at her then grinned at Max and then at Nick.

"Oh? And would that be before or after you thank me?"

"How's about that date you promised me earlier? You join us, sexy lady," stallion interrupted. His eyes were heavy-lidded with wanting and Allie's breath caught imagining having sex with this man and her sister.

"I've never had the privilege of pleasuring two sisters at the same time."

"Easy, stallion. Those two are her men," Sindie replied. "They don't share with anyone but each other. Besides, you'll have your hands quite full with me."

The man's gaze narrowed as he casually inspected Nick and then Max, who now wore their entire tuxedo outfits, if not a bit rumpled. "You two are a bit overdressed, aren't you?"

"And you're not underdressed?" Nick said coolly, eyeing the stallion's erotic attire.

Allie stifled a laugh. She sensed the hostility seething beneath Nick's calm exterior.

"She's off limits to you tonight, studly," Max said just as coolly.

"Another time then." Stallion looked hopeful as he winked at

Allie before her sister tugged him along with her down the hall.

When the three of them were alone again, she noted the tension in both men as they continued to watch the door where the stallion had disappeared with her sister.

"Hey, feel free to join them," she teased, knowing they were more concerned about Sindie like big brothers than lovers.

Both men turned to her and Max replied huskily, "I guess we should have left it up to you if you wanted to join them. Old habits die hard. This is a swingers club and you're free to do what you want."

Nick's gaze narrowed as he watched her closely for an answer. He'd never been much for sharing her with anyone else but Max so she knew he must be seething.

"I'd rather hang out with you two," she said truthfully. "I'm curious as to what else you've got in store for our business meeting."

"Curious, are you?" Max winked.

"I must admit I have enjoyed it so far."

"By all means then, let's continue," Nick said. From his breast pocket he drew a glistening gold key and inserted it into the door. When it opened, he bowed to Allie as if he were a prince and she a princess. She couldn't help but feel all bubbly and warm that Nick was acting so chivalrous. It was quite out of character for him.

"Your clothing awaits, my lady," he grinned.

She stepped into what appeared to be a large bedroom-sized changing room.

The two men crowded in around the open doorway. Both of their faces were flushed with excitement. The hot looks literally made her tremble with anticipation.

"Meet us in Room Three. One floor up, after you get dressed," Max whispered. "And we will make all your wishes come true."

The door closed and she was alone, surrounded with a vista of mirror-tiled walls. She caught the flushed redness of her cheeks, the windblown appearance of her red hair and her lips, full and swollen after sucking off Nick.

Tonight had turned into anything but the business meeting

she anticipated. While negotiating with her ex-lovers she sucked one of them off and had her nipples tended to by the other. And now she was in a changing room ready to have sex with them after all these years of being apart.

And she could hardly wait to be impaled by them. Just as she had barely been able to wait to have both of them inside her the night they'd become trapped in the elevator.

God! It felt as if it were only yesterday . . .

"We're trapped," Allie sighed as she finally gave up on pressing the red emergency button on the elevator panel and slumped heavily against the nearby steel wall. The elevator had come to a grinding halt a good ten minutes ago. There was no phone to call for help but surely at this late hour someone would eventually notice that it hadn't arrived at the first floor?

"Don't sound so down about it, Allie, I'm sure we can find something to do to amuse ourselves until the morning," Max said softly from beside her.

Her pulse picked up a wild speed as she looked up to find him watching her. Lust shone brightly in his blue eyes and she felt her heart flutter as it always did when she looked at him.

Oh boy. This was not good. She could not spend too much time in here with these two gorgeously sexy men. Since becoming their assistant, she tried like hell to remain aloof and professional around them but it was getting harder and harder. Especially in the almost overwhelming sexual way she felt attracted to both of them.

"That's right, sweet lady. We've got all night," Nick whispered in a strangled breath.

"All night? Surely there's someone around?" She tried hard to ignore the wicked way her pulse was picking up speed at the thought of being alone with Max and Nick all night.

"We're the only ones left in the building. Remember?" Max said in a tight voice. "Today was a holiday. No one is coming until the morning."

Her gaze snapped to Nick who suddenly seemed closer to her. Actually both men seemed rather closer.

Oh boy. It sure was getting hot in here.

"I think it's time we show her exactly how we feel about her. Don't you think, Nick?"

"Yes, we've been discussing you behind your gorgeous back, Allie," Nick agreed.

They'd been talking about her? She began to feel her face flush with heat.

"We've been talking about how nice it would be to get to know you a hell of a lot better." Max came closer. His dominant scent washed around her and pinned her to the wall. The intoxicating warmth of his body slammed through her thin summer dress and licked flames along her skin.

"We know you want to get to know us a lot better too, Allie. We can see it in the way your nipples peak whenever one of us is around you. Just like they're doing now."

She held her breath as Nick ran a finger down her bare arm. The heat of his touch made her moan softly.

"And the way your eyes sparkle when one of us looks at you," Max commented as he began to unbutton her dress at the collar.

She looked down. Watched in stunned fascination as Max's fingers quickly and efficiently popped the tiny buttons through the buttonholes with his long fingers.

"I . . . I don't do any such thing," she protested, knowing full well she was lying. Even now as Nick's hand slipped beneath her dress, she could feel her vagina cream and her nipples ache and swell in anticipation of their touches. The instant Nick palmed her pussy, she arched herself against him.

"Oh shit," she whispered as she bonded with his touch.

"We want you, Allie," Max growled hoarsely. "We've discussed our attraction to you. Talked about which one of us should pursue you. In the end we decided we both should."

"What . . . what about what I want?" she found herself asking, unable to keep her thoughts straight as Max pushed aside the opening to her dress to expose her bra.

All three of them were breathing heavily now. She could barely concentrate as Nick massaged her pussy with his palm, bringing out a long buried arousal.

"Do you have any lotion in your bag?" Nick asked.

"Lotion?" Confusion zipped through her.

"For later. Are you an anal virgin?"

She found herself shaking at the thought of anal sex and shook her head. She'd tried it with an old boyfriend a few years back and had enjoyed it. She couldn't wait to have Nick and Max taking her there.

"Yes, hand lotion. Yes, in my purse," she replied hoarsely.

"That'll do."

She felt her breasts jiggle and swell as Max undid the front clasp to her bra. A second later her breasts fell free.

"Fuck, you're so yummy-looking." Max grinned. She held her breath as he lowered his head. "I'm a breast man, Allie. And I have to admit you've got the most perfect breasts I've ever seen."

Fire zipped through her as his tongue caressed her nipple.

"We've wanted you for so long," Nick rasped as he got down on his knees before her. He hoisted her dress up around her waist. She trembled and automatically spread her legs as he lowered her panties and slipped them off.

"She's got a nice, nude pussy, Max. Just as we suspected."

Max made a guttural sound at her breast and just kept on sucking. His other hand cupped her breast and he began tweaking her nipples until she mewed.

This can't be happening, she found herself thinking as Nick's head lowered to between her legs.

This was the stuff her fantasies about her two bosses were made of. God help her, she cared and loved them dearly. Wanted this so badly.

In order to steady herself, she reached out and grasped Max's broad shoulder with one hand, placing her other hand on the top of Nick's head. It was an awkward position, being pinned to the cool elevator wall with a man sucking at her breast and another man about to go down on her, but it felt so damn good.

So damned right.

It was at that point she knew she could never go back to the way she'd been living. Never go back to avoiding her feelings for them because they'd just told her they wanted her. By her surrendering to them, they knew she wanted them just as badly.

She screeched when Nick's mouth latched on to her pussy and he began a hard, delicious suck that unraveled her.

She could smell her arousal now. A wild scent erupting from a woman who'd been craving these two men to fuck her for far too long.

"Fuck me!" she demanded as her emotions speared to the surface. She felt hot. Her body tight. Every inch of her on fire.

"Oh God, please fuck me!"

A low keening sound unleashing from Allie's throat snapped her from her memory.

Her breathing was rapid. Her body felt tight. So ready to be fucked. Just like she'd been that night.

She blinked wildly as she remembered what had happened between them on the first floor tonight. Moaned softly as she thought of what would happen when she left the security of this changing room.

Could she have sex with them tonight? An inner voice of doubt taunted. Would she lose her independence? Lose sight of her dreams? Would she lose her heart to them all over again?

Ah hell, her heart was already lost to them.

But were Max and Nick truly serious when they said they wanted her back? Would they end up ignoring her dreams again? Would she end up in their bed 24/7 because she simply loved having sex with both of them? But she also enjoyed the independence of running her own company and had grown used to living alone.

Why did life have to be so hard? Why couldn't she just be satisfied with having red-hot sex with the two men she loved tonight and see what happened?

She blew out a tense breath and watched a stray strand of her strawberry red hair flutter around her flushed face.

Yes, she was ready for a good roll with Nick and Max. She would think about other things afterward.

With trembling fingers she unzipped her dress and noticed the melted fabric of her bra around her rosy nipples. The sight of it made her even hornier.

Yes, she wanted sex tonight. Afterward she wanted more than sex from them. Being here with them had dredged up the familiar feelings of frustration again. She knew she should be pushing them aside, but she just couldn't seem to do it. They said they'd learned their lesson. She needed to trust them. Needed to follow her heart.

Her gaze dropped to the bench that extended along one mirrored wall of the changing room. A puffy pink terrycloth robe lay neatly there. She lifted it and spied the gorgeous outfit beneath the robe.

A bra and thong set she designed.

A leopard print dotted with delicate pink rosebuds. She knew the black spots were dark-chocolate-liquor-flavored. The beige-spotted areas were vanilla brandy and the white areas of the print were flavored with white Swiss chocolate. She added the rosebuds for romance and made them strawberry-ice-wine-flavored. This design had been her most challenging to date and her most expensive. She planned to have it in her European Fling line but she hadn't been able to bring herself to duplicate it for anyone.

It was *her*.

Sexy and playful. A sentimental reminder of Nick and Max who enjoyed calling her kitten and cat respectively.

Yes, she would kill Sindie for removing it from her factory. But first she would thank her for reuniting her with her men.

Excitement flared as she removed her jewelry, undressed and donned the silky bra and thong. The material felt as soft as a flower's petals and smelled delicately delicious.

Allie would cherish tonight. Cherish her memories of whatever developed as a result of making love with her men. If things didn't work out down the line, so be it. She would at least have given their relationship another try. No one died of a broken heart. No one got what she wanted either if she didn't at least give something she wanted badly enough a second chance.

Her breath stalled as she wrapped the toasty pink robe around her and stepped from the changing room. Several men wearing various shades of her edible underwear walked past with a gorgeous brunette.

The woman wore one of Allie's designs. A virgin white panty and bra set flavored in vanilla brandy.

Obviously the men were preparing her for a ménage. Allie's pussy creamed as she watched one of the men wink at Allie before leaning his head down to start licking at the cup on the brunette's right breast. The material quickly dissolved to reveal a plump burgundy nipple. The man moaned in pleasure. Allie imagined how the edible material burst sweetly against his tongue.

She wondered how the woman could even walk with the man nibbling on her nipple the way he did. The other two men were too busy to notice Allie was watching because one had attached his mouth to her earlobe and the other had his fingers inside the woman's ass, plunging in and out in a gentle manner.

Allie swallowed and followed them up the stairs to the third floor. Here the hallway was alive with sounds. Slurping noises. Flesh slapping against flesh. Hushed whimpers and hoarse moans.

Her pussy continued to cream warmly at the erotic sounds and she moved quickly along the hallway. Through one door she spied a young couple going at it in a doggie position. The woman's mouth was open in a silent scream while the man pummeled her with his huge cock.

Quickly she passed the door and found Room Three. Her legs trembled as she twisted the knob and entered. Nick and Max hadn't arrived yet and she found herself dazzled by the ultrahuge king-sized bed in the middle of the room. It was decked out with plush black satin pillows and leopard print satin sheets that matched the design of the edible clothing she wore.

She smiled warmly.

Bastards. Obviously they'd wasted no time in duplicating her rose leopard design. She should have had it patented. At least then she could have used it to blackmail them into hot sex whenever she wanted it. For a moment she smiled at that thought then frowned as another thought followed. Having that kind of control over her two men would only make things less spontaneous between them.

She looked around the room and didn't miss the racks lining a far wall. Racks containing different sizes of whips, packaged ball gags and other types of bondage gear such as leather restraints and handcuffs.

She wasn't into any of that. Neither were Max and Nick. The three of them had more than enough pleasure without the help of toys.

She noted the scent of freesia in the air and discovered a bundle of white flowers in a nearby crystal vase. A lone white candle flickered in one of the two windows. Her men still had a taste for romance. The thought made her smile.

She jumped as a pair of hot hands curled around her shoulders. Immediately she smelled Max's spicy aftershave and Nick's musky scent. Her senses jolted into awareness mode. Body heat slammed into her, making her nerve endings sparkle with excitement.

"You like?" Nick purred and quickly kissed the sensitive area behind her ear.

"It's gorgeous," she admitted, loving the tingles his kiss created. Loving his hot breath caressing her neck.

"You're gorgeous too, Allie," Max said softly from beside her.

She held her breath as Nick slowly pushed the pink terry-cloth robe down her shoulders. The robe didn't have a sash so it quickly dropped off her and puddled around her feet.

She watched Max's eyes widen with appreciation. Then she sighed as Nick's hands cupped her leopard-clad breasts. His palms felt like two white-hot brands, his fingers like fire as he boldly pinched her flesh with expert touches. He had her nipples scorched with pleasure and her moaning within seconds.

"I've missed being with you, kitten. I've missed us," Nick whispered hoarsely.

She found him pressing her forward, toward the bed.

"I have too," she admitted. "More than you know."

"Stand beside the bed, Allie. Bend over, grab the sheets for support. Spread your legs. I need to taste you, bad. I can't wait any longer."

Allie's heart beat wildly. She felt flushed. With fiery excitement she leaned over and took the required position while Max stood by and watched.

Nick's hands were hot as he cradled her ass curves.

"You smell so good, Allie. Such a succulent package."

His hot breath whispered between her legs. She cried out as his mouth nestled between her cheeks. His moist tongue dissolved the fragile material there and he began a mad lick against her labia.

Heat coursed through her pussy. Her fingers wrapped tighter into the leopard satin sheets.

"Oh fuck," she swore as Nick's tongue boldly stroked her clit.

"I can't believe I didn't go after you in Europe, kitten." He lapped harder. The velvety sensations of his tongue between her legs made her pussy clench with wicked anticipation.

"We thought we'd lost you forever," Nick growled. He grabbed her hips, holding her steady. Sharp, sweet pain zipped through her labia as teeth bit her delicate flesh. He rubbed the trapped ends with his tongue and she found herself hissing at the kiss of flames. Found her thighs tightening as his teeth let her pussy lips go and his tongue smoothed over her sensitive clitoris again. He began an erotic circular stroke, the firm pressure making her arch her back, making her mew and whimper for more.

She wanted to tell him he and Max had never lost her. That her heart yearned for both of them, but she couldn't speak from all the pleasure screaming through her. She waited for them to come for her in Europe. She knew that now. Why else had she been unable to start any serious relationships with the men she dated? She wanted to tell Max and Nick all those things but Nick's tongue was now drilling her clit so hard and fast it left her literally panting for air.

Her hips were moving now. Gyrating with need at Nick's every bold stroke against her sensitive flesh. She could feel the heat of her liquid gushing down her vagina toward him. His tongue expertly manipulated her pleasure center until her body ached and she literally felt the inferno of lust raging through her.

"I can see that Allie cat is being nicely primed," Max replied hoarsely as he came into her view. He was undressed and stood in front of her, breathing heavily as he massaged the huge bulge of his erection covered by a skimpy yellow thong.

It was one of her designs. She had to admit it looked very nice on him.

His body looked hard too. Every inch of him a perfect male. His abdomen was rigid and tight. Not an ounce of fat on either of her men.

His muscles were smooth and tanned. She knew they both worked out daily at the company gym. Knew they tanned naked up on Max's penthouse balcony every weekend. At least they had when she lived with them.

God! She couldn't wait to move in with them again. Couldn't wait to start fucking them on the balcony. In the elevator. On the kitchen table. In the whirlpool.

She jerked and moaned as Nick's tongue hit an extra sensitive spot on her engorged clit. It felt three times bigger—swollen and throbbed so hot against Nick's tongue.

Her breaths came faster and faster. The blood in her body heating with passion as she watched Max gingerly rub his covered erection.

"We've got lots to make up for," Max cooed. His eyes glittered darkly and his lashes lowered with a lusty-lidded look as he climbed up onto the bed in front of her.

"Now it's my turn to take that pretty little mouth of yours, cat." He pressed his thick erection close to her face.

Her mouth instantly watered as she smelled a wonderful scent wafting from the edible thong he wore.

Banana daiquiri. Her absolute favorite drink.

FIVE

She took a long lick and enjoyed the way the material disintegrated. Banana daiquiri flavor exploded against her tongue. Sweet and scrumptious.

She took another swipe. The hole in the fabric got bigger and her tongue found his hot, smooth cock head. A few more wet licks and she had the thong falling off Max.

His erection speared into the air at her. She couldn't help but moan appreciatively at the sight.

His penis appeared even bigger than earlier when they'd been down in Dining Room Seven. The plum-shaped head, swollen and needy. His cock flushed and rigid. She couldn't wait to have him thrusting deep inside of her. She found herself remembering the intense way Max's mouth had suckled earlier on her breasts. Her nipples still ached and she rubbed them back and forth against the edge of the mattress, loving the way every nerve ending sparkled with pleasure.

"You're more than ready, aren't you Allie cat?" Max hissed as he aimed his cock at her mouth.

She nodded numbly and parted her lips. His cock scorched her like a brand and her jaw ached as she opened wide to accommodate his big size. He tasted of man and lust and she eagerly slurped her tongue along the thick webs of veins that ran throughout the length of his stiff shaft.

"Oh yes, that's it, cat. Beautiful. Just fucking beautiful."

His soft guttural compliment made her blood sing. Made her slurp quicker. Made her suck his shaft harder. He groaned his approval and grabbed both sides of her head, trapping her as he took control of her mouth with his cock.

His solid flesh thrust deep and quick.

Silence followed, interrupted by intermittent slaps of flesh against flesh. A moan here, a cry there, as the two men kept a steady erotic rhythm. Her eyelids grew heavy with the haze of arousal from Nick's well-placed tongue strokes to her pussy and Max's plunges into her mouth.

"Sorry, cat, but your teasing licks are just way too much for me," Max growled.

Her fingers gnarled tighter around the sheets as the arousal snowballed. Her thighs tightened. She bucked against Nick and pleasure whipped through her at lightning speed.

She exploded on a scream. The sound a muffled alley-cat screech around Max's thick erection.

"That's it, cat," she heard Max soothe. "Ride the wave."

Violent spasms tore through her, ripping her body apart. Her pussy clenched as Nick removed his tongue and thrust two fingers in and out of her. Tremors gripped her hard and heavy.

All too soon the climax ebbed away. Max pulled out from her mouth and Nick withdrew his fingers.

An aroused after-climax daze drifted over her. She found herself being lifted onto the bed.

"Climb onto me, cat," Max whispered a few seconds later.

She blinked. Hadn't even realized he now lay on the bed beside her. She moaned at the sight of his huge erection. Mewed as she mounted him.

Crouching over his spearing cock, she cried out as she impaled herself on his stiff flesh. Slurping sounds ripped through the air as her vagina greedily clamped around him.

Max groaned hotly. Reaching out he popped the front clasp allowing her bra to drop open then he grabbed her pink nipples. His fingers twisted and pulled until the line of fire screamed into her pussy. She began a mad grind, gyrating her hips, crushing her pussy into his body, then lifting herself and coming down on him, her sheath enveloping his cock again.

In no time flat she had a nice steady rhythm going. Quickly she slipped her finger between her legs and over her swollen clitoris to begin a hard massage.

Ah, this feels wonderful.

She looked down and watched her breasts bounce erotically while Max continued to pull and squeeze her nipples. She saw the perspiration beading Max's forehead. Felt it dot her enflamed body.

Movement to her right made her aware of Nick. He stood beside the bed and through her sexual haze she watched as he greased his turgid penis.

Wow! He looked so huge. It made her remember that she hadn't been anally penetrated for so long. Yet she couldn't wait to feel the pressure of his penis inside her as both men impaled her. The erotic feeling of having two men double penetrating her. There was nothing else like it on Earth.

Max tugged harder at her nipples and her fingers frayed desperately.

She felt the climax coming and cried out as it rammed into her. She exploded on a scream. Max groaned as her pussy clenched around him. She drew air into her lungs in quick, labored gasps and continued to pump herself over him.

She whimpered as a warm pair of greased hands settled over her shoulders, moving her forward.

"I need to come, kitten. You two look too damned hot."

Nick's lubed finger pressed intimately at her ass. She cried out as the tight ring of sphincter muscles gave way and he slid into her. Pressure bit deep, throwing her off balance.

"So damned tight. Forgot . . . how . . . tight." Nick groaned as he slowed his intrusion. She tried to relax and immediately her anal muscles accepted him. A moment later he slid a second finger inside and began a slow erotic exploration that had her gasping.

"Your ass seems to remember me," he chuckled as a third finger entered. Pleasure-pain burst through her and her muscles eagerly gripped all three digits.

"Very nice," he cooed, and began a thrusting motion that made her squeeze her eyes closed. She panted softly and concentrated on the wonderful buzz starting inside her ass. Before long she was completely relaxed and enjoying the spearing rhythm.

When he withdrew, she opened her eyes and eagerly awaited his next move. A second later his generously lubed cock head slipped into her.

She moaned at the pressure. Fought for breath at the sweet, intense pain.

He bucked his hips and he sank deeper. Another thrust had her coming down on Max. Her mouth was inches from his and she suddenly realized they hadn't kissed each other for years. He must have realized the same thing for his eyes grew dark with lust and longing. His mouth parted slightly. She watched him lick his lower lip in a sensual swipe that had her heart skipping a beat.

How in the world could the sight of a man's tongue turn her on so much? But it did. It always did. His hot breath washed against her face breaking her from her fetish.

After years apart, should they not have kissed when they'd first met again? No, her mind reassured her. Kissing came when the time was right.

The time was perfect now.

She caught his mouth and his lips melted against hers. While Max and she explored each other's after such a long absence, Nick began a wonderful thrusting motion. Every plunge forced her clit against Max's hard erection. Another volley of pleasure lanced her.

She shattered and shook as the flames licked her body, screaming into Max's mouth.

Nick plunged deep into her ass. He kept up the demanding thrusts for a delicious eternity. She lay sandwiched between them. Her soaked cunt impaled on Max's cock. Her mouth fused and her ass filled.

The next climax came quickly on the heels of the last. Sweet and oh-so beautifully violent it rushed through her in one hot wave. Within seconds she became lost in yet another brilliant pleasure storm.

Max had never been able to get enough of Allie. Years without her just about made him crazy. Now she was back and the three of them would make up for all the lost time. He was stupid for not going after the woman he loved so badly. When she left, it felt like a knife thrusting deep into his heart.

Pride prevented Max from going after her. Over the years maturity pushed his pride aside and now he felt selfish. The three of them always had great sex and a loving relationship.

This time around he would commit to supporting Allie. Support her as a partner in their personal and professional lives. Why he didn't see it earlier, he had no idea. But now he knew what she needed. It was more than love and sex.

"She's quite a woman, our kitten." Nick grinned from the other side of Allie. Up until now they remained silent as they watched her sleep.

"She taught me a lesson walking away the way she did."

"Knocked sense into you," Nick chuckled.

"I won't be letting her get away again."

"We didn't know what we had until she was gone," Nick echoed his thoughts.

Max read the longing in Nick's eyes when he discovered Allie had walked out on them. He knew Nick loved Allie just as much as he did. Knew he wanted to go after her and bring her home.

But he didn't.

Neither of them did. Deep down they both must have known she needed space and the two of them needed to realize how much they missed her.

"It was only a matter of time before we hooked up again," Nick stated as he began stroking the length of his quickly hardening shaft. "She needed space to follow her dreams without us hanging all over her. I figured it would only be a matter of time before it sank through your thick skull that she's a jewel, inside and out."

Max nodded in agreement. He was stubborn, he admitted it. Sometimes something drastic had to happen before he came to his senses. And Allie leaving them had been drastic, that's for sure.

He reached down and began toying gently with Allie's exposed nipple. Both men watched as her nipple blushed a deeper shade of pink and hardened into a beautiful rosebud. Nick took her other nipple and pinched it.

She moaned softly and her eyes blinked open. Surprise crossed her face until she realized where she was. Then she smiled. Max could barely breathe at the beautiful sight of their woman looking so happy to see them back in bed with her.

She cocked her head questioningly and watched as they both played with her nipples.

"What are you two guys up to?"

"Ready to purr for us, Allie?" Nick cooed as he brought his mouth over Allie's exposed breast.

Max watched as she hissed and arched her back, making the sheets move lower on her waist until her nude pussy became exposed.

Fuck. She was simply too beautiful to ignore.

"Are you gentlemen ready to roar for me?" she moaned as Max's mouth latched on to her other tight nipple.

Both grinned and nodded in agreement.

Allie made them roar many times that day and for many years after.

VOYEUR

Shiloh Walker

ONE

A shlyn shuddered, a hoarse moan falling from her mouth. Her elbows gave out and her upper body collapsed on the bed. Behind her, Kye panted roughly while he pumped in and out of her shivering body. Looking down, he watched as he slid back inside the tight glove of her anus.

Ashlyn's fingers circled madly around her clit, and her knees started to quake. "Aw, hell. Kye, harder. Hard and slow," she hissed, her breath catching in her lungs as his thrusts went from short and quick to long, hard, and slow.

As always, the feeling of him buried inside her ass bordered on near pain, but each time she thought she couldn't handle it, her body clamored for more. The first climax caught her in its fist, and gushed from her vagina to soak her busy hand. Even as her body spasmed around the invasion in her butt, she ordered harshly, "Don't stop yet, Kye. Give me more."

He grinned and clamped his fingers harder on her hips, pushing her almost completely off before burrowing back in to the hilt, her agile fingers grazing the sac of his balls before returning to rub her clit.

Shuttling in and out of her tight little hole, he felt his own climax building at the base of his spine. Kye forced her hips down and dug in a little harder, angling his hips until he felt the tremors start inside her body again.

Just as he shot off inside her ass in vicious spurts, she screamed long and low, her anus clamping around his cock as she came a second time.

Black dots danced in front of her eyes as his hot semen pumped inside her butt. Her arms buckled and Kye fell against her as he rode her body down to the floor before he collapsed and rolled to his side, bringing her with him.

Some time later, he asked, "Who would you like to ride while I screw your ass?"

She stiffened, and buried her face in the pillow. They had moved to the bed after cleaning up and she had been drifting off to sleep.

It wasn't an unusual question, at least not from Kye. He seemed determined to share her with somebody, determined to slide inside her ass with tiny, invading thrusts while somebody else lay beneath her, fucking her in a more traditional manner.

As thrilling as the idea seemed, she wasn't about to let it happen. She knew herself too damn well and suspected if the time for such a treat ever came, she'd probably run scared. Ashlyn was not the adventurous type, or at least, she didn't think she was.

Anal sex was certainly something she had never considered. Kye had practically begged, and she still hadn't given in. It had taken him months to talk her into it.

And hell, the first time she had let Kye give it to her in the ass, she had been more than a little tipsy. And the second time. But by the third, and fourth times . . . she had come to crave it.

But another man in the bed? Not likely. She'd feel like a deer in the headlights—caught, fascinated—and then she'd turn into a rabbit and run like hell.

"Lay off it, Kye," she muttered, wanting to fall into the waiting maw of oblivion. With the exception of the past hour, the whole day had sucked. And tomorrow was going to be just as bad. The pediatric office where she worked had turned into hell on earth. Temporarily. One nurse on maternity leave. Another sick. And everybody just *had* to get in that day. Or the next. But only after four o'clock.

She snuggled into her pillow and yawned, the demands of the past few days catching up with her.

"Come on," he cajoled, fondling her breast as he propped himself on his elbow.

"Kye, it won't happen." With a sigh, she pushed up until she sat, and drew her knees to her chest. "Maybe I do want to try it, once. But I'm neurotic enough that it will have to be somebody we know, somebody we can trust. And I'd like it to be somebody I don't personally know. An anonymous stranger I know we can trust, how likely is that? It would also have to be somebody I'll never have to see again. I'd probably die from embarrassment. Facts, disturbing, distressing, embarrassing facts that I just can't get past, but hey, that's life."

Tugging her down next to him, he considered that while he rubbed her back. "Go to sleep," he murmured.

TWO

Three months later

Kye's hands were busy on her ass while he nibbled on her neck. Burning candles were scattered about the hotel room, the flickering light turning her pale skin to gold. She wore a silk robe and nothing else.

He was still dressed in a silk shirt she had bought that he rarely wore and a pair of khakis that showed his tight butt to perfection. Ashlyn's head was reeling from it all—coming home from work to have him stuff an overnight bag into her arms and usher her out to the car before she had even changed out of her scrubs.

Driving to this beautiful hotel nestled on the river and checking into a sumptuous suite. He had drawn her a bubble bath, she remembered, as his mouth closed over the hot point of her nipple. Urged her into it and washed her back, her hair, everything, in a gentle soothing manner that had aroused, and comforted at the same time.

And then he had left her alone, with a quiet order to relax. He'd left the robe in a gift-wrapped box. She had pulled the fine, rich silk over her soft, scented body while a goofy smile curved her mouth.

Her body looked quite luscious, she had thought as she smoothed the silk over her nipples, her gently rounded belly and curvy hips. She teetered between a size twelve and fourteen and took it as a matter of fact that she was, and would always be, a twelve something. With her broad shoulders and hips, she'd probably look anorexic in a size eight anyway.

Now, he tugged open the robe, sliding one hand down the length of her body to uncover her, but he left the silk on her shoulders. "Close your eyes," he ordered, sliding one thigh between hers, lowering his head to nibble on her shoulder.

Her lids drifted closed and her head fell back as he stroked and caressed, rubbing his cock against her belly. Of an equal height, Ashlyn and Kye were eye-to-eye, mouth-to-mouth when they stood facing each other. Right now, his mouth was cruising its way down her chest to lock onto her nipple with gentle teeth, as she arched her back over his arm. A sigh shivered out of her and she rubbed her hips insistently against his.

"Kye, please," she whispered, reaching for his trousers only to have hands close over her wrists. Big hands. Unfamiliar hands. Her eyes flew open and she stared into Kye's gaze while a big body pressed against her back.

Lowering his head, Kye whispered, "I know him, have for more than half my life. But you don't. And you won't ever have to see him again."

"No," she whispered as those big hands glided up and cupped her breasts, dragging the silk over the nipples, plumping them together, tweaking the hard points. A hard, long cock pressed against her spine and she caught a glimpse of a golden head swooping down to bite her along the side of her neck.

Kye grinned at her, hot and wicked. "No?" he repeated, sliding one hand down, into her wet, hot pussy. "Your little kitty just got wetter, Ash. Really want me to make him leave?" As he asked, his fingers left her dripping passage and both hands gripped her hips, urging her to turn around and face the man who had been fondling her breasts.

Her eyes stayed stubbornly straight ahead, which had her looking at his chest. It was covered by a nubby Aran sweater in some dark color. The candlelight made it hard to tell, but it was probably navy. That chest stretched the fine wool and rose up and down as he breathed.

One of those big hands came up to cup her face as he dipped his head and covered her mouth with his. Behind her Kye cuddled his cock against her silk covered backside, his hands stroking along her sides and hips as he nuzzled her neck.

The stranger—an anonymous stranger she didn't ever have to see again—seduced her mouth, nipping at her lip, gliding his tongue in to taste her, leaving before she could make up her mind to turn her head or kiss him back.

And he knew how to kiss. Between the two men—her husband and this stranger—her knees buckled and she started to slide, only to have those big hands catch her under the arms, one thigh going between hers to brace her weight with his. Behind her, Kye continued to rock his cock against her butt.

"Am I staying or going?" the stranger asked, his voice deep, rough, with a lyrical accent. *Irish. Oh, damn. He was Irish.*

Finally, *finally*, Ashlyn opened her eyes and looked up at him. He was *gorgeous*, almost too beautiful to be real, with a foxy, narrow face, large, intelligent, hot eyes that almost burned as he returned her stare. High cheekbones, almost hollow cheeks, and a mouth . . . hmmm, what a mouth.

Big broad shoulders strained against the dark wool of his sweater, matched by a broad chest before tapering down to a long narrow torso. Heavy thighs—strong thighs—she knew, remembering how it had felt just seconds ago as she rode one when he caught her weight.

"You got a name?" she asked, her mouth going dry as she stared up at him.

"Connor," he said, his hand stroking and kneading her breast.

"What do you want, Ash," Kye whispered in her ear. "I've known him most of my life. I trust him, with you, with this. He's a good guy, healthy and single. And you won't ever have to see him again." He nudged Connor's hand out of the way and wrapped his arms around her while she stared into the handsome, golden face in front of her. He had light eyes, probably blue and that golden hair fell almost to his shoulders.

Cuddling her against him, Kye said, "Or I'll ask him to leave and I'll let it go. I want to give you this—watch this. But it's your choice. Either way, it's your choice."

"Watch?" she repeated.

A grin tugged at his mouth and he said, "Yeah, watch. Watch you ride him before I take you in the ass. Watch while he plays with your nipples, and sucks on your clit." In a hot, smoky voice, he murmured, "Watch you suck on his cock while I eat you up. Then you can suck on mine and he can see just how good you taste." A hand drifted down, gathering moisture from her folds before bringing it up and painting her lips with his wet fingers.

Then he ate at her mouth, sucking and licking the cream he had rubbed onto her mouth.

"Yeah, I want to watch," he repeated after he lifted his head. "And you want it, too. You're almost ready to come just thinking of it."

Her body was hot, wet, and quaking at the thought of taking them both inside her. Before Kye had introduced her to the pleasure of anal sex, she had never before imagined it. But since he had . . . yeah, she had thought of it, in dark, wicked fantasies she never would have admitted, if Kye hadn't first suggested it over a year ago.

With her hands keeping Kye firmly against her middle, she stepped forward. A small grin curved Connor's mouth, a chiseled mouth that would have put Val Kilmer's to shame. One hand lifted, palm up and waiting. She put hers in it and let him draw her up against him.

While Kye's hands went to take her damp hair down, Connor lifted her hand to his mouth and pressed a kiss to it. "If you change your mind, I will leave," he promised, trying to ease some of the nerves he saw in her eyes. If it had just been nerves, he would have left.

But there were hot little licks of excitement there as well, darkening those eyes in that heart shaped face. He had been sitting in a chair in the corner of the room—hidden by the shadows—watching as his old friend kissed and stroked his wife.

She was adorable and sexy all at the same time, with her dark hair piled on top of her head, her body covered by the red silk of the robe. Beneath it, he imagined she had a soft, round, woman's body, with full, heavy tits, round hips, a firm but soft ass.

As he lowered her hand, he stepped forward until her soft, scented body was pressed between his and Kye's. Then he dropped to his knees in front of her and tugged apart the edges of the robe that had fallen back to cover her.

Yeah, a woman's body, Connor thought, leaning forward to nuzzle her belly as Kye's hands stroked and kneaded her breasts. This was a first for both of them, as well. Connor had been more than a little shocked when Kye had mentioned this to him on his last trip to the States.

Shocked and intrigued. He had seen pictures of Ashlyn, and there was something almost catlike about her, something feline in her small, smug smile, about her up-tilted eyes. She was sexy and inviting, and he had wanted her from the minute he had seen her picture.

But she belonged to one of his best friends, one of his oldest friends.

Shocked, intrigued.

Intrigued enough, that he had agreed to something he had never given thought to before.

And now, as his teeth closed over the hot little point of one rosy nipple, he was thanking his lucky stars he had agreed. A sexy little moan escaped her lips and Connor chanced grazing his knuckles over the patch of hair between her soft pale thighs. Drops of moisture were already beading in that downy thatch like pearls.

Her knees buckled and Connor supported her weight as she slid down to straddle his lap.

Kye propped his shoulder against the wooden entertainment center and stared, his cock tight, full, pulsing as he watched Connor bury his hands in her hair and drag her head back, eating at her mouth while his hips surged, pressing his cock against the wet folds between her thighs.

Her hands clutched at his shoulders, and her legs crept around his waist to lock behind his back, opening herself to him, purring when he started to rock and rub his shaft against her.

He kissed his way down her neck and shoulder, across her chest until he could feast on those tight, puckered little nipples. Through the heavy material of his jeans, Connor could feel her, feel how hot she was, how wet she was.

Kye went to his knees behind her, and Connor remembered he wasn't alone with this woman. Remembered the man behind Ashlyn was her husband and he had more right to be here, that he was the one who was sharing his wife. So he shifted his legs, shifted the panting, hot little bundle in his lap until Kye was once again pressed against her butt. Lifting his head from her wet nipple, Connor met Kye's eyes over her shoulder. "The bed?" he suggested softly, afraid to speak too loudly, to move too suddenly.

Kye nodded and rose, helping Ashlyn to her feet, nuzzling her neck and wrapping his arms around her, fondling her breasts while Connor stood.

Kye eased her onto the bed while Connor stripped, palming a rubber from his pocket and tossing it to the table before joining them. Ashlyn was seated on the side of the bed, her hands busily undoing Kye's shirt while Kye worked the belt and buttons of his trousers. Loathe to do it, Connor settled behind her, letting Kye go back to kissing and suckling his wife's pretty tits while Connor stroked and soothed her shoulders and spine as he cupped her body with his own.

He wanted to be in Kye's place, sucking on those sweet breasts, tracing his hands over her quivering, soft thighs. That is, until she squirmed against him.

From this position, Ashlyn's ass was pressing on his rock-hard cock and she kept squirming against it. He shoved back with a groan, his fingers digging into her hips as he thrust against her, a bead of moisture leaking from the tip of his cock.

They ended up with her straddling his hips as he nuzzled and bit and sucked on those pretty little rose nipples and the heavy white globes of her tits.

Kye's hands buried in her hair and he tugged her away from Connor—pushed her down until she could wrap those full lips around his cock. Connor shifted until he was propped against the headboard, watching as she sucked his friend off, his hand going to his own cock, and stroking it absently as he wished he was the one kneeling there with her in front of him, taking him deep in her throat.

While Kye might have mentioned her doing the same to him, Connor didn't see it happening. She wasn't going to wrap those lips around his cock and take him deep in her mouth. She was too damn skittish, too nervous. And damn if that didn't turn him on even more. She was hot and hungry for this, no doubt of that, which Kye had promised. But she was also jumpy, flicking him nervous little glances, her face flushing each time she looked at him.

Except for now. She was a little preoccupied with nibbling and sucking on her husband's cock, something she was turning into a work of art, from what Connor could tell.

Moments passed and then Kye's body stiffened. He came in her mouth with a groan and she swallowed, lifted her head and kissed his belly before turning her eyes to Connor.

Some of the nerves had left her eyes—now they held heat, and an endearing shyness. Her gaze drifted down to glance at his cock as he stroked it with an easy, sure hand. Her mouth parted and her tongue slid out to wet her lips, her lids drooping while her body started to lean his way. His hand slid up, briefly closing over the fat head of his cock, his thumb catching the moisture there and spreading it around, making the tip gleam.

His eyes closed as he had a visual of her mouth on him, sliding up and down, pausing to lick and suck on his sac. His whole body stiffened at the image and his cock jerked in demand as Connor resisted the urge to guide her mouth down to his aching flesh.

Ashlyn's breathing sped up as she watched Connor's hand work his cock in sure, unself-conscious strokes. His penis was big, long, and thick, rising from a thatch of golden hair. The smooth head of his shaft was ruddy and gleaming from the pre-come he had spread around, the shaft itself thick and straight. She wanted to feel those hands on her, and suspected he would be just as confident handling her body as he was his own.

Her gaze lifted to study the rest of him, lounging on the bed in all his naked glory. And talk about glory. His shoulders, just as broad as they appeared under his sweater, gave way to a sculpted, muscled chest, naked of any body hair, before tapering down to a narrow waist and flat belly where a fine line of blond hair grew, arrowing down to his cock.

Giving in, she went back to watching what intrigued her the most, his hand on his cock.

She wanted to taste him, she admitted to herself, licking her lips.

Glancing at Kye, she shifted and lay down on her stomach between Connor's thighs, turning her body so that Kye could stroke and caress, guiding his hands to the wet curls that covered her mound, moisture from her body gleaming like pearls on the short curly strands of her hair.

Then she turned her attention back to Connor, her attention and her mouth. He bucked in surprise when her lips lowered and engulfed half his cock in one swallow. "Aw, fuck," he gasped, one hand going to tangle in her hair, his eyes staring down in dazed delight as she slid her lips up and down his cock, one hand wrapping around the base, while the other stroked his balls. He held up her long curled locks of hair, staring at her profile, shuddering as he watched her take him in again, her lashes a dark fan against her ivory cheeks. Her mouth, swollen and red, slid wetly over his shaft and she paused at the head to nibble and swirl her tongue around him.

She glanced at him before turning her attention back to the task at hand. Kye stroked her clit, shifting her lower body so that she could open her thighs for him. Then he hardened his tongue and stabbed inside her waiting vagina, drinking down the musky cream before using his teeth on the hard little bud just atop her slit.

And Connor had a front row seat. His gaze tracked back and forth between what she was doing with her mouth and what Kye was doing with his. He watched, noting what had her hips rolling forward, what had her strangling a gasp while she deep throated his cock. Her breath caught and Connor felt it as it drew his length just the slightest bit deeper into her mouth before she pulled off and threw back her head, gasping and climaxing with a weak little cry when Kye started to thrust two fingers back and forth inside her, twisting his wrist slowly as he entered her, rotating it back as he pulled out.

He watched and ached, and remembered, because he was next. Connor wasn't leaving now, wasn't leaving this room without tasting everything this hot little woman had to offer.

Between her very talented mouth and the very hot show, Connor lost control and came inside her mouth, groaning as she swallowed his cock and his semen down before her head fell onto his thigh and she stiffened and bucked her hips as a second climax rolled through her.

"My turn," he muttered as Kye moved away. Without a glance at the dark haired man, he lay between Ashlyn's quivering thighs, cupped her ass in his hands and lowered his head. Still shaking, still sensitized from Kye's hands and mouth, she shrieked when Connor drew his tongue up the wet slit, lapping up the moisture from her climax, closing his eyes and savoring it.

Kye rolled to his side, lying crossways so that he could put his mouth to work on her torso but still watch everything. Connor paused, raising his head to stare up at Kye, his pale eyes going dark with lust, with need. "She tastes like heaven," he muttered, his mouth wet and gleaming.

"Eat her up," Kye offered. "You won't have this chance again."

Ashlyn's face flushed with embarrassment—with pleasure—

before she sank her teeth into her lower lip as Connor did just that, eating her up with greedy, thorough strokes of his tongue. He stabbed repeatedly at her wet aching cleft with his stiffened tongue, rotating his thumb against her clit until her hips rose and fell against him. Shifting a little, he nibbled and sucked on her clit, rubbing his tongue in circular motions against the hard bead of flesh.

Kye bit and sucked hard on her nipples, lifting his head he replaced his tongue with his hand so he could watch as she exploded again. A pleased smile curved his mouth as she fell apart beneath his hands, beneath Connor's mouth. He had given her this, he thought, quite pleased. That dazed, blind look in her pretty eyes—the flush that tinted her face and torso a faint rose—her heaving breasts as she gasped for breath. He had given her that. Her lids lifted and she stared at him with hazy, hot eyes as a pleased little purr fell from her lips.

And they were just getting started.

He stilled his fingers, turned them to soothing strokes as her breath shuddered out of her lungs. When Connor lowered his head, ready to burrow his tongue back inside her wet folds, Kye stopped him, holding him back with a hand on his big hard shoulder.

"We've got all night," Kye said mildly when Connor snarled at him.

But only tonight, Connor thought darkly. *At least for me.*

He wanted her, his friend's wife, for his own, and he wasn't certain if one night was going to be enough. "Y'got the rest of your damned life, mate. I've only tonight." But he shifted, coming to lie down on the other side of her, his cock stiff as a pike and eager to slide inside that hot little pussy.

Ashlyn's lids fluttered open and she stared at the dark, handsome face of her husband, into his beautiful dark eyes, at his high cheekbones—a gift from his Native American blood—at the black hair that fell straight as rain to just above his shoulders. "I love you," she said thickly, cupping his face in one palm.

Connor's gaze fell away, well aware of his intrusion, as Kye lowered his head and bussed her mouth gently, lovingly, as he murmured his own love. The jealousy that curled in Connor's gut startled him, enough that he almost got up and walked away. God, he wanted that—that connection, that certainty that your love was returned.

Feeling isolated, and slightly shamed, he started to move away when her hands caught his.

Ashlyn rolled to her knees, stroking her hand down the length of his torso, her eyes meeting his for a long moment before returning her gaze to Kye. "He's right; we only have tonight and I don't want to waste a second of it."

She shifted to straddle his thighs, catching Connor's cock in her hand as Kye came to cuddle against her back. He had retrieved a tube of lube at some point and she felt his movements as he spread it across his cock, smeared it between the cheeks of her ass as he stroked her, guided her into position over Connor's hips.

He was bigger than Kye, which was no surprise, being as he was close to a foot taller. His cock was longer, and thicker, and she eyed him a little nervously as he guided it inside her. The fat head stretched her tightly and she bit her lip and hesitantly started to work his shaft into her body. His hands came up to grip her hips and he rocked and thrust his way inside. She fell forward bracing her elbows beside his head, positioning her ass for Kye as Connor rolled his hips, burying his cock to the hilt.

She shuddered, moaned. He moved his hips in tiny little thrusts, so that the head of his cock rubbed against the mouth of her womb. With a shift of his thighs, he opened her further for Kye's penetration.

Kye pressed against the tiny rose hole, barely brushing it for now, waiting until it started to spasm. "Make her come," he told Connor. "I'm not fucking her ass until you have her moaning."

Connor stared up into the heart shaped face just inches

from his. Her eyes were glazed, pupils dilated. "She's ready now," he said softly, continuing to roll his hips against hers, loving the little flutters and ripples as her body worked to accommodate his.

"Make her come." Kye pressed his thumb against the rosette, smiling as she moaned hoarsely. "She's close." He reached between her thighs with his other hand, reaching around where Connor had entered her until he could press against the hard little knot of her clit.

Connor used his hands to lift her a little higher, well aware of what Kye was doing while Connor's cock eased in and out of Ashlyn's tight little sheath, knew Kye was stroking and plucking her clit. He could feel it as he pushed back into her creamy warmth and couldn't help but be startled at how erotic it was to fuck a woman while another man played with her body.

"Ashlyn," he whispered, hoarsely. He wanted her to see *him* when she came, wanted her to know he was the one inside her.

Her eyes met his—blindly, a little dazed—and he groaned when she lowered her sweet little mouth and kissed him. The tastes of each other's body lingered in their mouths and she whimpered as he bit her lower lip. Then he grasped her hips, pulled out, and drove into the heart of her.

Again . . . again—faster and harder—until she shattered above him with a hoarse little scream, bearing down on him while her vaginal walls milked him, dragging him much closer to orgasm than he was ready for.

Kye braced her hips and eased inside her anus as she rode the wave of the orgasm, feeling her flutter around him, the ripples from her belly echoing through the tight little sphincter so that he felt it as surely as she did.

"Easy," Kye crooned when she instinctively flinched away from the double penetration. "Easy, baby."

Still shaking from the orgasm, she collapsed on Connor's chest, staring up into his hard face, a will of iron keeping his body still as Kye worked his own cock inside her. Connor could feel it, could feel Kye's cock through the thin wall of flesh that separated them, felt her tighten around him as Kye started to work his cock in with slow, tiny thrusts and Connor couldn't help but wonder. "Does it hurt?" he asked roughly, reaching up to stroke her cheek. Over her shoulder and back, he could see the curve of her ass high in the air, held in place by her stiffened knees.

Kye was working his cock in slowly, waiting for her to accommodate him before easing further inside. She was stretched taut around Connor's shaft and the muscles of her anus were tighter than normal, fighting his slow intrusion.

The reddened flesh of her rosette stretched tightly around his cock and he groaned as he got past the tight ring of muscle there, gripping his flesh like hot, warm living silk. She whimpered deeply in her throat, a tiny pain-filled sound and he felt her body's slight, instinctive recoil from his possession. She had done that a number of times when they had first started this kind of sex play and he suspected it was hurting her a little.

But she was so wet, the cream from her vagina was apparent even to Kye. He could feel it, smell how hot and eager she was. The air was perfumed by the scent of her lust, so he continued to thrust inside with tiny, forward motions.

"A little. At first, but then . . . " her eyes fluttered closed and she flinched as Kye seated himself inside her ass, all the way down to the base.

"It's hurting her," Connor said, starting to pull out. "Back off."

"She likes it," Kye muttered, holding his position. "Ashlyn, do you want me to stop?"

"Don't you dare," she hissed, lifting her head to glare at him over her shoulder. Then she turned to look at Connor. "It always hurts, at first. Just a little." She rolled her hips as best as she could with Kye stuffed inside her ass and Connor buried inside her pussy all the way to the womb. She'd never felt so tight, so unbelievably full.

Something caught her eye, and she glanced sideways. Saw the unopened rubber on the bedside table. Her hesitation was minimal. And then she turned back, feeling Connor inside her, skin to skin, his cock snug against her vaginal walls.

"Feel good, Ashlyn?" Kye purred, rolling his hips against her, smiling as it sent a shiver quaking down her spine.

"Kye . . . Kye, please." She arched back, pushing against him. Ashlyn cried out when he pulled back, teasingly, keeping her from taking his entire length back inside. "Damn it, Kye, stop playing with me and fuck me!"

"Are you ready?" he asked, timing his slow thrust to match Connor's. It was enough to have him coming on the spot as he drove back inside her, feeling Connor's cock as it left her dripping pussy. Then as Kye pulled out he could feel Connor driving back in, the sensation sending a shudder down his spine.

Connor raised his head and he set his teeth in the curve of her throat, using that grip to hold her still while he slid inside the tight clasp of her body.

"Please," she gasped, rolling her head to the other side, giving better access as Connor continued to hold her flesh in the grip of his strong, even teeth.

Kye planted his knees and started to ride her, shuttling in and out of her ass, hard, slow, and deep. Connor released her neck when she started to lift her head—staring up into her heavy-lidded eyes, watching as her tongue darted out to lick at her lips.

"Connor, will you . . . " Her cheeks flushed and her eyes dropped away. Her whole body quivered.

"Fuck her, Connor," Kye finished for her as the ability to speak clearly left her. "That's what she wants."

"Ashlyn—"

"Connor, please," she gasped, twisting, trying to ride his cock, but unable to move well with Kye digging his cock into her ass.

"Want me to fuck you?" he asked, the words falling from his mouth in that lyrical accent, so that it sounded like poetry. Maybe he wanted to tease her a little, but he also wanted to make sure this wasn't hurting her. "You're so tight, so tiny. Are ya certain, now, you want me to fuck you?"

"Yeah," she panted. "Fuck me," she pleaded, feeling a climax just beyond her reach.

She was stuffed so full of cock—both front and back—she couldn't possibly reach down to stroke her clit, couldn't help bring the climax any closer. "As my lady wishes," Connor purred, quite satisfied that it would be his face she saw when she found the climax she was so obviously seeking. "Just let me look at you while I do it. I like the look of you."

She kept her eyes trained on his as Kye and Connor started to move in tandem, a reverse echo of the other's movements. Kye would fill her as Connor retreated, then Connor would thrust into her wet passage as Kye pulled back outside the tight grip of her ass.

"You're so pretty," Connor crooned, his voice low and gruff, as he pumped and rolled his cock in and out of her body. "I want another taste of you, Ash."

Kye chuckled breathlessly as he rode her ass, filling her, leaving, then filling her up again. "Con, my friend, we should have made a souvenir video of this. Then you could see it from my view.

"Her ass feels like silk when you're inside it. She's so tight around me, you have to . . . aw, damn . . . so tight, you have to work it in slowly or it hurts her too much. Then you're inside and she's tight and soft and hotter than hell. You'd fill her so full, she'd probably taste your come in her throat."

Ashlyn was beyond speech, whimpering mindlessly, rubbing her nipples against Connor's broad chest, as he fucked her pussy and Kye fucked her ass. Connor's hand joined Kye's on her butt, pulling the flesh apart, holding her completely open as they rode her hard.

It hit her like a monsoon, knocking the breath from her, and sizzling through her body like an electric shock. Both her anal and vaginal muscles locked down on the invading flesh.

Kye groaned and went off inside her, pumping her ass full of semen, filling her in hot, wet jets.

The orgasm took Connor by surprise. He'd been determined to make it last, to draw it out, but her vagina had vised down on him and tore it from him before he realized it was happening. He bellowed beneath her, closing his hands on her thighs and flooding her with a hot gush, plunging repeatedly into the hot tight depths of her vagina.

Kye collapsed against her, his weight bearing her down harder on Connor while the climax dragged on, tearing through him almost viciously. As their weight settled on Connor, he guided her body to the side so that she was cuddled against his torso, and spooned from behind by Kye.

"Oh, shit," Ashlyn mumbled after long minutes had passed. Her own fluids and their semen trickled down to dry on her thighs as she shifted, slowly sitting, then turning so that Kye's body cupped hers, propping her up.

Looking down at herself, and then at her two partners, she said, "We need a bath."

Connor remained sprawled on the bed, tempted to leave, unable to do so. Kye and his wife had retreated to the bathroom while he stayed where he was, fighting down the jealousy that was eating his gut.

She wasn't his.

She wasn't ever going to be his.

That hot, wild woman with the shy eyes and clever mouth would never be his.

And until tonight, he hadn't realized that she was what had been missing from his life. Until tonight, he hadn't realized that anything had been missing.

As the shower turned off, he rolled to his side. Spying his jeans, he grabbed them and tugged them on moments before the door opened and Kye and Ashlyn tumbled out—wrapped in the heavy cotton hotel robes—giggling like teenagers. He left them open, his soft cock uncovered and still damp from her as he strode past them, determined to shower and get the hell out.

When he stepped from the shower, Ashlyn was waiting for him, Kye standing behind her, watching her with hot eyes as she dropped to her knees in front of Connor.

"How can you share her like this? She's your wife. Does it not bother you, to see her doing this to another man?"

Kye met his eyes as Ashlyn took his cock into her very talented mouth.

Slowly, his mouth curled up in a smile and he shrugged, saying, "I'm giving her a fantasy, something she's dreamed of but would never ask for on her own." The answer was the same as it had been when Kye had first presented the idea that had been brewing in the back of his mind, the same one he had given to Connor as Connor stared at him as if he had lost his mind.

Wrapping his hand in her wet hair, he braced his back against the tiled wall. Groaning with pleasure as she deep throated him, shuddering when she pulled away to nuzzle and lick at his balls.

His head fell back against the tile, but he kept his eyes open, watching their reflections in triplicate from the walled mirrors. He could see the curve of her ass as she serviced him. With a flick of his eyes, he could see her face in profile, see as her lips slid down his cock. She paused as she came to the head and swirled her tongue over it, nibbling gently before taking his length inside her mouth again.

From the doorway, Kye watched before coming up behind Ashlyn, kneeling down, sliding his hand between her legs to fondle and play as she fondled Connor's heavy, hard penis.

She paused when she felt Kye's familiar hands stroking over her, paused and lifted her head, turning her body and catching his mouth with hers. Connor dropped to his knees behind her while she kissed Kye and ran her hands down the darker man's rib cage to grip his ass while she lowered her head to his groin and took his waiting cock in her mouth.

Staring down at her ass, thrust high in the air, Connor saw why Kye had wanted this position. The tight little hole of her ass beckoned. Her vagina had been made for that kind of penetration, yet she gloved him so tightly. What would it feel like to have the puckered little rosette open up and take him?

He knelt behind her and bumped his cock against her ass,

brushing and stroking. Ashlyn's body quivered and a whimper fell from her lips as she paused to bite delicately at Kye's balls. Connor repeated the motion, smiling when she quivered again. Every brush, every press against her anus made her moan and shake.

"I've made her come just by doing that," Kye said roughly, panting, taking her head between his hands and holding her still so he could plunge his cock in and out of her mouth at his pace, which grew frantic in mere seconds.

A muffled groan escaped her as Kye flooded her throat with hot jets of come, and Connor continued to rub his cock tauntingly against her ass. "Damn it, baby, I think you're going to empty me before the night is over," he muttered as she sucked on him like a straw, drawing the last few drops of fluid from him.

Kye eyed Connor over the naked expanse of her back, one black brow raised. Guiding her back up, he pressed a kiss to Ashlyn's mouth, and rose, easing her body back against Connor's before he left the room. "Are you enjoying your fantasy, Ashlyn?" he murmured, rocking against her butt, stroking his hands over her sides, her thighs, to graze over the wet curls before cupping her breasts and rolling her nipples between his thumbs.

She swallowed, savoring the taste of Kye's come in her mouth before she rolled her eyes to meet Connor's. "Hell, yes," she answered, her voice ragged and hoarse. Kye returned, watching as Connor palmed her breasts, rubbing his cock against her ass, eyes narrowed in pleasure—in need. He joined them, catching her face in his dark, work roughened hands and plundering her mouth.

Her head fell back with a sigh of surrender as he moved from her mouth to kiss and nip along the cord of her neck. "How sore are you?" he asked softly, lifting his head to look at her.

"Just a little," she replied, relaxed against Connor's chest, amazed at how easy, how natural it felt to be with these two men—together. Rolling her head on his shoulder, she pressed a kiss to Connor's neck, straining to brush her mouth against his jaw. His wet, golden hair fell across her face and neck when he lowered his head to meet her lips, kissing her with a startling hunger.

Kye leaned closer, whispering in her ear while Connor ate at her mouth like a man starved. "Think you can take another round?" Kye asked. Lowering his hand until he could circle his thumb around her clit. "I think Connor's wanting to switch around."

She tensed, pulling her mouth from Connor's to look at Kye. But he knew her well and cut off her hesitancy simply by rubbing her just the right way, sending her mind spiraling out of her body. Just a glide of his finger inside her wet vagina, a pass of his thumb over her swollen, throbbing clit while Connor rocked against her bottom.

"Just go slow," Kye told Connor, pulling Ashlyn up until she was straddling his hips. "She'll tell you if it's too much. She'll tell you how to do it."

"*She* hasn't told me she wants to do it," Connor growled as Kye offered him the lube he had used earlier.

"If *she* didn't want to try," Ashlyn interrupted sardonically, "*she* wouldn't still be in here." She took Kye inside in one quick thrust, a little hum of pleasure escaping her. "Do what you were just doing, put some lube on and I'll do the rest. I'll do it this time."

Connor hesitated, but he slowly took the tube of lubricant, squeezing it into his palm and smearing it over his cock until it gleamed under the bright lights. He squirted more into his hand so he could coat her anus with it, eased the tip of his finger inside her hole, preparing the tight ring of muscle there for his entry. She pressed her brow against Kye's, looped her arms around his neck and waited until she felt the broad head of Connor's penis press against her ass. Kye continued to roll and thrust inside her, pressing his thumb against her clit and whispering in her ear, "You're so tight, so sweet. When he gets inside your ass, he won't ever want to leave. Heaven knows, I never want to."

He continued to croon into her ear, distracting her with words and his shaft so she wouldn't get apprehensive about what was to come. He knew she was usually a little sore after anal sex, and suspected that taking Connor's cock inside wasn't going to be quite as easy as taking his.

Connor was taller than Kye, bigger, and it took a few moments and some shifts in position before she could take both of them. She started taking little increments of Connor's shaft as Kye rolled and flexed his hips, rocking his own cock inside her slowly, using his thumb to circle over her clit in slow, teasing circles.

At first, all she did was bump her anus against the head of his cock, while he used his hand to hold it steady. And then she started to slide herself down on him. Kye's hands came up to grip the cheeks of her ass, opening her as she slid down a fraction, working the head of Connor's cock into the tight little rosette.

Connor's breath was dragging out of his lungs, a fine sweat coating his body as she took him. Slowly. So damned slowly he thought he would die before she got him in. When she had him halfway seated inside, she gave a short little scream of frustration. "Damn it, I can't—" she panted, shifting, twisting, trying to get in a better position.

"Pull out, Kye," Connor ordered, bracing her weight by putting his hands under her thighs. As soon as Kye withdrew, he rose, holding her weight, holding her half-impaled on his cock.

Moments later, he pressed his back to the wall and spread his thighs wide, keeping her cunt low enough so that Kye could resume his position. Ashlyn hung helplessly with Connor half impaling her on his cock, her widespread legs opening her wet folds.

Connor could see it in the mirror and he lowered his head to purr in her ear, "I've never seen a woman so ready to be fucked, never in m'life." His accent had thickened as the lust consumed him. "Aw, darlin' girl, aren't you a sight?" He held her weight easily with his body, staring at the reflection until her gaze met his.

Kye hesitated, his attention caught by what he was seeing— Connor's big hands supporting Ashlyn's thighs, holding her up just with his grasp, leaving her wet and open, small drops of her cream seeping from her body, the lips of her sex red and swollen. Her breasts were heaving as she gasped for air, her nipples puckered tight and hard. After taking a long moment to enjoy the picture, he enthusiastically took his position, burying himself into her hot, silky little sheath with one hard thrust. Sandwiched between them, unable to move, Ashlyn whimpered as Kye filled her repeatedly. Connor stayed stubbornly still, holding himself back.

"Do it," she whimpered, trying to twist away from his restraining hands so she could work herself down farther on the hard length of him.

"I don't want to hurt you," he muttered, shuddering from restraint. It wasn't easy. Fuck, he could feel it as Kye rode her, feel it as he pummeled her hips, and drove his cock inside her. There was a maddening brush against his sac every time Kye drove in and Kye's balls bumped his. Each thrust caused her body to tighten around Connor and he knew he was going to go mad and lose it right there.

"I want you," she whispered, her head falling back against his shoulder as Kye's head ducked, his teeth catching a nipple and biting down hard enough to hurt—hard enough to leave a faint mark around the skin of her nipple. And she gloried in it. "All the . . . way . . . inside," she panted. "Just fuck me . . . okay?"

With a roar, he used his hands and drove her down until he was fully seated inside her snug, hot, tight little ass, causing her to shriek and writhe helplessly in his arms.

It was different from being inside her pussy, tighter, the skin seeming smoother, almost softer somehow. Definitely hotter.

He found his rhythm and matched it to Kye's so that she was being fucked simultaneously, as she had been earlier in the bed. They pressed her between them and fucked her endlessly, mercilessly.

His control flew out the window as her muscles rippled around him, working to accommodate him. And he forgot Kye's words, *"Just take it slow."*

He took her fast—hard and fast—the first orgasm tearing from him before either Kye or Ashlyn had reached their peak. As he spewed inside her hot little hole, he kept pumping in and out, his cock still as hard as it had been when he began.

God, he'd had some good fucks before, some good nights when he'd spent most of the time screwing, but never like this. Never needed a woman as desperately as he needed this one.

He felt like he was digging his cock into hot, wet, rich, *living* silk that moaned and responded to his every thrust. So good, so unbelievably good.

A keening moan fell from her lips and she whimpered. Some part of his brain whispered that he was hurting her, had to be hurting her, but Connor really didn't give a damn. She was coming now, clenching around them in tight, hot little pulses that set Kye off. Kye climaxed inside her with a groan—pressed in to the hilt—letting her milk his orgasm from him.

But when Kye pulled away, Connor didn't stop, he bore her to the floor—to her knees—and continued to fuck her ass, dragging another one of those keening moans from her.

Kye sagged to his knees in front of them and Connor wrapped his hand in Ashlyn's hair, dragging her head up and forcing her face to Kye's softening cock. "Suck him off, little girl. Make him hard again, make him come. Now, it's my turn to be watching," Connor ordered, shoving her head up and down as she opened her mouth to take Kye's soft wet penis inside.

Kye stared at Connor with wary eyes—at the animalistic need that was written naked on his face—but Connor didn't even notice as he watched her head start moving in rhythm with his hard, pounding thrusts. He had lost himself inside her body before, knew how easy it was for him to do so, but apparently she had caused his civilized friend to lose a little bit of himself as well.

Connor kept going until he pulled another climax from her—until she had licked all her cream from Kye's now pulsating cock—until another climax started to tighten her body. He could recognize the signs now. Her muscles would start to flutter around him in little seizures that gradually grew in strength.

"It's too much," she whispered, lifting her head from Kye. "Too much, damn it. Can't take any more."

"You will," Kye said, shoving his cock back inside her mouth. "You want it." It was written all over her, there in her flushed face, in the tight beaded nipples, in the submissive way she held her ass for Connor's deep penetration. His own balls drew tight against his body as he watched that long, hard dick ride her ass, as he watched her plump, swollen lips close over his cock before she tried to turn her head aside.

But the hand fisted in her hair wouldn't allow it. Kye took over, gripping her head as he had earlier until he was fucking her mouth as surely, as ferociously, as desperately as Connor screwed her ass.

When she started to come this time, Connor planted himself inside to the balls and refused to move until the quivers stopped. "You aren't coming yet. There's more," he purred, stroking the white mounds of her ass, leaning over to lick a wet path up her spine.

She started to pull her mouth from Kye to curse at him, but Kye grinned—just a little evilly—and clamped his hands on her head, refusing to let her stop. "Keep at it, baby," he said, meeting Connor's eyes over her naked back. "Suck me. Suck me off. I want you to; I want to shove my cock down your throat and come while he butt fucks you."

Connor still refused to move, watching instead, concentrating on watching as she deep throated Kye—as she paused to nibble on the head of his cock before sliding her mouth down the length of him.

After a time, Connor started to thrust again, pulling out and burrowing back in, using long, slow strokes that had her writhing around him. Each time her head started to slow, Connor would stop.

Taking pity, Kye took over, fucking her mouth—filling her mouth and throat with his cock so she could stay still. It was too much for her to suck on him with Connor buried in her ass.

He was big, and he was hurting her in a delicious sort of way, so that each time he retreated she followed with her ass until his big hands forced her to be still. He lowered his chest until he was cuddling against her body, so he could whisper in her ear, "You've had your fantasy, Ash. Now we'll have ours." His voice was a low, purring rumble in her ear. "He wants to watch me take you like this, while he shoves himself down your lovely little throat. And I want to fuck you like this, in your hot little ass until you come again and again, until you can't even remember your name," he finished, watching while Kye pumped in and out of her mouth. Her eyes rolled to stare into his and Kye grabbed her hair, turning her gaze—her attention—back to him.

Kye's cock in her mouth was a familiar, well-enjoyed thing. She knew how to drag out his orgasm, knew how to make it short and quick.

But the men weren't letting her do it her way. They controlled her with their hands, with their bodies, until she could only do what they wanted.

And she liked it.

She wasn't submissive, but she gloried at being controlled in this manner. A strong, confident woman in the outside world, she should have been shocked at how much she enjoyed them ordering and controlling her body—taking their pleasure—while withholding hers.

But she reveled in it. Reveled in how Connor's fingers dug into her hips when she tried to ride his shaft—reveled in how Kye's hands tightened in her hair in warning when she tried to turn her head from his pulsating cock—reveled in how Connor filled her with hard, fierce digs of his huge cock.

Holding her at his mercy, Connor reamed her ass hard, taking a dark pleasure when she flinched a little at his near brutal assault on her anus. "Such a good little fuck," he murmured, bending over to whisper praise into her ear. "So tight, so hot. Would you like to come now?"

She nodded as best she could while Kye forced her to take his cock all the way in, until her mouth could touch where his shaft joined his body. She started to gag and tried to relax her throat so he could do it again.

"What do ya think, mate?" Connor asked, his voice rough and tight as he watched how her anus would narrow when he pulled almost all the way out—the way it would stretch open around him when he drove his cock all the way in. "Should we let her come?"

Kye grinned, and said, "Might as well. The sooner she recovers, the sooner we can start again."

Again? She thought helplessly as Connor continued to ride her hard and rough, with none of the gentle hesitancy he had shown at first. Could she possibly take this again?

Hell, yes.

Connor shoved her hips down lower so he could bury his cock inside her anus in hard, deep thrusts, grabbing her hand and forcing it down until she could fondle her swollen clit. "Go ahead, Ash. Play with it." He shifted a little higher and pulled out—all the way—watching as her anus closed completely, then driving all the way back in and shouting out a ragged, "Aw, fuck," as she opened back up to take him eagerly—the pink hole widening and accepting him, closing around him like an eager little mouth to eat up his heavy surging cock.

She screamed around Kye's cock, mingled pleasure and pain clawing through her. "Want it harder?" Kye asked, feeling what it had done to her. "Fuck her harder, Connor." The words left him in a series of rough pants as he did the same, fucking her mouth harder than he ever had before. He could feel her throat close around him, trying to reject his invading shaft and it felt like glory.

Ashlyn didn't want it harder—it already was too much—but she couldn't say anything because Kye's hands held her head trapped, and his cock filled her mouth so that she couldn't speak.

Stop it, please, ohdamnit'stoo MUCH! Ithurtsithurts—

And Connor took her harder—harder and harder and harder—until she started to come. Long vicious spasms filled her belly, spiraling outward until she could barely breathe around the cock in her mouth.

And as her orgasm hit this time, it knocked her out, sending her flying off into the blackness while both men started jetting off inside her at the same time.

They took her into the large, enclosed shower—both of them—cleaning her bruised aching body with gentle hands. After cleaning the come and small traces of blood from her thighs and buttocks, Connor went to his knees in front of her, gripping her ass tenderly with his hands as he opened her swollen folds with easy strokes of his tongue.

Kye took her breasts, soaping her nipples and rinsing them clean before taking first one and then the other in his mouth.

There was no way she could come again, she thought cloudily.

No earthly way.

But they did it.

There in the shower and again on the bed, first with her straddling Kye while Connor watched. And then with Connor putting her beneath him and easing his way inside her swollen tight pussy.

This time with Connor it lasted nearly an hour—with him taking exquisite care, coaxing tiny little orgasms from her exhausted body before bringing her to a larger, mind shattering one as he flooded her body with his hot semen—as Kye watched from inches way, stroking his cock until his own climax erupted and come trickled down his cock and belly.

Connor collapsed to lay his head between her heaving breasts, staring at Kye with dull eyes. "Once I regain feeling from the neck down, I'll be moving," he said tiredly, feeling utterly drained, utterly spent.

Ashlyn hummed, a low thrumming purr deep in her throat, squirming out from under him until she could cuddle against his side, one arm draped low over his back. Kye pressed up against her from behind, his arm hooking over her hips. "No," she said simply, rubbing her cheek against his bare shoulder.

"No."

Kye pressed a kiss to her tangled hair, adding his weight to hers.

"Sleep," she muttered.

Connor laughed and said, "I've not the life for anything else, darlin'."

Within seconds, they all slept.

When she woke in the morning, Kye still slept beside her.

But Connor was gone.

THREE

Three years later

Tears burned hotly in her throat as she stared at the coffin covered with flowers.

Kye was gone, killed by some motherfucking drunk-driving bastard as he walked to his car one night after work.

He had held on until she had gotten to his side, held on until he could stare up into her face, and hear her tell him she loved him one last time.

He had mouthed the words back to her, the unbearable pain from his battered body darkening his eyes to black. The lids of his eyes had drifted closed, and in despair, she fell against the bed.

" . . . don't cry. Please, don't," he had whispered. "Love you, baby. God, always loved you. Don't cry. Don't cry. Love you." The words had fallen from his mouth in a hoarse plea while his face spasmed in agony.

And then he was gone, the internal injuries so severe death had been a blessing. His spine had been shattered from the waist down by the impact, and the internal bleeding had been massive.

Yeah, the death had been a blessing for him. The nurse inside of her knew that. He had been in agony and none of the morphine or Demerol or various other opiates they had pumped into him had touched it.

And for her, she supposed. That's what the logical part of her mind knew and accepted. She never could have watched him suffer through it. Each spasm that had gripped him had ripped through her as well. But the other part, the part that was only complete after she had found Kye, that part despaired. The ever-present tears burned her eyes, but she stubbornly refused to let them fall. If she started to cry, she wasn't sure she'd be able to stop.

He was gone.

"Ashlyn."

She whirled at the familiar lyrical accent. God knows, she had heard it often enough in the past three years. Just about every other time she tumbled into dreams with Kye's arms wrapped around her.

That voice, the one she had heard only one night, was almost as familiar to her as Kye's had been.

He stood behind her, his handsome, almost angelic face ravaged with grief. But he met her eyes squarely. "I came as soon as I heard," he said gruffly, moving up to touch his hand to the smooth metal of the coffin. "But if you aren't wanting me here, I will go."

"No. He was your friend, and you were his. I . . . I'm not ashamed of what happened. I think maybe I expected to be. But that's neither here nor there," she said, her voice hoarse and rough from all the tears she had shed.

Brokenly, she whispered, "He killed him, Connor. He took my beautiful Kye from me, destroyed his body, smashed him into pieces. And he sits in a jail, alive and well. And Kye is in . . . *there.*

"*Oh, God, I can't take it,*" she moaned, starting to fall to her knees, one hand pressed to her mouth.

Connor caught her against him and eased her to the floor, thanking God that Kye was still in the private viewing room. His own throat was knotted shut with grief. He'd never see his childhood friend again—never see the laughing, smiling man who had loved his wife enough to give her a fantasy most women would never have.

Never see him again—never hear him laugh and tell a dirty joke.

Ashlyn sobbed in his arms while he rocked her body back and forth, stroking one hand down her black, silk covered back.

He'd have the bastard's bloody balls on a pike—that was certain.

Nothing would ever bring Kye back, but the bastard would have to pay. And five fucking years for manslaughter weren't enough. A friend of his, an American lawyer, had told him in disgust that five years was sometimes optimistic for vehicular manslaughter.

Some sort of justice could be found, or bought, with enough money. Christ knew, he had more than plenty.

But he wasn't sure what to do for the woman who cried in his arms, her heart breaking.

Wasn't sure what to do for himself—he hadn't even had a chance to tell Kye good-bye.

Or tell him he was sorry for how he had pulled back. Or explained why.

Of course, the bloody bastard probably knew.

Knew that Connor had fallen head over heels in love, in lust with his wife that night.

It was too late. Too late to tell him anything.

Staring in stony silence at that flower covered coffin, Connor rocked the grieving woman in his arms, back and forth, stroking his hand up and down her back, rubbing his cheek against her soft dark hair.

"Who called you?"

"Da. My father. You knew, didn't you, that Kye's father was Irish? Moved here after he met Kye's mother?"

"Yeah, I knew," she said, taking the handkerchief he offered to wipe her eyes and blow her nose. Clutching the expensive silk in her hand, she settled back against him.

"Jacob called Da, and Da called me. I found out last night and spent the entire night in the air over the Atlantic."

"I found your number in his book. At least, I figured it was yours. I called, but some lady who sounded like Mrs. Doubtfire told me you were unavailable. I didn't want somebody else telling you."

"Da found me. They loved him too, Ma's heartbroken. They will be out here in the morning, I'm thinking." He paused, pressed his lips together until he was fairly certain he could go on without crying himself. "When will they lay him to rest?"

"Day after tomorrow," she said, swallowing the knot in her throat. *Rest? He was thirty-three years old. It's not time for him to rest,* she thought dully. "How am I going to live the rest of my life without him there, Connor? There's a part of me missing now, and it's in that coffin with him. How am I going to do this?"

Catching her face, he turned her until he could stare into those soft hazel eyes that had haunted him. "By remembering the last thing he'd want for you is to lay down and join him in the grave," he told her honestly. "Is that what you think he wants you to do?"

"He doesn't want anything from me. He can't. He's gone," she bit off, stiffening and jerking away from him, rising to her feet.

"He's not. He's just not here any longer," Connor disagreed, surging easily to his feet to stare at her while she paced the room in long, angry strides. "We're Irish—Kye and me—both of us believe in something beyond death. Don't you?"

She stopped and stared at the coffin. "I don't know. I think I used to."

"Even if there is nothing else, nothing beyond the life we have now, do you think Kye would be pleased to hear you saying you can't go on without him? Do you think he would want that?"

When she didn't answer, Connor said, "I know he wouldn't. So what you do is, take it one day at a time." Slowly, unsure of his welcome, he moved until he could lay his hand on her shoulder, rubbing it in gentle soothing strokes. "And the pain will ease. You will find a life beyond him."

She shuddered, her head slumping down. "I miss him, Connor. He hasn't even been gone a damn week and I can feel it inside me, that hole that being with him filled. It's empty," she said, her voice breaking. *"I'm empty."*

"I know. I miss him, too."

• • •

It was hell, being dead.

If it had been just . . . nothingness, it wouldn't suck so bad.

If he hadn't been able to hear, see, smell. Remember.

The pain had been indescribable. But he'd rather face that again, than what he was facing now.

He couldn't move beyond her.

And she was breaking his heart.

Kye watched impotently as Ashlyn sobbed herself to sleep. Again.

He had watched as his coffin was lowered into the ground—watched as Connor had driven Ashlyn home—as he led her to the bedroom and urged her to rest.

He had watched as she lay there crying silently so Connor wouldn't know she was awake, and hurting.

And now, he was stuck there. Watching. Again.

"Ashlyn, please stop," he murmured, pounding his head against the barrier that stood between them. The one that allowed him to see, hear and smell her, but kept him from reaching out and touching her.

Touching anything.

And he was stuck here, unable to go away, unable to go on to whatever happened after death. He had always believed in heaven, but being stuck in this limbo made him wonder.

She continued to cry, her face buried in a pillow, muffling her sobs.

The fury exploded through Kye and he punched against the barrier, roaring as the rage coursed through him. Over and over, until his hand hurt and throbbed and his throat was hoarse from yelling.

You could feel pain after death.

And then he sagged, limp and exhausted, until he knelt on the floor, his brow pressed against the barrier. "Ashlyn," he whispered raggedly.

"Ash."

• • •

A week later, she sat in the apartment they had shared, surrounded by his clothes, his books, his stupid video games. Connor sat across from her, silently boxing up what she turned over to him, rarely saying a word.

After that first day, he'd said as little as possible, stayed in the background, stepping forward only if she couldn't do something herself, offering assistance, a silent shoulder, and a comfort she hadn't expected to find, least of all, with him.

It should have been awkward, right? She had met him only once, on that hot night three years ago. A night that could still make her body wet and tight with remembered pleasure.

So why was it so easy for her to be with him?

Other than the fact that her body hadn't gone into hibernation, even if her heart was trying to. Watching him gave her a hot little thrill low in her belly that shamed her.

Kye not even gone a week and she was aching for another man. Aching, hell. She needed him so bad it was like an empty hole in her gut.

But Ashlyn shoved it aside, turned it off.

And she accepted his help graciously, gratefully—accepted his silent, comforting presence while she did what he had said, what Kye would have wanted. She took it one day at a time.

"I think this will do it," she finally said, using a roll of tape to seal off one last box. To her right was a pitifully small pile, all she would keep of him. A few shirts, a necklace she had given him—a silver replica of the golden Celtic knot he had given her the day they married—hoards of pictures—a couple of books. A thousand-and-one memories.

"You don't have to get rid of it all just yet, Ash," he told her, his heart wrenching at the pain in her soft hazel eyes.

"I can't keep it here," she said simply. "Seeing his things, day after day, will only hurt. He's gone, and keeping his favorite video games won't bring him back. Was there anything you wanted?"

An hour later, she walked him to the door, her hands tucked

into the back pockets of her jeans. The boxes were loaded in the back of his truck, boxes of books, videos, clothes.

"I can come tomorrow, if you like," he offered.

She shook her head. "I'm going back to work. The sooner I do, the sooner . . . the sooner I do," she finished lamely, unsure of what else to say. The sooner she'd feel better? The sooner she would start to heal? How did one heal an empty gaping wound in the heart?

He nodded, brushing his fingers against her cheek. "I'll be around," he said before leaving, his head tucked low against the cold winter wind.

Kye watched in disgust as Connor walked away from the apartment, behaving like a fucking gentleman.

"Come back," he muttered.

"Come back and make her stop crying, make her stop hurting," he snapped, pacing at his spot by the window, watching helplessly as Connor drove away. "You're dying to get inside her again, so do it."

Kye just wanted the pain in her eyes to ease.

It broke him to pieces to watch her, hurt and lost and lonely.

Because on the few times the pain started to clear, the invisible thread that bound him to her lengthened, and he was able to drift. Drift closer to a place where he couldn't see or hear her. Where he wasn't tormented with the sight of the beautiful body he couldn't touch, with the scent of the skin he had come to crave. Where he wasn't torn apart as he watched her cry herself to sleep at night.

Where he was safe and warm and happy.

She was why he was stuck.

Until she let him go, Kye's soul wasn't going to let go of Earth. Or her.

"Besides," Kye said wickedly as he watched Ashlyn settle down on the couch and flip listlessly through the channels, "it would be something that was actually fun to watch."

He moved closer, until he was as close as he was able to get.

The barrier kept him from coming closer than a couple of feet. Settling down on the glass top coffee table, he folded his legs Indian style and stared at her.

Sharp, bright pain ripped through him when the tears once more filled her eyes.

Stupid, miserable bastard, Connor thought to himself. She just buried her man, and you're wanting to crawl up her skirt.

Driving away to the furnished condo he had rented, he tried to shake off the frustrated desire. Tried to think past the guilt that wanting her was causing.

Tried to settle his mind.

Because somewhere, sometime, in the past miserable days, as he watched one of his oldest friends laid to rest, he had made a decision.

He was going to give her time to get past it, and then he was going after her.

He would have her, and damn anybody who got in his way.

The one person who could have kept him away—who had kept him away—was gone.

And if Connor knew Kye at all, Kye was smirking down at him from somewhere, telling him he'd better be thanking his lucky stars Kye had brought them together.

For now . . . for now, he had to wait. Had to lash this burning need down, keep her from seeing what he wanted.

FOUR

K ye watched with a grin, feeling something light enter his heart. This was new. Over the past few months—how long had it been? Three months? Six? He didn't know, but over time, something inside Ashlyn had started to shift, to lighten.

It was odd, how he could sense her moods so acutely now.

And the pain that had been starting to lessen wasn't clouding her eyes today.

Nope. Her eyes were clouded by pure and simple need. His heart pounded slow and heavy as he watched her step from the shower, and smooth oil on her skin until it was gleaming and soft.

Ghosts were perfectly capable of getting a hard-on.

Kye had become vastly familiar with the phenomenon. Of course, he wasn't able to come, which only made the whole business unbelievably frustrating. He couldn't reach out and touch her, couldn't kiss her, couldn't love her body.

Oh, but he could easily become aroused. Just watching her gave him a stiff dick.

She had turned the showerhead to massage and cried out in the shower while he watched, his hand stroking absently up and down the length of his cock as she whimpered and moaned.

He had whispered, "That's not gonna satisfy you, baby. You need a man."

Kye's eyes narrowed as he watched her step into a pair of thong panties, followed by a pair of very skimpy shorts. Fuck me clothes, he realized, as she topped it off with a push-up bra that did amazing things for her lush tits. The T-shirt she pulled on was thin and tight and showed the lacy bra quite clearly.

"Why, wife, you're looking to get laid," Kye mused as she painted her toenails a little while later. Murderous, bloody red on her toenails and her fingernails. Her mouth was slicked with a deep wine red, her eyes darkened and lined until that mouth and those eyes dominated her entire face.

He followed in her footsteps as she paced nervously up and down the hall of the little house she had bought. Just goes to show that ghosts didn't necessarily haunt houses. Some haunted people.

He flopped down on the couch as she continued to pace barefoot, rubbing her arms, stopping periodically to check her reflection in the mirror.

"You look tasty," he told her, even though she couldn't hear him. "I'd love to do you myself. If I could."

She was muttering under her breath, her eyes wide and dilated, her tongue nervously wetting her sexy little mouth. Under her bra, her nipples were hard little peaks that pressed into her shirt. The shorts stopped just below the curve of her ass and were tight— tight enough that he imagined the seam at the crotch was biting into her soft wet flesh. A picture of nervous sexual tension.

"Watching is going to have its advantages," he said as he saw Connor pull into the drive. "Maybe I can't fuck you, but I can watch him do it."

Her mother would have been scandalized, Ashlyn knew. Completely, totally scandalized.

It was August, more than six months since Kye had died.

And she was dying of unrequited lust.

Connor had never really left.

Oh, he flew back and forth to the States on business, but the art gallery in Ireland was mainly run by his younger brother now, while Connor concentrated on the one he had started here in the States. An Irish gallery, full of art and crafts by friends and family, and his own work.

He had remained, she knew, because of her, out of loyalty to Kye.

But he was treating her like she was his damn sister.

And Ashlyn wasn't sure how much longer she could handle it.

After that one single night when Kye and Connor had shared her body, something for Connor had worked its way into her soul. There had been nights when she had ached to be pressed between their two surging bodies again.

And while Kye was gone—forever gone—Connor was here. And the need inside her belly was a constant, burning ache.

Staring at her reflection, she tried to decide whether or not she was being too blatant.

The short, snug shorts weren't too obvious. Bullshit. But she was decently covered, and while she looked ready to get laid, she didn't look like a slut. And after all, it was hot. The short, sleeveless tank top was thin and white and while she had been tempted to go braless, she decided that was too tacky.

So she had donned a push-up bra that matched her thong panties and secured her hair in a loose, casual ponytail. She looked sexy, no doubt about it, but casual and not so blatant that it would bother either of them if Connor decided to ignore the invitation.

It was possible that he just wasn't interested, and she would hopefully be able to tell by the time the day was over. Before she embarrassed herself and stripped naked in front of him, begging him to take her.

She wasn't cut out for celibacy.

But she wasn't really into casual sex either.

An anonymous fuck might solve the immediate problem, but not very likely. She wanted Connor, in her vagina, in her throat, in her ass.

In her life.

She left the bedroom of the house she had bought a month after Kye had died. The little condo had been too full of memories, too full of Kye.

And this little house nestled on the hills of Floyd County, Indiana, overlooking the rolling Ohio River, was perfect. It felt like home to her, even before she had moved the first stick of furniture in.

In the backyard, there was a lazy hammock where she could read the day away and large oak trees that shaded the ground from the intense summer heat.

And the extras—the large master bath with dual shower-heads and a sunken tub—the large hot tub in the backyard—the fireplace she had spent so many lonely nights beside, reading, or just thinking.

The doorbell rang and she paused—pressing a hand against her belly to soothe the butterflies there—then she opened the door, smiling at the man who stood there waiting for her.

Always waiting for her, it seemed.

Connor's breath stopped in his throat, trapped in his lungs. When she had called and asked him to come over, he hadn't even let himself hope it was for anything other than friendship.

Not that he hadn't come to value that in her. She was a damn fine friend—funny, honest, with a biting humor that echoed his own.

But he was dying, bit by bit, every time he was around her without being able to touch her, every time he stifled the burning need he felt for her. He loved her, had been in love with her probably before he had ever met her, when he had seen a picture Kye had shown him.

Something about her eyes had called to him. And, after all, he was Irish, he believed in destiny, in love at first sight. Of course, he had never imagined he'd fall in love with a woman who didn't love him back.

Staring at her now, in a brief, snug pair of shorts that left her long, smooth legs bare, at the beautiful tits barely restrained by her white shirt, he couldn't stifle it. Couldn't hide it. Couldn't hide the raw, burning need in his gut, or the ache in his heart.

And when he met her eyes, he saw what he felt echoed in hers.

He reached for her just as she reached for him and they fell against each other, mouths seeking while their hands tore at their clothes.

He stripped the shorts down her thighs and jerked her shirt over her head, but didn't bother with anything else. She popped the buttons on his shirt and clawed at his belt before freeing his rigid, aching cock.

"Hurry," she panted as he lifted her, turned and braced her against the wall.

Shoving the shiny material of the thong aside, he drove into her, burying his cock inside her body, inside her wet pulsating sheath. Her head fell back and hit the wall as a cry fell from her lips.

"Bloody hell, Ashlyn," he muttered, staring down at her face— the half-blind need that glazed her eyes, her full, red-slicked lips parted as she gasped for air. The hot press of her breasts against his chest, the hard little points of her nipples against him, all drove him closer to the brink as he shuttled his cock in and out of her body, groaning as her tight wet tissues closed over him like a greedy fist.

He rode her hard, flooding her body with his semen before she had a chance to come. She cried out a protest but he stifled it with a hot, hungry kiss against her mouth, still taking her hard and deep, his cock as aching and full as it had been before he had even touched her.

He was nowhere near done yet. He had more than three years of need built up inside him and it wasn't going to be over just like that.

He dropped to the floor, pulling her with him, and he continued without breaking stride. She was tight, as tight as he remembered, and wet, her own cream mingling with his come as he worked her up and down his erection, as he shifted a little higher so that each thrust brought him against her clit.

He wrapped the back panel of her thong around his fingers, jerking it up so that the material bit into her ass, pressed against her sensitive rosette.

She shrieked, arched up against him, and tried to pull him completely inside her body.

But he had taken the edge off, and now he wanted to savor. Lowering his head, he used one hand to lift her breast so that he could reach it with his mouth. He sank his teeth into the plump mound of flesh while he rode her hard and slow.

Rising onto his knees, he grabbed her legs and shoved her thighs wide, her knees up, so he could watch as he worked his erection into her waiting, wet body.

God, she had missed this, missed feeling a man inside her, missed feeling a man's skin next to hers. Her fingers dug into the carpet beneath her as he dug his cock into her, as he shoved her closer to climax. He was big, so big and thick and long . . .

Every driving thrust forced her to take his cock so deep inside, the delicious pain in her loins blended with a pleasure so profound she thought it would kill her. She could feel the thick head of his cock as it breached the mouth of her womb, feel it as he passed over the bundled nerves deep inside her wet cleft, but he seemed to be deliberately withholding the contact that would allow her to come.

Of course she wasn't above begging. Or demanding. "It's been so damn long, don't make me wait," she whispered.

"You Americans," he teased, catching her earlobe and biting down gently. "Always so impatient."

"Impatient, hell. Damn it, Connor, let me come," she gasped out. "Please, please, please!"

He lowered his head to purr in her ear, driving her legs to her chest as his weight shifted. "If I do that, it's gonna take me with ya, darlin'. I donna wan' this ending so fast," he whispered raggedly.

"Make me come," she cried, straining upward, clenching her vaginal muscles deliberately so that she milked his cock teasingly. "Damn it, Connor," she panted as he pulled out just shy of hitting that spot inside her body. "Let me come. God, I've needed this."

"Needed it?" he murmured, kissing her silkily before telling her, "You don't know what need is. *Need* is what happens when you hunger and ache for a woman for years, ache and need to the point that nobody else will do.

"I've been wanting to fuck you since I left that hotel room, and I thought I'd never have you again." He rolled his hips, releasing the thong to slide his fingers upward until he could soak up some of her cream, returning to smear it on her anus and slide one finger in.

"Waiting to taste you," he murmured, bending his head to eat at her mouth. "Waiting to slide my cock inside your talented little mouth, inside your hot little pussy, inside that tight, tiny hole." As he spoke, he forced his finger in up to the knuckle. He rocked against her in tiny thrusts as he said, "Do ya know, darlin' Ash, that I'd never fucked a woman in the ass until you? Never knew what it was like?

"And I haven't done it since, and let me tell you, I've worked up a powerful need for it," he finished as he started to withdraw and plunge deep, while he pressed his finger upward inside her ass.

"Let me come," she pleaded, her head rolling restlessly against the floor. "And you can fuck me however you want."

He purred low in his throat and asked, "D' ya promise?"

"Damn it, yes. I swear . . . shit!"

He had pulled out and rammed back in, out and in, hard, glorious digs that hit that spot each time, and on the fifth brutal stroke, she climaxed, clamping down on him and milking his orgasm from him. She screamed as the orgasm caught her in its grip, as he leaned forward and bit down hard on her nipple while his other hand closed painfully on one cheek of her ass, the thong stretching and pressing ever tighter against her anus.

He flooded her vagina again, in spurts of liquid fire that had her shuddering.

K ye watched with hot eyes as Connor shoved her up against the wall and drove his cock into her body. Kye could see it as he pulled it out, wet and shining with Ashlyn's cream. A ripple of need rolled through Kye's belly as Connor plunged back into her, dragging moans and screams from her throat.

He watched as Connor bucked against her, his eyes closed in agonized pleasure as he came. At least, Kye assumed he was coming. "You better not plan on stopping just yet, buddy," he muttered, intense frustration ripping through him. But instead of stopping he took Ashlyn to the floor and rode her hard, shoving her thighs high and wide.

"Shit," Kye muttered, dragging his jeans open and wrapping a hand around his cock, pumping furiously. From his vantage point by the window, he could see as Connor's thick cock left Ashlyn's cunt, ruddy and wet and glistening—could see as he pushed it into her slowly until she was whimpering and straining against him.

"Shit," Kye repeated as he felt something he hadn't felt in months. A climax building at the base of his spine. His hand worked furiously at his hard dick while Connor whispered and murmured to Ashlyn.

She lay beneath him, begging and pleading, screaming when she came—again and again—under Connor's long fingers. One big hand went to cup her ass, and one finger . . . yeah, he was finger fucking her ass.

Just as Connor roared, Kye felt the come spurt from him, burning his hands and belly as it coated him.

A fter a long, hot bath, she cuddled against him. A sigh of pleasure rippled through her.

"You sound fairly pleased," Connor murmured, idly combing his hand through her damp hair.

"Hmm," she purred, nuzzling the smooth skin of his chest with her nose.

Smoothing his hand down her back, he cupped a round white buttock, slid his finger against the crack and said, "I'll be even more pleased in a bit."

She cocked her hips up, rubbing against his finger. From beneath the pillow, she grabbed the tube of *Wet* she had put there while he finished in the bathroom. "Hmm, me too. I think, in, oh, say five or ten years, I may be satisfied enough to go an hour in your presence without wanting you."

As she spoke, she sat up, flipping open the cap and pouring a small amount of lube into her palm. Connor watched—his eyes heavy lidded with lust—as she rubbed the lubricant on his turgid cock. "I'm needing more than five or ten years, darlin'. Ah, keep that up, why don't you?"

She slid her hand from the head of his cock, down to the base, back up again in a slow maddening rhythm while she covered his length with lubricant, pausing to tickle his sac with her fingers before getting more of the clear substance and applying another slow, lingering layer.

She grinned at him and slowed her strokes. "But if I do, you may not be any use where I want you," she teased, lowering her head to lick the tip of his penis.

"I've been hard since I saw you again, Ash. You jacking me off won't even take the edge off," he groaned, lifting his hips against her tight hand. He lifted hot blue eyes to stare at her, eying the way she perched by his hips, the sway of her full breasts as she moved, the tumbled red locks that fell around her shoulders, and splayed over her breasts, teasing him with brief views of her red, peaked nipples before shifting to hide them again. "I could stay here a bloody month and still be needing ya insanely."

But he rolled away from her, spying the lubricant and pouring some into his hand, warming it in his palm before smoothing it onto his fingers so he could prepare her ass. While he rimmed her anus with his fingers, he positioned his body so that he could use his other hand between her thighs and thrust his fingers into her wet depths while nuzzling and suckling at her erect little nipples.

She panted and strained against him, and as soon as he could feel her climax coming closer, he turned her onto her hands and knees and mounted her from behind. He brushed against her little hole, while his fingers sought and found her clit, hard and swollen, in her folds.

He could see it, in his mind's eye, that first time, how her anus had spasmed when she was ready, and he waited, rubbing and bumping against her until the edge of that tiny opening started to flutter against him.

Smearing the *Wet* on her rosette, he started to ease inside her, working his hard shaft in slowly, while she planted her hands and knees, her head hung low, like a pliant mare waiting for a stallion. The picture appealed to him, appealed to something inside him that enjoyed controlling and dominating her.

He crooned his praises while he stroked her ass and eased a little deeper, a little harder, grunting in pleasure when she started to rock back against him. "Hmm . . . Ash, oh, darlin', you're so tight, so hot. Are you wet inside, baby? It feels like it from here, so wet we probably didn't need anything other than you," he purred as he started taking her in long, slow strokes that had her arching against him.

Weak mewls left her throat as she strained harder against him each time he pulled out. "Connor, please," she gasped, rocking back.

Those long, slow strokes were driving her mad. She needed it fast and hard now, and she told him so.

"But I'm not ready for this to end," he told her, continuing at his own pace. "Fast and hard, and you'll start to come, then I will, and it's over." While he talked, he watched as his flesh joined hers, as her little asshole stretched so tight and hot around the head of his penis as he pulled out before shoving back into her, a little harder, dragging a weak cry from her lips. Her narrow passage was wet for him and eager, gripping his cock like silk while he watched his length disappear inside her. Each time he withdrew, she followed, seeking his cock, trying to keep him from pulling out. Her spine bowed up as she shuddered, as the inner walls of her ass clenched and convulsed around him.

She felt hot and cold at the same time, her body quaking around his intruding cock, shivering as he impaled her fully. A little harder, a little deeper with each stroke until she was screaming hoarsely with every thrust.

"Good, so damn good," he rumbled as the quivers started inside her ass. They grew stronger and stronger until the flesh gloving his cock felt like it was seizing around him.

When she bucked up high, screaming, he caught her around the waist, pinning her torso against his while he shoved her weight down, forcing his shaft in as far as it would go. And stayed there while her body vised around his, his semen flooding her.

They remained upright like that, panting, with her still impaled on his now softening cock, his arms holding her tightly against him. Silently, he mouthed against her hair, *I love you.*

And he stiffened when she sighed and settled comfortably against him, murmuring, "I missed you, Connor. After you left, I missed you. So much, it hurt."

He eased them down to the bed, stubbornly keeping his half-hard cock inside her anus. But before he could find a reply, she cuddled against him, humming in pleasure, before dropping into sleep.

K ye felt like a fucking voyeur but he'd be damned if he missed out on this. "This is the most fun I've had since that last night with you, darlin'," Kye drawled as he watched Connor smear lubricant on her waiting ass.

"It's almost as much fun to watch you fuck as it is to do you," he said. "Well, maybe. You need to tie her up sometime, Connor. Slap a pair of cuffs on her wrists and she'll be your slave. Willingly."

He groaned, moving closer, not realizing he had crossed that invisible barrier until he was standing by the bed, close enough to touch. "Oh, shit," he whispered as he watched Connor ease two fingers inside her tight little pussy, pressing his thumb against her rosy anus, probing until the muscles relaxed and welcomed his intrusion.

"God, that's good," he muttered, dropping to his knees to better see as Connor started to butt the head of his cock against her rosette. "Come, baby. Let me watch."

Kye's hand had sought his own swelling penis and was cupping his balls as he jacked himself off, watching in dazed, hypnotized pleasure as Connor started to ream her ass, slowly and almost gently.

He could see cream as it oozed down the lips of her sex to fall on the bed. He missed the taste of it, missed feeling her soft skin against him as he ate at her sex. *One last time,* he thought helplessly. *I want one last time.*

He grunted as a drop of pre-come started to leak from his penis. Connor was fucking her hard now, shoving her hips low so he could fill her hard and deep.

Ashlyn was writhing and shuddering underneath his hands,

her butt up-thrust and quivering. Kye grinned tightly when Connor's hand smacked sharply at her ass and the semen jetted from his body.

Kye's eyes widened in shock as a wet spot appeared on the sheets, spreading and spreading as his come soaked into the sheets.

"Oh, shit," he muttered.

It was there, wet and rapidly cooling, as real as the come that had soaked Ashlyn's ass and started to leak out to dry on her bottom.

And the two on the bed never even noticed.

L ooks like you've ended up in the right place."

"Kye?"

"Who else would it be?" he asked, his voice amused as he sat on the edge of the dresser, watching while Connor sat up, dried come and sticky lube on his soft penis. Ashlyn remained curled in sleep.

"I'm dreaming."

"Maybe," Kye said, grinning. "But that doesn't mean I'm not talking to you, mate."

"How can you be?" Connor asked. "You're dead." But he was staring right at him, at his golden skin, glowing faintly, as though he was lit from within. He could see that longish raven-wing hair that fell around his sharply cut facial bones, the warm, humorous, dark eyes and his wide, full mouth that seemed almost too damn pretty to belong to a man. How many times had Connor teased him about his almost pretty looks? How often had he ragged him about the hair that he stubbornly refused to cut?

Slowly, dumbly, he repeated, "You're dead."

Kye's eyes sobered and his mouth straightened. "I know. Dying does hurt, buddy. Don't think it doesn't. But it wasn't as bad as it could have been. Leaving her, I mean. I knew you'd be here."

"You know, don't you?"

"That you love her? Yeah, I know." Kye sighed, reaching up to run a hand through his hair in a familiar gesture. "I knew it that night. I didn't know what to do about it, though. Kept hoping you'd get over it."

He eased down off the dresser and came to stand beside the bed next to Connor, and stood staring down at his sleeping wife. "Don't know why. I never got over it, "Connor admitted. Kye eased down, until he could sit by her head and stroke her hair.

Connor could see it, see the way her hair moved and shifted, falling through Kye's dark fingers before he would scoop it up again. "You still love her," he said. Only his voice wasn't out loud. It was only in his head.

But Kye heard him.

Turning his head, he grimaced, and said, "Till death do us part. Death parted us, but it hasn't stopped the love I feel."

Well, fuck me, Connor thought helplessly. It was just as hard for Kye now as it had been—as it was for Connor. Two men, in love with one woman.

But now Kye was dead.

"And you're not." Kye continued to comb his hand through her hair. "Don't pull back on my account," he said, staring down at the curve of Ashlyn's cheek, leaning his head down until he could buss her soft, smooth skin with his mouth. "She needs you."

"I can't . . . "

"Don't—okay, Connor? God, she's so beautiful," he murmured, lifting a lock of hair to his nose. "I've been trying to get through to you for months, ever since I died. I can't cross over, you know. Not yet."

"Cross over? You mean . . . "

"I'm stuck in limbo. Don't know why. Hopefully it's almost over. It hurts, being able to see her, smell her, but not touch her. Not talk to her."

"Why haven't you talked to me before now?"

Kye shrugged and said, "I've tried. Haven't been able to." He rose, turning to face Connor, seeming somehow larger in death than he had been in life. They stood eye to eye and Kye raised a black brow. "Are you going to take care of her, Connor?"

"If she'll let me."

"Do it," Kye ordered, his eyes glowing and hot, authoritative. "She'll fall in love with you. She already needs you."

"I need her. I love her. But I won't force my way into her life, mate. For any reason."

Kye smiled sadly, as he turned back to study the woman on the bed. Her mouth puckered and shifted in her sleep, as if she were seeking something. He could feel the need, the lust, the love coursing through his body, and wondered, if she opened her eyes could she see him? Touch him?

"I forced you into her life, Connor. Remember? You've been inside her ever since, and she's been inside you."

"Regretting it now, are you?"

Kye laughed, the happy, wild laughter that Connor remembered so well. *"Regret it? Hell, no. That was every bit as good for me as it was for her. Not as good for you, in some ways, I know. Knowing she was leaving with me, that she was mine."*

"But," he said, shrugging, *"now she is yours. Take care of her."* Leaning forward, he hugged his friend hard and whispered, *"You were always a friend, Connor. One I was proud to have."*

"Kye, wait . . ."

But he was gone. And Connor went tumbling back into sleep.

When he woke, he wondered if it had really happened.

He curled around Ashlyn, his heart pounding, his eyes stinging. Her sweet little ass pressed against him as he wrapped his arms around her, holding her tightly against his body. Lowering his face to her silken hair, he let out a shaky breath as a tear managed to escape and roll down his cheek.

Damn you, Kye.

This is not how things were meant to be, mate.

And he could almost hear Kye's dry voice asking, *How in the hell do you know?*

• • •

When Ashlyn's eyes flew open, it was dark out. She wasn't sure what had woken her. Connor was sprawled against her from the back, his face buried against her hair. It was silent, save for the hum of the fan beside the bed.

Swinging her legs over the edge of the bed, she peered around her in the dark room. When her eyes landed on the door to the bathroom, she shrieked.

Or at least she thought she did. Her mouth opened but no sound came out. And then she felt exceptionally silly for doing it.

It was Kye. Only Kye. The love of her life.

"Hey, beautiful," he murmured, unhooking his ankle from behind his leg and moving out of the doorway, walking until he was standing right in front of her. Close enough to touch.

"What took you so long?" she asked. Then she frowned, and pressed her fingers to her still mouth. Her lips hadn't moved.

" 'S okay, I can hear you," Kye said, reaching out and pressing one finger to her full lower lip. "I think maybe it is so you don't go waking anybody else up." Slowly, he knelt in front of her, staring at her as if memorizing her face.

"Don't know if you're going to remember any of this, darlin' girl. I'm here to tell you good-bye."

"I figured that out," she said, a sad, heartbroken smile trembling on her lips. "I've been waiting. And hoping. Kye . . . "

"Shh, beautiful," he crooned, dropping to the floor before he took her hips and eased her naked body down on his lap. His blue jean covered lap.

God, he feels so real.

"I am real," he told her softly. "You aren't dreaming this. I am here, I am touching you." Jealousy flared in his eyes. "I'm sitting here with you naked on my lap and I am smelling Connor all over you." A brief smile came and went on his mouth.

She flushed, feeling the blood rising from her chest, up her neck, until her face flamed. "Don't," he whispered roughly, cupping her cheek. "I don't want you to stop living. If you had lain down beside me after I died, I would have never forgiven you for it. Or him—for letting you. Connor was right about that."

Her eyes widened, remembering that conversation in the private viewing area of the funeral home, months earlier. "You saw . . . ?"

"I've been watching and trying to talk to you ever since it happened."

Watching . . . ? Guilt, shame, pain all pooled in her belly, a vicious cramp seizing her.

"Don't," Kye ordered through clenched teeth, one hand fisted in her hair and forced her face back up to his when she would have looked away. "Don't. You're alive, damn it. Alive. You're supposed to be making love, going to work, eating supper. You're supposed to be living. Don't feel like you shouldn't." With a wry smile, he said, "Hell, this has probably been the most fun I've had since that fucking car hit me." Gently, he stroked a finger down her cheek. "It was good, watching you. Almost as good as being with you myself."

"If I'm supposed to be living, why do I feel so guilty? And why are you here? Aren't you supposed to be somewhere else? Or are you just lingering on earth to watch me screw?" she asked acidly, dashing one hand across her damp cheeks.

God, she could feel the aftereffects of hard sex on her body, muscle aches, dried come on her thighs, and she was sitting in her dead husband's lap.

And unless she was mistaken, he wasn't . . . unaffected by her naked body.

With a sigh, Kye said, "I can't pass over, Ash. I've tried. I'm stuck here for some reason, and I'll be damned if you add to this hell by feeling guilty." With one finger, he lifted her chin up until he could stare into her eyes.

"I've always loved you," he whispered gruffly, lowering his mouth to hers. "You made my life worthwhile. Without you . . . "

"Life would have been empty," she finished when his voice halted abruptly. "You were my life. If it . . . "

"Don't stop saying what's on your mind, Ashlyn. Not to me—not to anybody."

"If Connor hadn't been here, I think I would have lost myself," she said honestly. "He's been so good to me. Such a good friend."

"A friend? Is that how you treat your friends? Damn." A quicksilver smile lit Kye's face, the familiar one she had loved so well. "He'll be even more, if you will let him. Don't let me get in the way of that." Pulling her close, he kissed *her gently. "God, I wanted, want, so much for you. A long, happy life. Kids, grandkids. Connor can give you that."*

"I don't love him," she said, a sob sounding in the air. "I love you."

"I'm dead, baby. I'm gone, dust in the ground. Please, for me. Go on, live your life. The one I wanted to share with you. I want that. I need that." Kye's eyes were wet—with desperation—with sorrow—with grief. "Ashlyn, if I don't know, in my heart, that you'll be okay, I'm gonna be stuck here. I can't pass over with things unresolved. And you were the only thing in my life that mattered."

"I don't love him," she repeated, a knot in her throat." I can't!"

"You will," Kye said with simple certainty. "He loves you already."

Before she even realized it, he was on his feet and she was in the bed, with him leaning over her, handing her over to Connor's waiting arms. In sleep, Connor wrapped his arms tightly around her, as if he had missed her presence in the bed.

"Be happy. Live your life, Ashlyn," Kye whispered, lowering his head, pressing his lips to hers in a sweet gentle kiss. A tear spilled from his eye, just as one leaked from hers. "For me, Ashlyn. If you won't do it for yourself, then do it for me."

The last thing she saw, felt, remembered was his lips, brushing hers one last time.

In her sleep, she turned in Connor's arms, seeking his body, his warmth, as she sobbed in her sleep.

K ye was still reeling from the shocks he had just received. First, when he had spewed his come all over the bed. He had been immaterial for so many weeks—no substance— no ability to touch or be touched.

And then he had reached out and touched Connor, rousing him from a sound sleep.

Then he had touched Ashlyn.

Spoken to both of them.

And some instinct inside him whispered that his time here had come to an end. He was running out of time.

• • •

Ashlyn awoke to a sensation she thought she would never feel again. Pressed between two hard, surging male bodies. Connor's long length was pressed against her back, where he had fallen asleep.

In front of her was Kye.

He was slightly glowing, slightly transparent.

And solid.

She gasped, reached out to touch him, to be sure, even though she could feel him pressed up against her body, hard and tight and firm. "Kye?"

"Hey, beautiful," he purred, grinning that cocky, arrogant grin that managed to be little boy sweet at the same time.

Then his grin faded and his face swooped down, his mouth closing over hers like a man starving. She was dimly aware of Connor's body stiffening behind her, dimly aware that he was no longer asleep.

Her moan died in her chest and she threw her arms around him, rolling atop his so very solid body. Connor remained lying on his side, watching with blank eyes.

"Kye," he muttered, reaching up to rub his tired eyes with a shaky hand. The loose, liquid feeling that spiraled through him wasn't shock though. It was joy, pure and simple. But the joy faded slowly as he took in the faint glimmering form of Kye's body, the near translucence to his skin.

And his eyes blanked again as confusion raced through him.

Blank eyes, until Kye rolled Ashlyn back between them and whispered, "One last fantasy, beautiful. One last time." Over her shoulder, Kye looked up and pinned Connor with hot, hungry eyes, his face stark and harsh and full of a desperate need.

Ashlyn gasped when she was flipped to her back and ravaged by both men. Kye's mouth went straight for her pussy, while Connor focused his attention on her breasts and neck and mouth. As Kye parted her with his tongue, she screamed, shocked and startled, as she flew straight into orgasm, ejaculating into his mouth as he ate at her.

"Missed you, missed this more. Damn it, Ashlyn, do it again," Kye muttered roughly, pulling away to blow a cool puff of air on her swollen clit before burying his face against her a second time.

Kye controlled them this time—both of them. He shoved Ashlyn so that she sat between Connor's spread legs, Connor's hand cupping and massaging her breasts as Kye returned to lap up the juice that started to trickle from her. His hands were everywhere, massaging her ass, lifting her hips, plucking at her nipples until she cried out.

Snatching her from Connor, he tumbled to his back and guided her mouth to his hard swollen cock. And when Connor started to rub his dick against her exposed entrance, Kye snarled and pinned her beneath him so he could again fuck her orally.

Starving. He had been starving for her and was being offered one last banquet.

When he finally lifted his face from her cunt for the third time, his mouth and chin were wet from her climax, and her tissues were swollen and sensitive from his teeth and tongue. Rising to his knees, he pulled her up, effortlessly, draping her across his lap as though she weighed nothing. Some new strength flooded him and he lifted her easily, holding her above his cock, her vagina dripping her juices all over it. Then, staring at her, he dropped her, forcing her to take his entire length in one brutal stroke. When he was fully embedded, his eyes drifted closed and he shuddered. "Beautiful," he whispered, holding her tightly against him, reveling in the euphoria of being buried inside her one last time.

His eyes flew to Connor who knelt on the bed, only inches away. Gutturally, he said, "Just me this time. This time, she is mine."

Connor only stared and nodded, his own erection hard and pulsing. Closing his hand around his flesh, he stroked it as he watched Kye and Ashlyn.

"Later," Kye whispered in her ear, shuddering as her wet slick sheath squeezed his cock. "Just me, this time. Look at me."

Her hands lifted and cupped his cheeks so that they stared into each other's eyes as he rocked her slowly into climax, a wash of hot fluid filling her only moments after she cried out in pleasure.

His cock stayed hard and firm as he pulled it out of her, lifted her off and guided her head down until she eagerly took the fat swollen head of his penis in her mouth and sucked him down. His hands closed over her head, buried and twisted in her hair while he muttered, "You always knew how to suck, baby.

"Oh, shit. Do that again," he ordered when she swallowed his length down her throat. Turning eyes that burned to Connor, he whispered, "Fuck her, Connor."

She was wet from her own climaxes and from Kye's, and it felt hotter than normal for some reason. Shoving his cock inside her roughly, Connor groaned and grunted as her overly sensitized sheath started to convulse around him. "Harder, harder, fuck her harder," Kye was rasping out as she deep throated him and shot him closer to climax. "Give it to her harder, until she can't see."

And to her, he kept saying, "Suck it, baby. Take it in your throat like you're taking him in your pussy. Like you're going to take me in your tight little ass. I'm going to fuck your ass, beautiful. Hard and slow, until you're begging me to stop."

Ashlyn groaned, trying to lift her head. She could barely breathe. And she wanted to see Kye, wanted to stare at the skin that glowed a soft mellow gold in the dim room. But his hands kept her head low, kept her working on his cock while Connor pummeled her from behind.

Talk about simultaneous orgasms. All three came at once. She closed tightly around Connor, her pussy going into spasmodic clenches as Connor's seed flooded into her vagina and he roared out her name. Kye's come filled her throat as he gasped out, "Beautiful."

But when she pulled away and collapsed, exhausted, to her side, Kye shoved her thighs wide, startling her when he started to lap Connor's seed from her thighs before turning his attention to her throbbing cunt.

Connor stared and swore softly when his cock started to twitch, then throb as Kye ate and drank from her pussy. "Trying to kill me, he is," he mumbled, rolling until he could close his hot mouth over her hard pouting nipples as she thrust them high.

"Kye, stop," she whispered when his tongue laved roughly against her swollen clit.

Connor laughed when Kye ignored her; he could hear Kye's eager, hungry sounds as he sucked and licked at the cream she gave him. "He can't, darlin' girl. You're so tasty," he purred, one hand going under her thigh to rub into the fluids that soaked the cheeks of her ass, her anus, and the sheets beneath her. Then he slid the two fingers inside his mouth and licked them clean before returning to suckle at her nipples.

Her eyes fluttered closed and she whimpered as Kye speared his tongue inside her, stabbing repeatedly before working on her clit with his teeth and tongue. "Kye, I can't," she pleaded even as her hips lifted invitingly.

"You'd better," he replied before lifting her up, and placing her astride Connor. "Because it's time to do a little double penetration. I have to fill your ass with my cock again, beautiful. I have to."

And so he did, smearing lube all over her ass, rubbing her anus, probing with his finger until she was bucking and squirming against him. With that uncanny strength, he lifted her, holding her steady while Connor rolled to his knees so he could work his cock inside her tight little vagina, so swollen and sensitive from being ridden all night.

"Poor baby," Connor murmured, working his shaft inside her, feeling how tight and swollen she was. "Are you sore?"

"Yes," she gasped, quaking when Connor used one hand to shove her breast high so he could close his teeth around her hard, tightly beaded nipple.

Releasing it, he reached down and grabbed her ass, fondling and massaging the firm white globes as he whispered, "You're so tight. And even though I've been fucking you most of the day, I feel like I can't get enough of you." He kissed his way down her face and neck, sinking his teeth into her flesh and biting when he was all the way inside.

She felt Kye's fingers probing the tight pink rosette, then the thick head of his cock. He started to work his cock into her anus, shuddering as the tight ring of muscle relaxed just slightly, allowing him to slide inside a bare inch. Connor's hands closed tightly over the cheeks of her ass, spreading her wide and open. "Thanks, mate," Kye said with an unsteady laugh as he thrust a little farther, until half his cock was buried inside her. The faint glow that still emanated from his body cast faint shadows on Ashlyn and Connor. Leaning back, he watched as he forced a little more of his length into her anus. The pink hole stretched wide and tight around his penetration, the skin of her ass so pale and white and lovely against the darker gold skin of his body.

Her nipples ached and the oddly tight, hot feeling was spreading throughout her loins, until she was shivering and shaking with combined hot/cold feelings. Connor's mouth closed over one nipple, taking it gently between his teeth and pulling it long and tight away from her body before releasing it.

From behind her, she heard Kye rasp out, "Fuck it." And that was all the warning she had before he fucked her, ramming his length into her and pulling out before doing it again, and again, and again, and again until she was screaming and begging for more.

"Harder! Harder!" she screamed mindlessly, clutching at Connor's shoulders while she rode him, while Kye rode her. When she lifted off of Connor, Kye pulled down, leaving her rectum almost completely, and when she dropped down on Connor's impaling dick, Kye would ram his cock back inside her.

"Harder," Connor muttered harshly. "Fuck her harder. Fuck me harder," he ordered Ashlyn grabbing her face and eating at her mouth savagely. He nipped at her lip, hard enough to hurt and then he sucked at the tiny bead of blood as her tight, wet pussy shot him closer to oblivion. "The best little fuck," he gasped, smacking her sharply on the ass as he started to pump his aching cock inside her.

She climaxed, but begged for more. More of Kye's rod in her ass, even though it hurt. More of Connor's cock in her vagina, even though she ached.

Connor's seed flooded her, but he, too, needed more. More of her hot, pulsating little pussy—more of the breathy moans and wild screams that fell from her tasty mouth.

And Kye continued to pound into her, even after his climax faded, until his cock was hard and firm and long once more, filling her ass completely. *He* needed more of everything—more of her sweet cream in his mouth as she ejaculated—more of her pleas and demands for more.

And he knew time was running out.

So he fucked her slowly, then harder, gently, then roughly until her waning body stiffened and bucked and arched in the circle of their arms. When she started to sag, he lowered his head to whisper in her ear about how tight and hot she was, how good her ass felt around him, or to order Connor to play with her clit or her nipples.

He lowered his head and set his teeth into the soft fleshy mound of muscle atop her shoulder, biting, moving to another spot, marking as he screwed her ass, shoved her a little closer to the edge. "I'd like to tie you up, standing in the middle of the room, with your arms stretched overhead, so you're helpless. While we take turns fucking you," Kye whispered. "We wasted three damn years and we'll never get them back and now we only have tonight."

She whimpered as his hands closed over her breasts, his thumbs rolling her nipples, lifting them to Connor's mouth. Her head fell back against Kye's shoulder, one arm clutching Connor to her, the other wrapping behind her to hold Kye close.

"You like that, eh?" Kye asked. "You like the thought of him watching while I eat your pussy? It *is* tasty—hot and creamy and yummy. Do you like the thought of me making you eat his cock? You want some cock in your mouth now?"

She started to shake her head no, she just wanted this to continue.

"*I* want some cock in your mouth," Kye told her, whispering directly in her ear. "I want to watch you suck him off while I fuck you senseless."

But he only closed his hands over her hips, whispering, "Not yet, not yet, not yet!" With an agonized groan he climaxed, flooding her ass with hot wet seed while she screamed blindly—Connor's teeth sinking into her nipple, Kye's into her shoulder—stuffed full of cock and unable to move; pinned between two hard bodies. And she felt Connor's come jet off inside her vagina, flooding her womb.

Dark stars and rainbows filled her vision, and she went limp, slipping into unconsciousness for a few brief seconds. When her eyes opened, she was lying on her side, facing Connor, Kye draped over her shoulder, his face pressed against hers. "I love you," she told him quietly.

He grinned—sad and bittersweet. "I know. But I think it's time to move on. Both of us."

And then he started to fade. Panicking she struggled out from between them, to turn and grab him. When she reached out, her hand went right through him. He grimaced, solidified only briefly, long enough to reach out and catch her hand.

"It's okay, beautiful. It *will* be okay," he promised.

And then he was gone.

Ashlyn buried her face against Connor's chest and sobbed.

T
he sun was edging up over the horizon as Connor stood by the bedside staring down at Ashlyn's sleeping form. *Time to move on*, Kye had said.

It finally dawned on him that he had to move on as well. Ashlyn wasn't letting go of Kye. After she had cried herself to sleep last night, he had made the decision to go back to Ireland.

Maybe in a few years . . .

"Don't, mate," he told himself, pressing his palms to his eyes and rubbing.

Quietly, he tugged on his clothes and found his keys.

Should he leave a note? he wondered as he pulled his boots on. Say good-bye?

She'd figure it out sooner or later.

A deep tide of self-pity washed over him as he left the house. As Connor drove away, it damn near drowned him. Bloody hell, he loved her. Loved her so much it was damn near killing him, being so close, spending the night holding her while she cried for Kye.

He was going to be noble about this if it killed him.

He was going to step away, step aside, while she took some time to heal.

Hell, she didn't love him, now did she? Had she ever said so? No.

Hell, she wasn't ready to love him yet. Probably never would be. She had yet to let go of Kye. Not that he held that against her. Kye had been the kind of man most people would never know—kind, loving, honorable through and through, a good man, a good friend. Connor had never known another friend like Kye, and knew he never would again.

How could he expect her to let Kye go when Connor could barely do it?

Ashlyn might need Connor, but she still loved Kye. And that wasn't going to be changing any time soon.

And he wasn't going to fool himself into believing she would come searching for him.

Ashlyn awoke to the sound of the door closing quietly behind Connor.

She lay alone in the middle of the tumbled, tangled sheets, her body aching and sore. She groaned when she rolled up to her side at the edge of the bed.

It was so quiet.

Completely silent.

Reaching up, she rubbed her hand against her breast, feeling the slow steady pounding of her heart.

Alive.

She was alive.

And she wasn't going to lie down beside Kye and die.

"Not my time," she whispered softly.

But she figured she knew what time had come.

Sunset found her standing at an old cemetery nestled in one of the numerous valleys of Floyd County, Indiana. The marble headstone said so little about Kye, his name, his date of birth and his date of death. *Beloved.* And he had been beloved, to her, to his family, to his friends.

But it said so little. Nothing of his life.

Nothing of the joy they had found in each other— nothing of the love—nothing of the fun—nothing of the life they had shared. Nothing of the emptiness his death had left inside her.

The gaping hole in her heart was by no means healed. But she also didn't feel as if she were slowly, and endlessly, bleeding to death inside. It no longer hurt so badly to think of Kye.

He was okay.

And she had gotten to say good-bye.

Maybe now it was time to see what else she could find in her life.

She knelt down, settling on her heels in front of the stone, laying a white rose down on the grass. "I loved you," she whispered quietly.

A soft gentle breeze drifted by and she smiled.

"I'll find what it is you wanted for us. And I'll remember you, every day. But I won't stop living."

S he waited a few days to let her aching body recover. Gave her spinning head time to settle. Let her wounded heart take a breather.

But when she went after Connor, he wasn't there.

The house was closed up.

He had turned his booming new business over to the very hands of his very shocked office manager.

Gone back to Ireland.

After waiting for her all this time, he had gone back to Ireland just when she had started to realize exactly why he had been waiting.

Ashlyn stood on the sidewalk in front of Celtic Concepts, the trendy little shop of Irish art, music and lore that Connor had started and had flourishing in less than five months.

The shop he had left behind.

She was shaking and trembling and angry.

And hurt.

Both her heart and her pride.

Just like that?

She paced back and forth on the sidewalk while the new shopkeeper stared at her through the windows, watching her with worried eyes, as the pedestrian traffic flowed around her, some giving her a curious glance, others muttering in annoyance as she blocked their passage.

Couldn't he have given her a little more time?

Then she stopped.

Maybe he hadn't realized she needed it.

Maybe he hadn't realized that she needed him.

FIVE

It took three weeks.

Three long, lonely weeks while she waited for her passport and cleared her schedule at work. Well, maybe cleared wasn't the right term.

They hadn't wanted to give her time off.

So she had quit.

After all, Kye's life insurance policy had covered her very nicely. Even after paying for the little house in the Knobs, if she wanted to spend the next twenty years at home, she could.

Working out two weeks notice, she packed and planned and pouted. Ashlyn alternated between being angry and hurt. Between sulking and brooding.

What if she was wrong? What if Kye had been wrong?

Maybe he didn't really love her.

And what if she got there, looked at him, and realized she didn't love him?

She laughed at herself. She was already in love with him and had been for quite some time. Maybe even since that first night, maybe it had started to grow then.

• • •

Now she stood with her feet on Irish soil, staring at the River Shannon, her hands cupping her elbows in the cool air. Even though it was well into August, it was cool. Probably only in the fifties this early in the morning.

Her eyes were gritty from lack of sleep. Her body stiff and weary from trying to sleep during the flight. *Should've brought some Xanax,* she chided herself. And she was seriously starting to question her sanity.

Now what?

Find him, the saner part of her insisted. *You sure as hell didn't come this far just to turn back, did you?*

Maybe. She had a wide streak of cowardice in her, and it was rearing its ugly head.

Wimp.

Definitely should have brought some Xanax. Maybe she could have shut up the voices in her head.

Ashlyn forced her feet into motion and plodded back to her hotel. She needed a few hours sleep.

Then she'd try to find her way out to his house.

This has to be the wrong place.

Ashlyn stood outside her little rental car, which, thankfully, was still in one piece after driving on the left side of the road. The little narrow, winding paths that served as *roads* here. And the roundabouts.

Oh, the roundabouts.

Maybe she was still stuck on one of the roundabouts and had driven herself straight into an unconscious state and she was dreaming.

That huge, towering stone structure in front of her couldn't possibly belong to Connor. If so, she was seriously out of her league.

A man who owned a house like that wasn't going to want a mousy, overly curvaceous nurse from America. He needed a French supermodel. An English lady. An Italian heiress.

Just get the hell out, now. This time, both voices in her head were yelling the same thing. Maybe that cowardly streak was wider than she thought.

"Can I help you, miss?"

Resigned, she thought, *Too late.*

She turned and faced the speaker.

C onnor threw his bag down and tossed his jacket over the newel post. The silence of the house washed over him and he dropped to sit on the lowest step and stare into nothingness.

When had his life become so meaningless?

Had it already been that way and it took leaving Ashlyn to realize it?

God, he missed her. Missed smelling the soft scent of vanilla and lavender on her skin. Missed the little touches, the friendly smiles.

Missed sinking into her tight, welcoming body. Feeling the press of her breasts against him, the tight wet glove of her sheath on his cock.

Two nights with her.

Very little, by the way, with just him and her.

But two simple nights and he had gotten addicted to her.

In the three weeks since he had left her, he had come to realize a few things.

He wasn't ever going to be able to fuck another woman without seeing her face, without smelling her skin—and he wasn't sure he wanted to.

And . . . he had been an idiot to leave.

She had said good-bye to Kye, whom she had loved more than life. Had he expected her not to cry? Expected her not to mourn?

He had, hadn't he? He had expected her to cheerfully say good-bye to Kye and turn straightaway to him. But because she cried herself to sleep after saying good-bye, he had taken it to heart and decided she was still too in love with a ghost and she'd never love him. Then he had walked away from her, left her sleeping with dried tears on her face, her thighs sticky with their combined climaxes.

"Stupid bastard," he muttered, grinding the heels of his hands against his eyes, then shoving his hands through his long hair as he shot to his feet and started to pace.

Call her.

It wasn't the first time he had tried to talk himself into it. But he usually talked himself out of it. She needed time. He needed time. She would be too mad to talk to him after the way he'd walked away. She was at work. He had an irate artist waiting.

"Next thing you know you'll have to wash your hair, you stupid, brainless fuck," he mumbled, dashing the back of his hand against his suddenly dry mouth.

"Any other excuses now?"

The phone was in his hand before he realized it.

"Won't hurt a bit to call, now will it?" he muttered to himself, randomly punching buttons here and there.

A friendly voice kindly advised him to call the operator if he needed any assistance.

"Fuck off," Connor said easily as he tapped the button to disconnect.

He finally dialed her number, holding his breath. She wasn't going to be happy. He had walked away from her when she most likely had needed him the most. She would yell, or cry, or hang up. Or all three.

Or . . . she wouldn't be home.

As the phone rang on endlessly, he lowered it and stared at it. Not home.

"Bloody figures," he said with a wry laugh.

On an oath, he hurled the phone across the foyer and watched as it fell to the floor in a number of pieces. Christ, he was falling into just as many pieces, going absolutely fucking insane without her.

He forced himself to his feet and climbed the stairs. And as he climbed he moved faster, until he was jogging up them. He was going to pack.

He was going to go to the airport and fly back to the States.

He was going to get her back.

If he had to wait, then bloody hell, this time he would wait until the moon fell out of the sky. He loved her—needed her—had to have her. He was going to get her back.

He was going . . .

. . . to have a heart attack.

Ashlyn stood in the middle of his room.

Wearing nothing but an unbuttoned shirt, her wild red hair falling halfway down her back in a riot of curls.

"Holy Christ," he whispered, falling back against the door. *Have I lost my mind completely?*

"Ash?"

"Surprise," she said, taking a step in his direction. The movement pulled the edges of the shirt farther apart, revealing her pale body, the red curls between her thighs, her lush tits.

He reached out, grabbed and whirled her around, pinning her between his body and the door while he captured her face in his hands and took her mouth roughly, greedily, drinking down her sweet taste liked a man dying of thirst.

Ashlyn's hands were at his waist, loosening his belt, unzipping his slacks, freeing his cock. He lifted her without ever taking his mouth from hers and shoved his length completely inside her.

She tore her mouth away, her head falling back as she gasped for air. He gripped her round butt in his hands and spread the cheeks of her ass, forcing her legs farther apart while he pulled out.

She closed over his cock, a slick wet glove that clamped down around him as she started to shudder, climax building in her loins. Lowering his head, Connor caught one beaded pink nipple between his teeth and bit down as his hips pistoned against her, faster and faster.

He dropped to the floor, taking her with him, riding her to

the down. He rose to his knees, draped her thighs over his and grasped her hips in his hands, flicking his thumb over her swollen clitoris from time to time as he fucked her hard and deep, holding tight to his control as she tightened around him in climax, sobbing out his name as she clamped down on him so tightly he had to work his cock back inside her each time.

Her back arched up, lifting her breasts high, her nipples tight and hard and red, a long lock of hair curling over her shoulder to lie between her breasts. A delicate flush pinkened her cheeks and her lips parted on a shuddering gasp as he pushed back inside her.

His gaze trailed down her body to her sex, to the neat thatch of red curls that shielded her, to the swollen red lips that spread tightly around him. Her clitoris rose stiff and swollen from her folds and he reached out, rubbing it with his thumb and groaning when it caused her to tighten around him.

"Again," he purred, lifting his hand to lick the cream from his thumb before he leaned back over her body, one hand burying in her hair, the other circling endlessly over her clit.

She cried out and gripped him closer, trying to lock her legs around his hips. "No, you don't," Connor muttered, catching her thighs in his hands, hooking his arms under her knees, using his weight to force her thighs wide while he shuttled his cock back inside her wet sheath.

"Connor . . ."

"I love you," he whispered in her ear as he shifted his weight and rode her slower, deeper. "I love you."

Her arms closed around his neck and she whimpered, straining to move faster on him.

"Say it back," he rasped, sinking his teeth into the exposed flesh of her neck. "Even if you lie, say it back, Ashlyn."

He pulled out and thrust his cock deep inside, and held there while she shuddered and bucked against him, screaming out as her climax grabbed and held her, cream pouring from her body and coating his balls, while she clamped rhythmically around his penis, pushing him closer and closer to the edge. "Say it," he pleaded desperately, his own heart shattering inside him, his own need for her driving any and all thought of sanity from his mind. "Damn it, Ashlyn, say you love me."

Bloody hell, he loved her. He had this insane need to stay right here inside her body for the rest of his life. And she was here. That had to mean she felt something. *Give me something, damn it*, he thought, starting to move inside her wet, slick passage.

Her clouded eyes drifted open a few moments later, when he started to rock against her again. His heavenly blue eyes were hot and full of need that she was just now recognizing. It had always been there, every time he had looked at her, that need had been there. He had just tried to hide it from her. A sweet, sexy smile curved her mouth while she reached up to cup his cheek. His golden hair spilled over his shoulders, his narrow handsome face naked with emotion. His whole body was tight and stiff with tension as he waited, his cock throbbing inside her, causing her muscles to contract around him.

She trembled under the exquisite pleasure that was racing through her, lifting her hips to take more of him as she said raggedly, "Connor, I can say it without lying. I love you. Why else would I be here?"

His hands tightened on her painfully and his control shattered as he drove into her mindlessly, filling her tight wet sheath repeatedly until he came inside her with hot flash-fire intensity, a dull sense of relief sliding through him as he felt her climax around him.

He wanted to fall asleep against her, to rest his weary body and take comfort just in her nearness.

But first . . .

He lifted himself off her slowly, settling down next to her before drawing her into his lap. "Did ya mean it, darlin' girl?" he asked roughly, cupping her cheek and lifting her gaze to his. "Did ya?"

She nodded slowly, staring up at him. "I meant it," she answered, leaning into his hand, rubbing against him like a cat seeking a caress. "I meant it. Do you think I'd fly thousands of miles to see you if I didn't love you?"

He only stared at her, his eyes nearly dumb with bewilderment.

And then—shock as she plowed her fist into his gut, her blow glancing off and causing no pain, thanks to her shitty leverage. But she got her point across, both with the blow and with how she shot off his lap and flounced away, grabbing the discarded shirt and pulling it on before glaring down at him with wounded eyes.

"You could have waited," she said, softly. "Given me a chance."

He watched as she lifted her chin, stiffened her body and prepared to argue. And he watched the fight drain out of her when he said, simply, "I know." Slowly, he rose and closed the distance between them. "I know. I was coming up here to pack, and then I was going back to America, to you."

A smile spread across her face as she asked, "Seriously?"

"Seriously," he echoed, reaching out and pulling her up against him. "Fuck me, but I love you. I have for all m'life. I pulled away from Kye, after that night, because of it. I didna want to hurt him, but it hurt me too much to be around him, knowing he had what I had always wanted."

He fell silent, as his eyes darkened with guilt and regret and his mouth tightened. Three years wasted. He had lost three years with his best friend and the man was gone forever. "I hate myself for that. If I had known . . . "

"Don't," she whispered. "He knew. Please don't be sad. Kye doesn't want that for us." Slowly, she drew him to the bed and urged him down, straddling him, stroking his shaft as he lengthened and hardened before she took his cock and slid down on it, impaling herself.

Her wet passage closed tightly around him and she rode him eagerly, hungrily. She was starving for him, trying to fill the ache he had left inside her when he had left.

His hands gripped her hips tightly, hard enough to bruise as he took control, slamming her weight down on him as he arched up, driving as deep inside her as he could go.

The climax hit them both suddenly, and Ashlyn screamed his name before she fell forward against him, nuzzling his neck as she murmured, "I love you."

When he exploded inside her, he rasped it back in his lyrical poet's voice, "I love you always, Ashlyn."

SIX

Kye went from hovering beside the stone while Connor and Ashlyn stood over it, straight into nothingness. Where he drifted for what felt like eons, in a fog that had no shape—no color—no scent. Where he was just an insubstantial thought with no body—just his memories.

And anger.

Impotent rage and immeasurable frustration.

Is this what he had hurried to? What he had told her she needed to let him go for?

Had he left watching her for this? To just hover in this nothingness?

And right when he was getting really pissed, he was thrown in a well of pain. Sharp biting teeth worked over his body, and icy winds blew right through him. Bright lights burned his eyes and his naked flesh felt cold. Was he being born?

Again he was thrown back into the limbo, only it wasn't his world. And it wasn't Ashlyn he was watching.

A lithe, sultry brunette with a mouth made for sex, a tight, round little butt, full breasts, long legs . . . and a lover. And Kye didn't know either of them. Didn't know what in the fuck was going on.

Each time he muttered that out loud, there was an answer. Of sorts.

A deep aristocratic voice, almost familiar, that would sigh inside his head. *A mistake. So sorry lad, but this is your life. And that is your woman.*

"No. Ashlyn was my woman.

"And my life is over.

"Let me go on."

We can't. We can't change what is meant to be, or what is. This is where you were supposed to be all along. We brought you here, and here is where you must stay. With her.

With her? Granted, she was a sexy little bundle, with big almond shaped eyes, full, golden breasts, a body that would have made a Playboy model jealous, but it wasn't Ashlyn.

Ashlyn isn't yours any longer. Let her go.

"*I have!*" he shouted into the nothingness. "Now let me go!"

Another rippling sigh sounded through his head and the voice whispered, *We cannot. She needs you.*

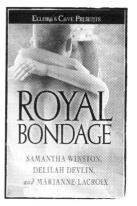